Though I d... transformation, the evil greediness of the disease, the insatiability of it. The cancer had taken everything from him until he had nothing more to give. And then, in the end, it would take one thing more.

Max was thin. So thin.

His skin had a yellow tinge, and his hair was sparse and gray. He was asleep. His rhythmic, noisy breathing was shallow but consistent. I put a hand over my mouth to bury a gasp and kept it there to choke down a sob.

The man Max was, was no more. He was a frail silhouette of the man. A tall, strong, swaggering Max, now unrecognizable under the thin cotton blanket. Seeing this was nearly too much for me to bear.

I walked to his side, gently took his hand, and turned it over in my own. "Max," I whispered. He didn't move. I came in closer and whispered again, so my breath caressed his cheek. "Open your eyes, it's Sofie."

His eyes fluttered. He coughed and took in a deep breath, winced, and coughed again. I leaned in close to him, held his hand tighter, and whispered through quiet tears, "Max, open your eyes. I'm here."

His head turned to the sound of my voice, his eyes quivered, then finally opened. The disease had taken nearly everything, but his dark eyes were still his, the whites a bit yellow, but still his. They danced with pleasure. All the pleasure he couldn't show with his body was in his eyes.

"My darling…you came."

Praise for E. Graziani

"Sofie and Max's impasses were authentic. Their dialogue—easy, inciting, passionate, soul-baring. ... Their predicaments were genuine and convincing. The decisions and choices they made were relatable and rational, yet compellingly draw the reader in. ... *EVERYTHING THAT WAS US* is magnificently written. Filled with raw and visceral emotion. Passionate, compelling, heartbreaking. Makes you want to chase a love like that wherever in the world you need to go to find it, keep it, and never let it go. Like Heathcliffe and Cathy…Sofia and Max share a true, rare and everlasting love that transcends time."

~Gia of @GiaScribes 2020

"An evocative story of a love that never ran its course, and, therefore, became unrivaled—the eternal predicament of choice and what could have been. Intense and heart-wrenching. I could not put it down."

~Lu of Lu Reviews (lureviewsbooks.com @lureviewsbooks)

"This story is the depiction of everyone's fantasy of going to a foreign country and meeting someone you would fall head over heels for. And the realistic undertones of that fantasy…of having to leave that someone…another 'right person, wrong time'…love doesn't always conquer all…both heart-wrenching and exhilarating in more ways than one."

~Hazel Pagador (Zel from @grimreaderx)

"Such a beautifully written book!! …It made me smile and cry at the same time."

~Musfira Sultana Siddiqui (@musfira.)

Everything That Was Us

by

E. Graziani

This is a work of fiction. Names, characters, places, and incidents are either the product of the author's imagination or are used fictitiously, and any resemblance to actual persons living or dead, business establishments, events, or locales, is entirely coincidental.

Everything That Was Us

COPYRIGHT © 2021 by E. Graziani

All rights reserved. No part of this book may be used or reproduced in any manner whatsoever without written permission of the author or The Wild Rose Press, Inc. except in the case of brief quotations embodied in critical articles or reviews.
Contact Information: info@thewildrosepress.com

Cover Art by *Kim Mendoza*

The Wild Rose Press, Inc.
PO Box 708
Adams Basin, NY 14410-0708
Visit us at www.thewildrosepress.com

Publishing History
First Edition, 2021
Trade Paperback ISBN 978-1-5092-3421-9
Digital ISBN 978-1-5092-3422-6

Published in the United States of America

Dedication

To my parents, Edo and Bruna,
who loved Italy and made me fall in love with it, too.

~

For my beautiful daughters,
Julia, Alicia, Michaila, Chiara.
Love you to the moon,
four times around and back again.

~

For my husband, Nanni.
Thank you for your patience and unending support.
Tuscany awaits!

Acknowledgments

Thank you, Kathy, for reading it first and for your honest reflection on what was barely the second draft.

~

Thank you, Gia of @GiaScribes, for your encouraging and heartfelt valuation and recommendations as my beta reader on this project. I owe you a box of tissues!

~

Thank you Priya at @WriterlyYours for your unwavering support of all my work.

~

Thank you to my wonderful editors, Judi Mobley and Roseann Armstrong, for your guidance and direction in making *Everything That Was Us* the best it could be.

~

Finally, thank you to The Wild Rose Press for picking this manuscript out of the slush pile and trusting it.

Chapter One

Long Island, New York, Present Day

This is a ghost story.
Not all ghosts are dead.
My ghost was very much alive.

It was a cold, clear day in April—too cold for the time of year. Folded laundry sat in piles all over my bed in my Long Island home. I had finished folding a pair of jeans when the phone chimed on the bedside table.

"Hello?" I tucked the handset to my ear and then grabbed a sweater from the laundry basket.

"May I speak with Sofia Romano?" The man on the other end spoke Italian. The voice held urgency requiring no translation. I wouldn't have needed interpretation anyway—being an international investment banker, I'm fluent in Italian, along with a few other languages.

"This is she." My eyes rolled impatiently, but my tone remained businesslike. "Sir, I'd be happy to discuss any concerns you have about whatever file in question…on Monday. Call my office Monday and—"

"*Signora*," he interrupted. "This is Vittorio Gennari. I am an end of life counselor at the St. Joseph Hospice near Lucca, Italy."

My chest tightened. "Hospice. Yes. What can I do

for you?" I still had a cousin in Tuscany.

"I am calling on behalf of someone you know, one of our patients here at the hospice. His name is Massimo Damiani."

Silence hung in the air like a wisp of smoke across the four-thousand-mile expanse.

"*Signora?*" he repeated. Another long pause.

"Yes. Excuse me," I murmured. Stunned, I sat down hard on the bed and tried to put words together. "I haven't heard that name in—many years."

"Of course, Mr. Damiani said you may be surprised. I beg forgiveness, but he insisted. I had to do some digging, but I suppose now with such an abundance of information at our fingertips I was able to—"

"Excuse me, Vittorio, is it?"

"That's right."

"I'm sorry—what about Mr. Damiani?" My cheeks burned as the prickling threat of sweat teased the back of my neck.

"As I said, this is St. Joseph's Hospice and Mr. Damiani is a patient here. *Signora*, he is very ill."

Through the confusion already swirling in my head, I heard the distinct clunk and thump of the mudroom door open and close downstairs. "Mom? I'm home." My daughter's voice drifted up to the bedroom.

My hand snapped over the receiver. "I'm upstairs. Be right down." Then to Vittorio in a hushed tone, "Why are you calling me about Massimo?"

"He was admitted here from Mercy Hospital in Lucca a week ago." Hesitancy permeated his voice. "I am obliged to tell you he is in palliative care."

As fast as my face flushed, I felt the blood drain at

the last two words. *Palliative care*. "He's dying? Max…" I whispered, transfixed at the realization, then gulped and fashioned the question. "Uhm, can I ask…from what?"

"Pancreatic cancer." Papers shuffled on the other end. "I read in his chart he was diagnosed some months ago." A sigh. "I will be forthright and advise that he doesn't have much time."

The crushing news knocked the breath clean from my lungs. "Does he want to talk to me, or…what does he want?"

"He has asked me to find you—to ask you to come here. Mr. Damiani would like you to be with him." Then in a hushed voice, he repeated, "He does not have much time."

I squeezed my eyes shut. "Uh…where is this hospice?"

"We are north of Lucca, in the hills outside of Pescaglia."

Pescaglia. Long buried memories came rushing back to me at the mere mention of the place.

I grabbed my iPad from the night table and swished furiously, legitimizing the hospice location. *Find the website, find the website.* "Okay, I've got it. The phone number on the site, is it the best one to contact you?"

"It is." Vittorio cleared his throat, then, "What shall I tell Mr. Damiani?"

I drew in a breath. "I'm going to have to think about this—I mean…I want to speak to him. No offense, but how do I know this is even genuine?"

"Of course, I understand. However, you should also know Mrs. Romano, there is no one else here. No family."

"Wait, I know he had—"

"Mom? What are you doing?" My daughter's footsteps sounded on the stairs as she ascended. "Who are you talking to?"

"Wait a second, Cara. I'm almost done," I called out away from the phone, then turned my attention back to the counselor. "He had a son, he was married."

"No. No one. Mr. Damiani is alone," he said empathetically. "He asked me to tell you, you promised you would come. 'When we are old and gray,' he said to tell you. Does it make sense?"

The words made the back of my throat tingle. I tried to swallow but couldn't. If I didn't get hold of my emotions fast, I would have to explain to Cara, who was now leaning against the door frame of my bedroom, weighing my every expression.

"What's wrong, Mom?" she asked, surveying me, her phone momentarily suspended in her hand. "Your face is like…green."

Again, I put a hand over the mouthpiece. "Please, Cara. Give me a moment."

Cara raised her brows, her face betraying slight insult. " 'Kay, just wanted to tell you I was back from the mall." She refocused on her phone and left.

I listened for her bedroom door to click shut, then resumed the conversation. "Please, I need to speak with Mr. Damiani." My voice quavered tensely.

"One moment." The line went mute.

As I waited, the dizzying emotions inside me churned, and the questions spun out of control.

Max. His memory…hell, his name still had this effect on me, a tempest of images swirled around me, delicious and passionate, enraging, and hurtful, all slamming into me at once like a colossal velvet fist.

The line clicked live again. "*Signora?* I have Massimo here. Please, hold one moment."

My insides jumped, thinking he was as close as the other end of the phone. I heard shuffling sounds and then finally, "Sofia?" It was him. His voice was rasping and weak, but the throaty quality it had in its youth still lingered.

I was speechless, yet to ask him what in hell he thought he was doing, was my first instinct. My common sense wanted to admonish him for making his caseworker call me; to tell him his dying did not justify dragging my soul through hell, yet again; to shout it wasn't fair he was making my daughter suspicious, and I would have to tell James to swallow his frustration and deal with it. But in my heart, I wanted to cry out with the full force of my lungs when I heard his voice speak my name after so many years.

"Sofie, it's Max," he repeated.

I held back a sob, then declared, "You're a bastard. You know it, don't you?"

A bout of coughing followed a faint chuckle. "I am. Always have been. And no one knows it better than you, my darling."

My eyes welled up, and tears spilled over onto my cheeks. "What are you doing to me, Max?" I whispered.

"I can't help it. I'm not only a bastard, I'm a selfish bastard." His words drifted to me on barely a wisp of a breath. "I'm dying, Sofie. But I swear to you, hearing your voice gives me strength."

"Jesus, I'm so sorry," I murmured. "But I'm wondering if you woke up this morning and decided to turn my life upside down."

"Now, you're the selfish one."

"I don't know what you expected. It's been so many years. I have a daughter. I'm married. Why, Max?" I wanted my anguish to turn to anger, but my efforts were in vain. It was surreal, bizarre, like a scene from a bad movie.

"I need…to see you. Talk to you."

"Oh, God," was all I managed. The self-absorbed side of me shone through, I'm ashamed to admit. The words *this couldn't have come at a worse time* kept playing through my head. "I want to. I want to help you, but I'll have to call you back. I need to arrange things. I have to talk to James."

"I know, Sofie," he assured, his voice fading. "You talk to him. I need to rest now. I'm going to hang up."

My head bobbed as I put a hand over my eyes, sensing they were sufficiently red by now. "Okay. I'll call, and if I can't get you, then I'll leave word. I promise. Talk soon."

"I'll be waiting." The line clicked dead.

I pressed the off button and dropped the phone on the bed, breathing deeply to settle my adrenaline. Through the onslaught of old emotions, I knew I had to think clearly. I wiped the wet from my cheeks and sweat from my palms before my daughter could see me, a pang of gnawing guilt already settling into my soul.

Jesus Christ. Goddamn you, Max.

I wondered what my husband's reaction would be and thought of all the reasons why I should refuse to go. My job, James, my marriage, my kid—my life.

How dare you, Max!

The negotiations were endless.

In the isolation of my bedroom, I concocted myriad

excuses why it was impossible for me to go all the way to Italy at a moment's notice. I would politely apologize to Max, albeit his impending fate, but firmly and calmly tell him I couldn't possibly drop everything to support him at his most vulnerable.

I would cordially offer to help in any other way, hire someone if needed, to be kind and so he wouldn't be alone. But to haul ass across two continents to be at his side, to fulfill his last wish? Sorry—no can do. I would bid my final goodbye over the phone and hope he would understand.

He's alone. What are you doing? I got up and paced.

But James—what will he think about it all? Really, though, he's got no right to think or say a goddamn thing, not after North Carolina, that's for goddamn sure.

Certain it would be too late to get a flight, I scooped up my iPad and Googled furiously. *Damn, there's space on that one.*

I thought of Cara. How would I tell her? How could she understand the reasons why I had to do this? How could she understand in my longing to tidy up the loose threads of my emotions, maybe pulling on those threads would unravel the tapestry of our lives?

The pacing and deliberating held me captive for a while, but in the end, I could have debated with myself into the next day and still come up with the same decision. Whatever James' reaction would be, and despite my fiery protests to the contrary, I had made up my mind the second I'd heard Max's frail voice. I would do what I had to—exactly what he asked.

****

"What?" James' shout jarred me out of my reverie and back to reality. With a confused grimace, he raked a hand through his thick shock of red hair and asked again. "You're doing what?"

Outside, the peaceful stillness of an early spring evening hovered over the Long Island suburban neighborhood where myself, Sofia Romano, and James O'Halloran, my husband, made our home. Local kids rode home on their skateboards, hungry from the day's activities as a hush of moving sunlight and lengthening shadows lay upon our front lawn. There was a promise of a clear evening, which made the skeletal shade of the maple tree in our front yard a place to be desired.

But inside the house, the scene was somewhat different.

"I know it sounds crazy, but I have to." I walked briskly back and forth in front of him, from the closet to the suitcase, putting another pair of pants in, lighter cotton ones this time—in case the weather in Italy took a mild turn. April was unpredictable there.

"Are you serious? You're going to drop everything and go?" My husband was putting away his socks from the laundry basket when I dropped the bombshell. He shadowed me back into the closet. "Because this 'friend' asks you to? I've been trying to get you there on holiday for years, but he snaps his fingers and you go running."

I sighed impatiently and pushed the hangers aside, one by one. "Don't be so selfish!" I snapped. "And don't make it sound like I was the one who made it inconvenient. You seemed to be busy enough with work." I paused for effect. "…and a few other things lately." My glare pierced his stare like ice picks.

"Besides, I told you, he's dying. He's at the end of his life, and he's asked me to go there and be with him. He's alone. It's as if my mother asked me to be there. I can't say no."

"Are you trying to tell me this guy is on the same level as your family?"

"Yes, for chrissake James, I've known him longer than I've known you."

"Yeah, but you're married to me." He stopped me from flicking through the hangers and held my shoulders.

"I know I'm married to you—and for this reason, I'm asking you to understand this is important to me." My stare bore into my husband. In a saccharine-sweet voice, I added, "Did you remember we were married when you were in North Carolina?"

He swallowed hard and let go of me, casting his gaze to the floor. As he stuffed his hands in his pockets, he asked, "What about the office? What did they say?"

"Rolfe said they'd be okay for a couple of weeks. He's splitting up my files among the team. They have four new analysts. It'll be a good way for them to get their feet wet." I walked back to the suitcase with a pair of jeans, a couple of T-shirts, and a sweater.

"Look…I know it's sudden, but I have to do this. I'm obligated to do this." I managed to push my bitterness aside for a moment and channeled all my sincerity into his gaze. "I'm not going there to punish you. He's dying, and he's alone. If I don't help him, I'll have to wrestle with my conscience and guilt for the rest of my life. It'll all be done before you know it. His caseworker said he has days, a week at the most. I-I'm sorry, I need to move fast. Please, try and understand."

It didn't take a psychiatrist to sense he wasn't convinced.

James breathed out heavily. "Okay, listen."

I knew him well enough to know there would be a proviso. "It's spring break next week. What if I take time off and...and Cara and I will meet you there? We can spend time together—you know, as a family." He took my hand clumsily. "I want to make things right."

I sensed ulterior motivation. "You're taking a week? For us? You can't even take a Saturday off. Can they survive a week without you? Or will your office and the New York State Bar Association crumble to pieces in your absence."

"They'll be fine," he answered, his jaw tensing. "You will alleviate your misguided guilt, and Cara and I will do some sightseeing. We've never been, and it will be a great chance to do some father-daughter bonding, spend time with her before she goes off to college. When you're...done, you can join us. For whatever time is left."

"Yes." I sighed. "I think you'll be alleviating some of your guilt, too, though yours isn't misguided." The last comment was somewhat unnecessary, but I couldn't help myself.

"Sof, we've been through this—"

I put a hand up. "Okay, sorry. Maybe I'll catch up with my cousin while I'm there, too. Maybe afterward..." Afterward. My voice trailed as I thought about what "afterward" actually meant.

"I get it," he said, saving me the trouble of finishing the sentence. "Besides, when I retire," he added, "I might buy a house over there. Maybe we can spend the summers in Tuscany."

I looked away, not even wanting to consider it. "We can talk about it later." My voice was wistful. I knew deep down this was the one way he could feel comfortable with my going.

The trauma in our marriage was still too fresh, too raw. I had a crazy thought he was probably afraid if I went there, I may decide to take Cara and stay for good.

We ended the negotiation there. A compromise. So civilized, and so like us.

At the end of the day, I was emotionally and physically exhausted. Having broken the news to my husband and daughter and just managing to secure a seat on the 6:30 p.m. flight to Pisa via London the following evening, all I could do was hope Max's suffering would be mercifully brief.

Chapter Two

At first, Cara seemed mildly interested that I had to leave for Tuscany. When she discovered she would get a trip to Italy over spring break out of the deal, she was elated.

James drove me to the airport the next day, still unsympathetic, still questioning whether it was the right thing for me to do. He reminded me of a toddler expanded to adult size, irritation in his anger, a sort of impetuousness, and gaspiness in his arguments. "How did he know where you were anyway if you haven't heard from him in years?"

"He had his caseworker find me," I responded icily, watching a man in the car next to us eat a hamburger as we drove down Woodhaven Blvd to JFK.

"Wow." James' tone was disparaging. "He must really want you there to go to such lengths to track you down."

My head snapped around to look at him directly. "How dare you," I growled through clenched teeth. Without another word, I rummaged in my purse and pulled out my phone. I scrolled through my pictures and within seconds I found what I was looking for.

I made my voice mimic what I thought was a birdbrain.

"—*hey James, miss you, loved our dinner. Pick up when I call.*—"

"—*James.*—"

"What the hell, Sofia," he interrupted.

I looked up at his face. It was of a man who had lost what he knew he must lose, but the knowing didn't soften the desolation.

"Why? You took pictures of them?"

"—*James, call me when you get to Carolina for the tort conference.*—"

"Okay enough." James' voice was thunderous. "Did you take a shot of the one where I asked her to stop texting?" He threw a hand in the air, signaling he was done with it all. "Fine! I'm the asshole in this marriage…you got me. Congratulations."

"Believe me," I murmured. "It's no treat for me either."

"Look…Sofie…it came out of nowhere. One minute we were…engrossed in discussing case briefs over the other side of the dinner table, the next we were—"

"Oh, God." My gaze shot up to the ceiling of the Subaru. "The thought of it makes my stomach turn—"

"…after a few seconds, I broke away…I promise."

"Shut up, James…shut up," I interrupted. I took in a breath to steady myself. "Just drive."

We were silent in the car for a long time. The only sounds were the road noise and Miles Davis, belting out a live version of *Stella by Starlight* on the radio.

Then, without warning, "Sofie, your apathy is killing us both. You act as if my love is owed to you, but all you give me is indifference," James blurted out the declaration in one breath.

He was again, trying to blame me for his near miss. After thinking carefully, I answered, "I see it's been there a while now, this...whatever it is—this anger, escaping from you."

A heavy silence settled over us, thicker than the uneasy tension in the atmosphere. James gripped the steering wheel until his knuckles were white. I pulled my lips in so thin they became a gray line. Both of us shifted uncomfortably in our seats for the rest of the ride to the airport, with our unsettled eyes glancing around, trying to avoid catching each other's gaze.

After what seemed like the longest ride to JFK in history, James pulled the car in front of the terminal, put it in park, and calmly opened the door. I exited on the other side, and we met at the trunk. He opened it, pulled out my carry-on, and placed it upright, handle out, ready to go. I already had my tote bag slung over my shoulder.

We stood there, nose to nose, neither wanting to speak first. We stood there with nearly twenty years of a packed-full marriage between us, yet a great empty space keeping us apart.

I caved. "Well...I should get in." I motioned to the automatic door.

He nodded. "Yeah." Sheepishly, his hand reached out and grasped my arm, then he kissed my cheek like he would kiss his mother. "Be safe."

With a nod, I grabbed my carry-on, turned, and melted into the crowds inside.

I knew if I stood a chance of surviving this, I had to push James and the associated shitstorm out of my head.

I had to focus on Max. One day at a time, focusing on Max.

Once I was on the plane, I had time to think about

what I had undertaken. Sitting back in the cramped airplane seat, I assessed the last twenty-four hours. It was still sinking in that I had agreed to do this.

I thought about preparing myself for the change in his appearance, self-cautioning that I must expect to be shaken, to be taken aback by the toll cancer had taken on Max. How thin, haggard, and weak he must be at this point. My mind meandered to the way he would have aged had he not gotten sick. Would he still be the Max I remembered?

My thoughts wandered, pondering life and death, existence and energy, and the way living had a tendency of speeding up when you were doing all right and working and raising a family, and before you knew it, days and years sped by quite literally unnoticed.

Last weekend was Easter Sunday—the holiday was early this year. Being a good Catholic family, the three of us had gone to Mass. Children in the congregation prattled on in the background, eager to get home to their chocolate chickens and bunnies as the priest on the pulpit read from John.

It was a woman's story really—Mary Magdalene's. It was Mary who, before dark, found the stone rolled away from the tomb, the sepulcher empty. She ran to summon Peter and John, that first Easter. The two raced competitively to get to the sepulcher and concurred on its emptiness, but for the neatly folded linens, then raced away again.

Men. Why are men always bound to rush off to the next thing? To leave women behind, wondering why? Instead, Mary, the woman, stayed behind and wept. Mourned.

"Woman...why are you weeping?" the angels

asked her.

Why, indeed, do women weep? I supposed we wept for ourselves, for our husbands, our children, and our own transgressions, our deepest secrets, and our even deeper disappointments.

Disappointments. I brushed the word out of my mind and instead thought of my triumphs. My daughter, whom I love beyond words. Cara is an impetuous, tempestuous personality, fiery at one moment, then kind, thoughtful, and cerebral the next. She was dichotomy made flesh, and I loved her even more for it.

My work. I loved my work. Most days it was nerve-wracking, but I adored every minute of it from the very beginning. Long hours and stress aside, it wasn't at all about the money, it was the win I loved most.

Because I work for one of the largest investment banks in the country, I have clients around the globe. The languages and cultures I've come to know in my line of work often give me a unique perspective on some of the most profound topics. Something stuck out in my mind one day while meeting a client in Beijing. I inquired about what a few markings meant on a poster in the room. One of the interpreters read the line to me. He said the one word I pointed to meant "crisis." He then went on to explain the two Chinese characters in combination, made up the word crisis—one meant "disaster," the other meant "opportunity."

As I looked at the cottony tufts of clouds below, these thoughts brought me back to Max, back to our early years. Our beginning would be our undoing. Our immaturity to handle the greatness of what was supposed to be us, our great love, would be our legacy.

We had managed to resurrect it twice from the depths of timelessness only to waste the chances we had been given.

Chapter Three

Near Pescaglia, Tuscany Italy

"*Buon giorno*," I said to the clerk at the reception desk. "I reserved a room last evening, online. Romano?"

The lady smiled pleasantly and clicked her computer mouse to check.

"*Buon giorno* and welcome to Hotel Barberi. Yes, here we are—Romano, presently booked for two weeks?"

"Correct. I parked out front but—"

"There is guest parking in back…" I listened as the clerk went through the usual welcome prattle, but all I wanted to do was unload my suitcase in the hotel room, splash some water on my face, and seek out St. Joseph's Hospice.

She handed me the room keys. "You are in 310. It has a nice view of the valley."

"Thank you. Um, can you tell me the best way to get to the hospice? I have a GPS in the car but—"

"Very simple. Follow the road to the roundabout and then up." She indicated with a slim, toned arm. "It's the big white stucco building about a kilometer up—can't miss it. You speak Italian very well by the way. Are you originally from here?"

"My parents…Pescaglia."

"Hmm, not too far from here. Oh, I'm sorry. Are they…at the hospice?"

"No, my parents passed away years back. I have a cousin in Pescaglia now, but I don't want to impose, so I'm staying here. Plus, I needed to be closer to the hospice."

"I see. A loved one?" The lady inclined her head sympathetically, anticipating my answer.

I smiled without humor. "A loved one. You can say that." I picked up my bag and headed to the elevator. "*Grazie.*"

Once in the room, I did a quick scan. Clean and simple. I set my suitcase down on the desk, walked to the window, and opened it, craving fresh air. The lady at the desk wasn't kidding when she mentioned the view—it was breathtaking, a poem written in landscape.

Standing there, listening to the quiet, the peace, and taking in the scenery of whitewashed houses spilling down the hillside like icing on a cake, I felt as though I was betraying my purpose. I shouldn't be allowed to enjoy the beauty of nature, not when nature ravaged someone I loved.

Back to business. I needed to call James and let him know I had arrived. I didn't want to, but I had to. I dialed his cell, expecting him to be at his Madison Avenue office.

He picked up on the second ring. "Hello?"

"Hi, James, I'm here…safe and sound."

"How was the flight?"

"It was good. Weather's nice here. I got a Peugeot for a rental."

"Nice cars…safe. Have you seen him yet?"

"No, I barely stepped into my hotel room. I'm headed there after I talk to you. Listen, I texted you the address and phone, but I put the information on the fridge too—for both the hotel and the hospice. Cara okay?"

"She's good. Don't worry, all's fine here." There was a pause. I pictured him in my mind's eye, deliberating over his words. "I'm worried about you, though."

I wanted so badly to snarl back *well you have a funny way of showing it*, but instead, I said, "You have nothing to worry about here, either." I ensured my words held a matter-of-fact clip. I didn't want him to think he had wormed his way into my good graces yet. "I'll call back when Cara's home."

I hung up and considered if my tone was too cold. I concluded it was just cold enough to send a message, but not so cold as to set back our "mending of the fences" too far. My good graces were not a friendly place for my husband of late. I couldn't shake that a couple of months ago, after a conference out of state, I found incriminating text messages on James' phone. I confronted him outright, and after persistent prodding, he confessed. Though comparatively speaking, there wasn't much to reveal.

The argument that followed was ugly. It was ugly yet illuminating in a strange kind of way because my sweet, unflappable, even-keeled James dropped a bombshell of epic proportion on me I didn't expect, which sent unpleasant cold shivers up and down my spine.

I had just accused him of disappointing me in a way he could never imagine and of being like every other male in the species—thinking with his dick instead of his brain.

"How could you do this, James? Now you're like the rest of them…you're a horny, needy, walking cock."

"Hey, now that's not fair—"

"No, it's very fair and very true. All these years I've never once given you a reason to question my fidelity. Nev—"

"Bullshit!"

"What the hell are you talking about? Who the hell do you think you're talking—"

"I'm talking to you!" His breathing escalated, and what were probably years of pent up tears began welling up in his eyes. This was not like James.

"What…you're trying to pin this on me now? Typical. I expected more from you. It's my fault you were this close to having sex with another woman?" I squeezed my thumb and forefinger together.

"No," he said, in a softer tone, his gaze now downcast. "That's not what I meant."

"Well, what do you mean?"

He breathed in deeply. "I don't know what's making me think this…I swear, Sofie, I've pushed it away for so long. I don't even think it, I feel it…I feel like—like…"

"What?" I said, my face a twisted grimace. "What is it?"

"I feel like…" He struggled to form the words…like if he said them, they would have to be true. "Like you've never really…fully been mine."

I shook my head. In my heart, I felt shame, but on my face, I made sure he saw disbelief.

"It's not often, and I can usually always push it away, but sometimes." He licked his lips and looked away. "It's like…you're with me, but you're not with me at all."

Those were words I thought I'd never hear from my husband. All I could do was let them sink in. Let them float out to me, into my ears, and settle into my brain, and then just as easily reject them as bullshit and not admit right now, I hated him and loved him in equal parts, and I wanted to punish him for what he almost did to me.

I realized all these years, I convinced myself everything was normal. That my feelings were a part of the natural progression of marriage, and everything was in place. But my husband knew better. And though I wouldn't have admitted it to myself, his supposition was bang on.

James O'Halloran was always too busy or too wrapped up in his own matters to notice…or he was just plain blind. But despite all evidence to the contrary, he wasn't.

I was speechless.

James looked up and stared straight through me. "You're a million miles away."

"Maybe I'm preoccupied with work. Ever think of that?" I sputtered.

"No," he said, shaking his head. "I can tell it's not." He clumsily brushed the tears away. "Maybe, it's why I did it—because I've always sensed a part of you was somewhere else."

His statement packed a powerful punch. Carefully spoken, without drama, his words had an air of finality to them.

No way, you are not going to do this to me. Faraway looks? Bullshit! "Oh no you don't—this is all you. You're full of crap." My mouth was almost too dry to speak.

My husband regained his composure and swore up and down and back and forth on his mother's grave and good name he hadn't had sex with the woman sending him the texts. He bought her dinner and drinks. She put her number in his phone, and she took his. He had come to his senses before anything happened. But in my mind, even the consideration of an idea that maybe at the outermost millionth of a percent he would have even thought of having sex with her…then the damage was done.

James begged me to believe him because he'd never given me a reason not to. I was rattled by what he had said—my occasional lapses into reveries in the past, yeah, okay—all women have fantasies. We all have secrets. Take that, James O'Halloran. It was no excuse.

So I took care of it. I called her and advised her if she didn't stop texting and calling my husband, I would drive to North Carolina and file an "alienation of affection" lawsuit, which is when an "outsider" interferes in a marriage.

I warned her it could cost her hundreds of thousands of dollars, if not millions. Because it was my lucky day, and I knew these suits are allowed in seven states, Hawaii, Illinois, Mississippi, New Mexico, South Dakota, Utah, and North Carolina, I would give her an out if she didn't contact him again.

Still, the nagging thought he sensed something all these years was unsettling. I wondered if it was an excuse other spouses used to explain away their errant behavior. Then it got me thinking; how many other spouses got caught because they were plain stupid enough to keep texts, emails, and pictures on their phones?

****

I was tired and jet-lagged yet determined to see Max. After freshening up, changing, and spending more time on my makeup than I would ever admit, I made my way to the Peugeot and set the GPS for St. Joseph's Hospice.

The closer I got, the more nervous I became. As bizarre as it sounded, I was equal parts excited to see him again, panicked as to how I was going to handle this desperate situation, and guilty for feeling anything but mercy and compassion for a human being suffering through his last days on planet Earth.

Prepare for the worst. Breathe and prepare.

As I turned into the parking lot of the converted palatial Tuscan villa, I thought of the last time I had butterflies in my stomach. I swallowed them and checked for parking. There was a spot across from the main entrance. I veered into it, turned off the engine, and took in a calming breath, wondering how I could prepare myself. After some hasty soul-searching, I concluded there probably was nothing I could do to be ready for this. This wasn't exactly commonplace, taking care of a former lover in his last days after so many years of no contact whatsoever between us.

Then I thought of James. Thinking of James always grounded me, brought me back to earth.

I checked my hair and face in the visor mirror and decided Max probably didn't give a fig how I looked. I buttoned up my sweater, grabbed my purse, and started up the path.

Once inside, I spotted a reception desk to the left of the front double doors. A lady with a "volunteer" badge and perfect skin smiled up at me as she filed papers in a cabinet.

"*Buona sera*. Can I help you?" Her tone was toasty warm.

"*Ciao*. I'm Sofia Romano—here for Max…Massimo Damiani."

"Welcome," she said warmly. "My name is Grazia. I'm a volunteer here. I can take you to Mr. Damiani's room. I believe his caseworker may have gone home, though—it's after five." She circled around the desk and ushered me to the elevator.

"I think I spoke with him—a Mr. Gennari?"

"Yes—Vittorio. He's excellent. Massimo is in very good hands." Grazia pushed the up button. "We are pleased he has company—there hasn't been a lot for him."

The doors glided open, and we entered. "So I've heard." I raised my brows. "No one at all?"

"I think a brother may have called, and a co-worker? Two or three times, but…" Grazia pushed the number "4."

"I see." I shook my head, suddenly ashamed of myself for even considering not going. "I suppose his family is scattered or away or…" My voice trailed off nervously. There was silence as we watched the numbers climb until a soft *ping* sounded our arrival.

"Here we are," said Grazia. The doors glided open to a gracefully decorated reception area, with statues, potted plants, and lots of light, reminiscent of a *pensione* rather than a hospice.

A gentleman sitting behind a desk looked up. "*Buona sera*, Grazia."

"*Ciao*, Alberto," she replied, then turned to me. "*Signora* Romano, this is the fourth-floor charge nurse, Alberto. There is a nurse on each floor, with three personal support workers, and an on-call doctor, twenty-four hours a day. Eight patients per floor, usually. Everyone is very well looked after."

"Good to know," I said to Grazia, then offered my hand to Alberto. "Nice to meet you."

"You as well," he replied as he extended his hand. He had a strong grip. "Who are you here to see?"

"Massimo Damiani."

Alberto's face lit up. "So you are his Sofie? A pleasure. He hasn't stopped talking about you since he found out you were coming."

"His Sofie?" I smiled as I felt my face color. "I hear there hasn't been much support…in terms of family."

"A brother came for a few weeks when he was in the hospital, but other than him…"

I squeezed my lips. *How could his family abandon him like this?* "Can I see him?"

"Of course. Please, come this way." He indicated the hallway.

Incredibly, my heart jumped. "Thank you."

"He'll be so glad to see you. Now, remember, if *you* need support, we are always available." I listened as we moved down the hall. "We have a small team of caring, experienced counselors who offer psychological and emotional support to patients and caregivers, individually or in family groups…"

As he spoke, my mind worked.

Now brace yourself, Sofie. He's got cancer, he's probably a shadow of himself and weak. Breathe deep and prepare.

"...who are either attending the Hospice or living with a life-limiting illness in the community. If you are here tomorrow, I'm sure Vittorio will come by to chat." Alberto halted in front of the last room at the end of the hall. A large balcony with French doors was the only place left to go. "Here we are." The door was ajar, and from my eyeline, I discerned feet under a blanket.

"Thank you." My voice was barely above a whisper as my stomach churned both in anticipation and sorrow.

Alberto nodded and, with a pleasant smile, turned toward the nurse's station. I watched him walk away and wondered how many times he had done this. How many times had he walked down this very hall, uniting family with someone, who in a short time, would cease to be?

For Alberto, I was just another visitor for another patient. But in my heart, I knew this was more than a visit.

Pausing to breathe in a last calming breath, I licked my lips with a dry, papery tongue and grasped my handbag for strength. After what seemed like an eternity, I knocked lightly on the doorframe and stepped over the threshold.

"Max?" My call was soft. As I inched further into the room, his frail body became more and more evident. "Max, it's Sofie. I'm here."

As I fully entered the homey space, his body and face came into full view. IV drips, monitors, and tubes surrounded him, but it was Max.

Though I didn't let it show, I was struck by the transformation, the evil greediness of the disease, the insatiability of it. The cancer had taken everything from him until he had nothing more to give. And then, in the end, it would take one thing more.

Max was thin. So thin.

His skin had a yellow tinge, and his hair was sparse and gray. He was asleep. His rhythmic, noisy breathing was shallow but consistent. I put a hand over my mouth to bury a gasp and kept it there to choke down a sob.

The man Max was, was no more. He was a frail silhouette of the man. A tall, strong, swaggering Max, now unrecognizable under the thin cotton blanket. Seeing this was nearly too much for me to bear.

I walked to his side, gently took his hand, and turned it over in my own. "Max," I whispered. He didn't move. I came in closer and whispered again, so my breath caressed his cheek. "Open your eyes, it's Sofie."

His eyes fluttered. He coughed and took in a deep breath, winced, and coughed again. I leaned in close to him, held his hand tighter, and whispered through quiet tears, "Max, open your eyes. I'm here."

His head turned to the sound of my voice, his eyes quivered, then finally opened. The disease had taken nearly everything, but his dark eyes were still his, the whites a bit yellow, but still his. They danced with pleasure. All the pleasure he couldn't show with his body was in his eyes.

"My darling…you came."

My emotions overflowed. I lifted his hand to my cheek and brought my other hand around to hold his face. Every part of him looked frail like it would yield under the slightest pressure.

"Of course. I promised I would." I laughed softly. Max nodded, not taking his eyes from me, scanning every feature of my face, seemingly renewing its imprint in his memory.

"How can it be you are even more beautiful now than you were when I first met you?"

"You're so full of shit." My smile never left my lips.

"Now, now—I'm being truthful." He breathed in, coughed, and continued to study my face.

"Are they looking after you all right? The pain management and all?"

"Couldn't ask for better. See that little guy up there?" He pointed a finger to the IV drip. "He's my best friend, Mr. Morphine. He visits me regularly."

I nodded and sat on the edge of the chair beside his bed, lightly massaging his arm. "I see. Well, hello up there, sir. Nice to meet you."

Max smiled a beautiful smile. "My God, Sofie, it's so good to see you. Why didn't I call you before? Why did I wait so long?" His speech was labored.

I shook my head slowly. "I don't know why...maybe because we had our own lives. It's been a long time, Max, but I'm here now."

"Look how lovely you are, still a beauty."

"You're not so bad yourself, you know."

"Liar," he said simply as he worked his hand to twine his fingers through mine. "You look the same as the night we first met. Do you remember? The night I first saw you, in the *piazza* at Pescaglia. You were so young, so precious. You were the most beautiful thing I had set my horny eyes on."

I burst out laughing, and Max laughed weakly with me. "Your hair, your eyes—your beautiful backside in those tight blue jeans."

"Hey, you know, you're not too sick to get slapped there, Maxxy."

"Oh, yes I am. Only a few days left to live automatically exempts me from any reprisals due to socially inappropriate comments."

I winced rather obviously at his last remark, prompting Max to tighten his weak grip on my hand.

"I'm sorry." He sighed shallowly. "I say things like that too often."

Wiping stray tears from my cheek, I nodded in acknowledgment. "You're going to have to give me more time to get used to this, Max. Not at a point where I can joke about it. My head is spinning right now."

"Agreed. I promise I will behave." After taking a few breaths, he continued. "How was your family with all this?"

"Well, I think they understand. Cara is old enough to realize it's important to me. She's in her last few months of high school, going away to college in the fall."

"And your husband, Jones, is it?"

"James. He's well. Works all the time. Sometimes I don't see him for days between my job at the firm and his commitments." I shrugged as Max's eyes narrowed. "He's busy at his law office, and he has a position as a board member with the local—"

"You are still on Wall Street?"

"Not at Goldman Sachs anymore, but yup—they're going to bury me next to the bull, I think." We smiled at the light conversation, and then there was a pause. It wasn't an awkward silence, though. Even then, our silence was never awkward.

Suddenly, Max blurted, "Does James make love to you every day?" The question was asked unapologetically.

Taken aback by it, I paused for a moment. After which, "Sweetie, at our age, nobody makes love every day."

He let out a chuckle, followed by a punishing cough, then, "I would make love to you three times a day if you were mine."

"You probably would have." My gaze settled on his. "We never had trouble in that department, if I recall correctly."

Max took shallow breaths to calm a rattling wheeze. "If I hadn't thought I was going to live forever, I would have come for you. And if you had argued with me, I wouldn't have listened. I would have—" A sharp bout of coughing shook Max to his core.

"Now stop." I frowned. "Don't get yourself all worked up. That was all done a long time ago. It's done."

Max paused and closed his eyes. "I know. Sorry. I'll stop."

"Let's forget about it all and talk. Are you up to it? Can I get you something? Some water?" I reached up to brush a few stray hairs from his forehead.

"I have a cup of water over there…with a sponge." He motioned with his index finger to the night table on the other side of the bed. I rose and quickly scooped up the cup, dipped the sponge, and touched it to his lips. I imagined the full lips I had kissed so often in the past, now replaced with a parched, cracked slit.

"There. Better?" He nodded as he licked his lips. I dipped the sponge again and brought it to Max's mouth, but he turned away. Uncertain, I asked, "Are you tired? I can come back."

"No." He shook his head vehemently and closed his eyes. "No, don't go."

"I won't." I sat again, but instead of the chair, I sat on the bed and soothingly stroked his forehead. "So, Max, your family…what about your son? Your brothers and sister? Gabriela?"

Max sniffed and opened his eyes. "My older brother and sister are dead. My younger brother lives in Belgium. He has a wife, family, a job. He came to France…when they discovered cancer, and again when they first put me in hospital in Lucca, stayed two weeks, but he had to go back. Gabriela and I divorced years ago. My son…I haven't heard from him in over five years. When my ex-wife died, he moved away. I ran into one of his old friends and they said something about him moving to Australia. I figured if he wanted me to know where he was, he would have at least emailed me." Max tried to laugh, but hardly managed to sputter. "Why burden him with this now?"

The news his son had abandoned him made my heart twist with anguish. "I'm so sorry about Michael. What about Conti? Is he still at Eni?"

"Retired and living in the Bahamas. He came before I was transferred here. The last time he called, we said our goodbyes."

My heart ached for him. "It doesn't matter. I'm here. I'll stay here as long as you need me."

"My Sofie." His eyes closed again. He looked so

consumed, so tired. There was a long pause. I thought he had drifted off, but then he spoke, barely over a whisper. "We'll go for a walk in the piazza later. To Camillo's…" He stopped there, and his breathing slowed as he nodded off, shallowly moving in and out of his lungs.

The piazza…Camillo's in the Frescobaldi. Oh my God, he's thinking of Pescaglia…and of Florence. When we were in Florence. Jesus.

As we spoke, Alberto strode into the room, with a tray of medication giving me a cursory smile as he worked. He checked the IV drip, replaced the bag, and checked Max's pulse. "How is he?" he asked.

"Okay. We talked and then he took some water, but his last remark was strange. He wanted to go to a place in Florence we used to go to years ago."

"He may be dreaming, hallucinating," Alberto whispered. "Usually at about this time, the liver starts to fail. There may be ammonia in the blood, hence unclear thinking."

I nodded, pretending to understand. "How long will he be conscious?" I asked in a low voice. "Like, be able to talk, comprehend?"

"It's hard to say. I find everyone's end of life experience is unique. Right now, he's still taking fluids. Sometimes even after they are out for a while, or very weak, they can have lucid moments. Almost like they know it's time to say goodbye."

Stinging tears were threatening to emerge again. "Can I stay a bit longer?"

"Stay as long as you like." He smiled and turned to go. "I'll be back before the end of my shift." Alberto headed for the door with his stainless steel tray and then paused. "You know if you need to talk to someone, we have counseling sessions for family here, at the Hospice."

Offering him a quick smile, I said, "Thanks. I'll keep it in mind," then turned my attention back to Max, watching him as he struggled for every breath. He had given me ten minutes of solid conversation today, and I couldn't help but wonder how much more he had in him to give.

I closed my eyes and touched his arm, remembering him in his prime, but I shook the thoughts away as I reckoned maybe it was wrong on some level or other.

I sat nearby, stayed with him, hummed to him, and prattled on about work, my flight, and other ordinary, mundane things as he slept. I massaged his hands gently with some lotion I had in my bag.

He was still as stone for a long time, then I noticed his eyes moved under his lids. *My God, he's dreaming. What could he be dreaming about? Pescaglia? Florence? Of us?*

The picture window in the room was adjacent to Max's bed. Above the monitors and machines, birds sang outside, in the long shadows of late afternoon. My gaze was drawn to the countryside, to the picturesque beauty which lay beyond it.

I gave Max's hand a gentle squeeze, watching him as he slept. His face was peaceful. I breathed deeply and walked to the window, to draw some strength from the splendor. The view was awe-inspiring. It looked out over the entire valley with rolling patchwork hills in the distance, dotted by the occasional cypress tree.

Eventually, involuntarily, my gaze focused on a

faraway spot. Anyone who saw me would have thought I was taking in the remarkable view, but I didn't see a thing, because my mind had wandered to another place, and another time.

Chapter Four

Italy, July 1976

There were bicentennial celebrations all over the country, and what did my parents do? They took me back to the country of their origin, Italy, to connect with my "roots." My mother had read a book that was sweeping the nation called *Roots*—she was inspired.

My parents, Rita and Tony Romano, immigrated to America from Italy in 1958, from a mostly agrarian little community in rural Tuscany, before modern agritourism and expensive B&B's swept the nation. It was their first trip back since then. My father was a welder and my mother worked in a bakery—we didn't have a lot of money, but they had high hopes for me, which meant I was under a lot of pressure as they lived for me, their only child.

At fifteen, skinny, naïve, and virginal, I remember having mixed feelings about leaving my friends for a month and going to a strange country. I was nervous about my scarcely adequate command of the Italian language and anxious I would sound like an idiot, but once off the plane and through customs at Fiumicino, I realized I wasn't the only anglophone in the country.

We got our rental, and my father drove through Rome as though he was navigating a go-kart through an amusement park. Red stoplights were merely a suggestion here, and one quickly learned to adapt; my father was right about one thing: it was the survival of the fittest. If someone got in your way, you honked, swore at them, and moved on.

Soon our journey brought us close to my parents' ancestral village, outside of Lucca in Tuscany. When I caught sight of the medieval walls wrapping themselves around the city like protective wings, the romance of the old provincial town beguiled me.

"Promise we'll come back and see Lucca?" I begged.

"Of course, but we have lots of people waiting for us in Pescaglia," countered Dad in his "Joi-Zee" dialect mixed with an Italian accent.

I believed him.

My dad's dream car, a red Fiat, wound its way up a hillside about thirty minutes outside of Lucca, my anticipation mounting with each turn of the wheel as we clung to the edge of the steep slope.

Then with a slight left turn around a sharp rise, the valley opened before us displaying Pescaglia, an ancient settlement perched on the mountain, carved into the hillside as if by a giant's chisel. It was no small village, but rather a sprawling town on the side of the Apuane Alps, the surrounding landscape accented by centuries-old olive trees and vineyards.

Our reception was a momentous affair, in what seemed like the entire town came out to the main piazza, to greet the Americans who had come home to their origins.

Once introductions and reacquaintances were done, a supper fit for royalty awaited us at the local restaurant, the owner and cook proud to feed the

Americani from New York. Uncle Mario raised a small tumbler filled with red wine and toasted us, me, and my parents, who finally caved to liberally let me have a glass of wine at dinner, at my aunt Carla's prompting.

"What's wrong with you Americans—it's only wine," said my uncle. "Don't tell me you've bought into that legal drinking age nonsense, my brother."

"Give the girl some wine—don't you know forbidden fruit is ten times as tempting?" A wise woman, my aunt Carla.

I met my cousin for the first time that night, Simona. She was eighteen and looked very much a woman. A more athletic version of me, with a thicker build in straight-legged Levi's. Next to her, I looked like a skinny, pale milquetoast, with a mass of light brown ringlets and baggy bell-bottom jeans.

Simona introduced me to some of the other girls in the village, and despite my homesickness for my friends, I found I easily adapted. Simona took me to the bar adjacent to the piazza, which was basically a café, and got me gelato. Raucous sounds of laughter and snatches of songs from the bar jukebox filled the humid night air.

As I slurped my gelato in the piazza, conversing in broken Italian with one of the boys—one of many who I noticed, to my delight, jockeying furiously to catch my attention—I felt a sudden sharp jounce from the side. I jerked my head around and caught sight of an attractive, young man, reaching out to steady me, grasping my upper arms.

"Careful," he said, his voice deep and husky. "You don't want to drop your gelato."

I barely had time to react before he strolled into the

bar, taking a long drag from his cigarette.

Sensing I probably had a limited repertoire of curse words, Simona responded for me. "Watch where you're going, Massimo—asshole."

He shot an over-the-shoulder glance at her as he exhaled the smoke and gave her a half smile. *Sigh.* I was the local oddity.

It was the first day, and I received a confusing mixed bag of hormonally charged messages from the males. This for me was a novel experience because back home I wasn't exactly the belle of the ball. Most of the time, I faded into the background and was positively happy to do so. But here, it suited me. Here, I was someone else.

Two days later, I sat on the patio of my aunt's white stuccoed house under a canopy of ancient grapevines, my gaze feasting on the Tuscan countryside. My attention was focused on the lush valley opposite us, dotted with miniature villages. Above them, there were terraced vineyards reminiscent of giant pieces of lace placed on steep hillsides.

Deep in my daydream, I didn't notice Vanessa, one of my new friends, strolling down the steps and onto the patio, until she was nearly at my side.

"*Ciao*, Sofia." She flashed me a smile, then waved to the adults.

"*Ciao*, Vanessa," replied my aunt. "Have you come to visit Sofia?"

"Yes," she answered. With a slim build, blonde hair, and blue eyes, she looked no more Italian to me than Olivia Newton-John. "I thought I'd come to take Sofia for a walk down the road to the sanctuary." Then to me, "Want to come?"

"Wonderful idea," gushed my mom. "Go and enjoy yourself. Explore the village, see new—"

"I'd love to," I blurted, not allowing Mom to complete her sentence and grateful for the opportunity to converse with someone my own age. "Thanks, for thinking of me," I offered.

"My pleasure," she said. "I figured you would be ready for a break."

We climbed the steps and rounded the corner to the main road. "Your presence could not be more welcome," I said, wincing at my Italian.

"Don't mention it." She laughed softly, then she bit her lip and gave me a sideways glance. "You don't mind if another friend tags along, do you? You met him in the piazza the other night."

Despite my newfound pseudo-confidence, I experienced a surge of intimidation. Deep down, I was still not the most confident when it came to boys. Plus, one person listening to me butcher the Italian language, I could handle, but some boy now, too. *Ugh!*

"No, I don't mind." I shrugged. "Though I'm nervous about speaking."

"Oh my God—you are doing beautifully. If you want to hear a language massacred, you should hear my English." We laughed as we ambled down the incline and out of the village, onto the main road. Chattering and giggling and talking about boys in America and what they were like there, and about how stupid boys were all over the world.

We turned the corner around a great stone house and stepped down the ramp to the clearing in the road and there, leaning against a signpost waiting for us, looking deliciously buoyant, was the boy who "accidentally" slammed into me, my first evening in Pescaglia.

He took the last drag from his cigarette, then crushed it underfoot. I watched him as he swaggered over to us, his hands in the pockets of his tight Levi's 501's, black hair blowing carelessly in the light breeze. His aquiline nose was perfectly placed above full lips, and a corner of his mouth was curled up in a half smile, with an endearing little space between his front teeth—he was perfection with the right amount of imperfection to make him real. The boy stopped halfway up the ramp and met us midway.

"Massimo, *ciao*," Vanessa said, smiling broadly.

"*Ciao*." He nodded to Vanessa, still stuffing his hands into his jean's pockets, not acknowledging me directly. Naturally, I figured this was because he and Vanessa were an item, and he probably resented me being there as the third party.

"Massimo, this is Sofia. Sofia, you remember Massimo—from the piazza?"

"Yes." My gaze met his, and we both smiled cordially. "You were the one who nearly knocked me over," I blurted as we strolled.

A slight smile formed on his lips. "Allow me to apologize. Sofia, is it?"

I nodded as the three of us walked down the incline and passed the tall retaining wall under Pescaglia.

"My senses abandoned me. Beautiful name, Sofia." He was confident, his tone almost cocky. "Where do you come from? I know from America, but someone said New York?"

"Close to New York. New Jersey, across the river."

"New York, New Jersey, everything is new in

America." He waved the notion away and then pulled out a pack of Marlboro's from his shirt pocket, offering one to Vanessa, then to me. We both declined.

"What do you do in New Jersey?" asked Vanessa.

"Go to school—high school. I'm in—" I thought about the Italian system and compensated. "I'm in my second year."

"Wow. High school." Vanessa was clearly impressed.

"And you?" My glance focused on both.

"I work in a shoe factory near Lucca. We make Fendi, Gucci—" Vanessa said matter-of-factly.

"I work for my brother-in-law," said Massimo. "He has a heating oil business. It's slow now. Go figure, it's summer."

"So cool," I offered, smiling affably. They both looked so young. I thought of my life back home and what my life would have been like if my parents never left Pescaglia. I'd probably be looking for work next year.

"Are you joking? It's shitty." Massimo flicked the ash from his cigarette. "I hate working for my brother-in-law, he's an asshole."

"Aw...poor Massimo, you're so hard done by," cooed Vanessa.

"Maybe you and I should get together again, Vanessa." Massimo's arms wrapped gently around her neck, then he leaned in to give her a quick peck on the cheek.

I admit an unwelcome twinge of jealousy rose in my gut. I looked away pretending to be fascinated by the gnarled apple trees growing wild on the side of the road.

"What do you say, *bella*. Maybe we should get back together, you and I?"

"Hmm...one word...disaster." Vanessa rolled her eyes and shook her head as she grasped his tanned forearm. "Come on now. We're better as friends."

I watched the two joke and tease as the afternoon meandered. Massimo's jokes made me laugh, and I even allowed my eyes to linger on him once or twice, in appreciation. His features had character, his eyes onyx black. He was tall, his body lean and muscular, accentuated by his Levi's and tailored linen shirt, the sleeves rolled up past the elbows. He was young, I knew this much, but he carried himself with the assurance of someone much older.

Eventually, we found our way back to the town's main road and climbed the last few steps back to the street leading to my aunt's house. As we stopped to say goodbye, Massimo combed his fingers through his hair and lingered while Vanessa stepped gingerly up ahead.

"I'll see you around then." His words were confident, but his gaze hardly met mine. The tone in his voice made my knees turn to water. "Come to the piazza tonight. I promise I won't slam into you again."

"Sure, uh..."

"I'll come to get you around eight," Vanessa called to me, waving. "Come on, Massimo. I've got to get my sister's stuff."

"See you later. *Ciao*." He smiled at me and turned to follow Vanessa.

I ambled back down to my aunt's house feeling mildly confused, somewhat nervous, and extremely excited.

What just happened? Was Massimo interested in

me or not? And what was going on between him and Vanessa—what kind of a weird relationship did they have? And incidentally, what did her sister have to do with them?

The questions swirled in my head the rest of the afternoon. By dinnertime, I had made up my mind his attention was purely amicable, and he was trying to make me feel welcome.

Stop fantasizing and making so much out of nothing. Boys like him are not interested in girls like me. I'll go to the piazza tonight, be friendly and cordial and it'll be normal.

My family ate dinner, alfresco, under the grapevines on the patio, with the sunset in the background, playing up its mix of lavender, red, and yellow, creating yet another palette of otherworldly colors in the sky. I found myself fighting giant butterflies in my stomach, the closer it got to eight o'clock. After the espresso was served, I heard nimble footsteps descend the stone path.

"*Buona sera!*" said Vanessa cheerfully. My heart jumped as I turned to face her.

"*Ciao*," I said anxiously.

"*Buona sera*, Vanessa," replied Mom and my aunt Carla. The men were busy smoking and discussing politics.

"It's nice to see Sofia has made a friend so soon," said Mom with a smile.

"And you were afraid she would be bored," Aunt Carla concurred. "What are you girls doing tonight?"

"Hanging out in the piazza." Vanessa shrugged and cast a side-glance to me. "There's not much else to do around here."

"Well, have fun. Not too late now," my mother cautioned.

"We won't, don't worry," assured Vanessa. My newfound friend smiled and linked arms with me, which totally freaked me out because you just didn't do that in New Jersey. "Let's go."

When we were halfway up the stone path, Vanessa turned to me, her voice filled with excitement. "Oh my God—I have to tell you Massimo likes you—he told me today after we left. He wants to hang out with you."

"What?" I stopped in midstep. The butterflies in my stomach had suddenly become giant sparrows. "Seriously?"

"Yes, seriously." Vanessa pulled me along again as I was in shock. "I knew he liked you right away. I can sense these things—sometimes I think I'm a clairvoyant."

"I'm stunned. Just like that? I thought he was into you—you two looked so comfortable together. Like there was history there."

"There is," said Vanessa as we reached the top of the rise and turned right. "We dated last year for a couple of months, but it didn't work out. His older brother is dating my older sister now. It was a little strange."

"Yeah, I can see how it would be odd. But what did he say exactly…about me?" I still couldn't fathom it…a boy like Massimo, interested in me? My face wasn't exactly striking. With brown hair, hazel eyes, and a body that could have stood to gain a few pounds, I saw myself as actually quite ordinary.

"He said you were cute, and he likes you." We stepped in rhythm and slowed down to a composed, casual pace as we approached the piazza. "What more do you need? Just go with it."

Just go with it?

I mused on *it* for a moment. *Go with it.* "One thing for sure," I added, leaning into Vanessa. "My mom and dad will definitely not go with it. They won't let me date until I'm sixteen."

"Neither will mine, but I've been dating for two years." She giggled through an impish grin.

The sun bid its final farewell to the day and sank slowly behind the mountains, allowing a thin pink sliver to linger above the horizon. There was a lavender hue in the air like the valley had been swathed in mauve with a giant's stroke of a brush.

Vanessa and I scanned the piazza, sauntering arm in arm, strolling by the dozen or so other teen boys and girls who had gathered to socialize in the freshening evening breeze. I tried not to give away that I was looking for Massimo, peeking subtly into the bar. I had nearly given up, figuring he had thought twice about coming out tonight, when a distinctively deep voice behind me made me start.

"Looking for me?"

I gasped, then spun around and came nearly nose to nose with him.

"Whoa! You've got good reflexes." He laughed at my reaction.

"Oh my God," I said, stepping back a few paces. "You might want to make some noise before you sneak up on someone and give them a heart attack."

"Sorry." He held up both hands. "Didn't intend to startle you. I've been watching you—looks like you were searching for someone. Thought it might be me."

His appreciative eyes traveled from my sandals to my tight tank top.

"I bet you say that to all the tourists?" I arched a brow and allowed a smile to play on my lips. Then it hit me—I was being flirty. Me, flirty—not like me at all.

"No—just you." He pulled his pack of Marlboro's from his shirt pocket and offered me one, and again, I shook my head no. "Let me make it up to you." He gestured toward the bar. "Let me buy you a gelato."

"No, thanks," I said, once again, self-conscious and looking desperately around for Vanessa. I spotted her sitting on a nearby bench holding hands with one of the other boys. Our eyes made contact. She nodded her encouragement and sent a playful wink my way, then turned her attention back to nuzzling the boy who was stroking her hair.

Okay then. I guess I'm on my own here. "On second thought, why not. A gelato would be nice."

He gently put a hand on the small of my back, and guided me toward the bar. That simple gesture was enough to send wild signals to my brain.

"So how long are you here?" he asked casually as he inhaled a puff.

"Four weeks. Until the end of August."

"Only a month?" He paused a moment. "Not much time."

"It's just a holiday." I shrugged.

"True." He took another drag. "Still, I hope we can get to know each other better—spend some time together."

Massimo's remarks left me speechless. Candid and open, his approach was so different from the boys back home. But I supposed one couldn't mince words when

47

one only had four weeks with a girl. "I'd like that, but I should warn you—my parents won't like it. They're old-fashioned."

"It's all right. We're just hanging out." He slipped his fingers through mine and led me into the café. Again, I tapped into a weird sensation, a floaty, syrupy feeling in my stomach. "There's nothing for them to know." He guided me to the gelato bar and pointed out the selections over the sneeze guard, smiling an irresistibly crooked smile.

"*Fragola*," I said to the attendant. Massimo declined one of his own. "Ti Amo" was playing on the scratchy radio behind the counter, the singer's gruff voice belting out his lament over a lost love.

An awkward silence hung between us, as the girl prepared the ice cream, but it was mercifully brief. Before long, we were outside in the night air, walking through the peaceful streets of Pescaglia.

"So tell me about your life in America?"

I had to think a minute as I slurped my gelato. "I go to school, hang out with my friends." *Say something exciting.* "Go into Manhattan every so often and shop with my mom—"

"Do you have a young man?"

"A young man?" When I translated it in my mind, it sounded positively medieval. "No, no young man."

"I'm surprised. A beautiful girl such as yourself—what's the matter with the men over there." His hand confidently took mine.

My ingénue's heart raced, and my stomach turned somersaults. "What about you," my voice croaked. "Tell me about you. Your work."

"Nothing to tell. I quit school two years ago to help

support my family. My 'work' is working for my brother-in-law. He has an oil and propane company, but supplies wood fuel, too. That's where I come in. I cut trees and chop wood." He looked to the ground and I got a distinct impression he was embarrassed. "My father's sick and can't work anymore. My sister, the oldest, is married, hence my brother-in-law. I've got one younger brother. My older brother is engaged to Vanessa's sister. End of story."

I was silent, but I wanted so much to say, "I'm sorry." Then, I thought it might be offensive. He might misunderstand and think it was meant for him. "How very kind of you—quitting school and all, to go to work and support your family."

"Who else is going to do it?" He shrugged. "My sister has her own family, my brother is about to start his, and my little brother is a pain in the ass."

I giggled. He had an extraordinarily charming sense of humor. "Well, I think I should be getting back. It's late."

Massimo turned toward the piazza. "Anyway, if you can, come by my house tomorrow," he blurted. "I'll introduce you to my little brother. It's the last house at the top of the village. Near the cemetery."

I thought a moment about how I could pull it off. "I'll try to. After lunch, all right?"

"Perfect."

We walked through the quiet streets of Pescaglia, the windows now darkened. Silence once again became the specter taunting us with awkwardness.

Think of something to say. Ask him something. "How old are you?" I winced at the banality of my question. *You couldn't have come up with something more clever?*

"Eighteen." His gaze drifted to the half-moon high above us.

Eighteen, I mused. Yet he seemed older than his years, in every way he carried himself, his body language, his confidence, and coolness; I sensed he had lived as a man since he was a small boy.

"And you?" he asked.

My gaze dropped shyly to the cobblestone walk, but I sensed his eyes were now focused on me. "Fifteen. Just fifteen. Painfully, only fifteen." *Where did that come from? Painfully? God! you're so lame.*

Massimo's long strides halted. I fully thought he would grimace and leave me right then and there. My bogus imitation of a confident young woman had given way to sounding like an insecure, silly little girl, with self-esteem issues and problems filtering out my thoughts before they became my comments. *This is it, you dope...he's going to guide you back to the piazza and you'll never see him again.*

Instead, he cupped my chin gently and lifted my eyes to meet his. He smiled empathetically as he grasped my other hand and held it. Then he moved slowly toward me, leaning in so his face was so close to mine our noses touched, and our lips were no more than a breath apart and waited.

I hesitated, but for a second. Then I stood on my tiptoes and closed the distance between us. It wasn't my first kiss, but it was the best one, the sweetest.

I opened my eyes and wondered how something could feel so right, so easy, so soon. Without words, he draped his arm over my shoulder, as my hand reached across his back. He rested his head on mine, as we walked the remaining distance to the piazza, unaware this seemingly innocuous moment would affect the rest of our lives.

Chapter Five

The next afternoon, I nearly bolted out the door after I convinced my parents I was going out with some girls from the village. Only Vanessa knew where I would be, a plan we hatched once back at the piazza the night before.

I wore a simple T-shirt and slim jeans. Vanessa walked me up to Massimo's place, and once I reached the doorstep, she turned and promptly left to go out with her own young man.

Massimo's house was an ancient-looking place, all stone, and heavy wooden beams, in the middle of an open meadow, with age-old chestnut trees surrounding it like silent sentinels.

Though I was characteristically timid and nervous about this visit, the thought of seeing this boy forced me to push myself to my limits. I approached the door and knocked softly.

"*Avanti!*" A disembodied voice floated to me, through the open window.

I grasped the latch, twisted it, and pushed. "*Permesso?*" Reticently, I poked my head over the threshold into a kitchen, which looked like it was plucked from the last century—a wood-burning stove, a fireplace in the corner with glowing embers, and a copper kettle whistling over top, with an old-fashioned hand pump at the sink for a tap.

A woman in a well-worn day dress stood at the sink, washing dishes in a plastic tub, a cigarette pinched between her teeth. She looked like an overworked Anna Magnani.

"Yes, come in. Are you Rita's daughter? Jesus, you look exactly like her." She craned her head toward the back of the house. "Max—your friend is here." She glanced back at me. "Sit down. Do you want a camomile tea?"

"No, no, thank you." I peered about, marveling at the snapshot in time.

"I have camomile tea ready—Max's father's stomach won't tolerate anything stronger, but if you want, I can fix you an espresso."

This was Max's mom? She looked more like his grandmother. "Thank you, I'm fine." I heard footsteps coming from the back of the house, and in seconds Massimo stood framed in the doorway.

"*Ciao*, Sofia. You made it." His voice drew a smile from me, as he walked over and took my hand.

"I did. I think I've been talking to your mom?"

"Excuse me." He gestured to his mother. "Mamma, Sofia, Sofia, this is my mother, Maria."

"A pleasure." We nodded simultaneously.

Massimo grasped my hand. "I'm going to show her around the farm, Ma," he said, leading me through to the back of the house. "Come on with me."

"Watch the cow pies," Maria yelled after us.

Massimo shook his head and flashed me a half-smile. "She's all class."

"Never mind. She seems very sweet and down to earth."

He pulled the side door open for me. The simple,

rustic wooden door opened to a breathtaking vista of the valley. My gaze was drawn to the snowcapped mountains in the distance, with the occasional village dotting the thatched landscape. "Wow. The view is stunning."

I was gushing at the view, but the scenery seemed lost on Massimo, who walked behind me. "The view is pretty good from this angle, too."

His openness excited me.

We chose a spot close to a makeshift abutment, where we sat and watched the clouds roll lazily by, offering us the occasional respite from the hot summer sun.

"Tell me what an ordinary day is like for you, in America," he asked, pulling at the grass while his eyes remained on my mouth and eyes.

I shrugged. "Nothing special. It's very centered around school right now. I'm going into my junior year, and after high school there's college."

"College?" he questioned. "Is it like a university? Here we have university or trade school—you know apprenticing."

"Oh, understood. Are you ever going to go, do you think?"

"I want to apprentice if my father gets better and can work. But with the way he is…someone's got to work…make money to pay the bills, buy food—you know." His gaze focused on a far-off spot.

"It doesn't seem fair. What's going to happen when you have a family of your own?"

"Wasn't planning anything anytime soon—unless you decide to stay." His sideways glance made my heart melt, and my belly felt warm and tingly.

"Oh, you're good, Massimo." My smile was playfully coy, my words surprisingly forward. I was disarmed from the beginning by him. "My friends warned me about Italian boys. I know you'll say anything to get your way." I gently nudged him with my elbow.

"American women are so suspicious." He put a hand to his chest, exaggeratedly faking great disappointment. "Now you're hurting my feelings, Sofia."

"Please, call me Sofie—everybody does. And I'm sorry I offended you."

"Don't be. Your friends are right." He laughed. "And you can call me Max. Everyone does."

The way he spoke pleased me. He was refreshing, outspoken, real, not too serious, yet not a fool. And it sounded as though he had lived more in his mere eighteen years than any of the boys in Jersey will live their entire lives. "Okay, then…Max." I allowed myself to be lost in his words.

"In any event"—he stood and pulled me up—"I can't hold my family responsible for my ends. When I was younger, I had an idea that one day I would go to school and become an engineer, but I probably would have flunked out anyway. I've got a hard head." He tapped the top of his skull with a closed fist. It produced a *bonk, bonk* sound, which made me giggle. "Come here, I want to show you something."

Max stepped behind me, resting his hands on my hips, pointing out various landmarks in the distance. I nodded and listened carefully without hearing a word, only thinking about how close he was to me and hoping I wasn't turning red.

"See…over there is San Pellegrino." I followed his forearm with my eyes as it indicated a flat-topped mountain, bearing a few structures. "It's a monastery."

"Hmm, I see." I wasn't looking at the monastery. I was watching the muscles flex in his arms as he moved his hands. Even the veins under his skin were sexy. As my eyes feasted on his extremities, I discovered my hands had developed a mind of their own. They found his hands and wrapped them around my waist in a tight embrace, letting my head hang back on his chest.

He welcomed this with a throaty, "Sofia," his warm breath on my temple. "Turn around," he whispered.

I eagerly obliged. At first, they were polite kisses, mannerly and restrained, then my kisses deepened, and his hands tangled in my hair, pulling me closer.

Suddenly, "Hey! Max—who's your friend?" a young voice called out, piercing through the heavy breathing.

All hands were at rest in an instant. "Franco," mumbled Max. "It's my little brother."

We looked around to see where the voice came from.

"Franco, where are you?" he called out angrily.

I nodded and smiled my appreciation of little siblings catching their older siblings in the act of making out. He must have had a transistor radio with him because I distinctly heard the song "Shake Your Booty" drifting down to us. Our gazes followed the sound up, and there he was, perched on an old knobbly chestnut tree, not twenty feet away from us.

"How long have you been up there, you little shit," snarled Max.

"Long enough," replied Franco, winking at me. He wrapped his arms around himself and made kissing noises with his mouth. "Oh, Massimo…Oh, Sofia…"

"If I catch you, I'll strangle you, you little—" Max started for the tree.

"Oh, come on, leave him alone." I grabbed his arm and laughed. "He's just having a little fun."

"Yeah, Max. I'm just having a little fun." Franco's laughter echoed through the hills. "You're such a hothead."

Max and I looked at each other, defeated. "Let's walk." He locked fingers with me. "He'll end up following us anyway."

I drew in a breath as we turned toward the house, my gaze shyly cast downward. "It's okay. I should be getting back. It's getting late, and my parents are probably wondering where I am."

Teasingly, he intercepted my stare as he squeezed my hand. "I'll walk you as far as the lookout, Sofie. Do you know your way from there?" His lips touched the tips of my fingers.

"Yes, I can find my way back." Then reticently, "If I go to the café tonight…will you be there? I'll have to see what we're doing, but I think I can get out."

"Try and keep me away. Until tonight then—I'll meet you in the piazza."

****

Time simply was not cooperating and had decided to slow down to a crawl. My wistful sighs and finger tapping punctuated an otherwise leisurely dinner.

"What's the matter with you?" Mom whispered to me while the others were engaged in a spirited conversation about the state of the Italian Democratic

Party. "Why are you so jumpy?"

"I'm bored, I guess." I huffed out an impatient breath. "I want to go meet my friends."

Her face broke into a warm smile. "Well, my daughter, I have a cure for boredom—tomorrow we're headed to the seaside for a few days. Viareggio! Exciting?" She playfully poked my ribs, producing a gasp and a burst of giggles.

"Oh, so cool! When did you—" And suddenly, the realization hit me like a wave of murky water, if we were away, I wouldn't see Max. In a span of time already too short, we were barely getting to know each other. "When did you plan this?"

"This afternoon. And by the way, who are your new friends?" asked Daddy. "I bet we know their parents?"

I processed the questions and came up with a believable answer. "Vanessa and a couple of other girls. I forgot their names, but they're from around here."

It was the '70s and a different world, and I hated that I had no control over my own life and even more so that I had to keep my budding relationship with Max a secret.

Finally, I had found a boy who understood me, who appreciated me, who found me desirable and attractive, and he lived four thousand miles from New Jersey.

****

I couldn't get to the piazza fast enough that night. I spotted him first, casually leaning against the ancient retaining wall, smoking.

When he saw me walking up the incline, he straightened and started down the cobbled path to meet me. Soon we were locked in a loving hug.

As he held me, I couldn't help but marvel at the speed I had fallen for him. With gentleness, his strong arms wrapped around me. There was a safety in his embrace I'd never experienced before. A new emotion, a satisfyingly rich sense of belonging to someone and finding safety and yearning in that belonging, which built me up so completely in a span of mere hours.

"*Ciao,* Sofie," he murmured, as he kissed my forehead.

"*Ciao,* Max," I whispered, my core fluttery and giddy all at once. I pulled away and looked up at him.

He grasped my hand in his and kissed the palm. "What?" His unknowing smile was torture for me.

"My parents are taking me away for a few days starting tomorrow." A punch in the stomach would have produced the same expression on his face.

"So soon? Where?"

"Viareggio, on the Riviera. I'll be back Friday in time for the weekend, though."

He let go of me and pensively pulled his cigarettes out of his pocket. "Nice. But a week is already done—then there are three left."

"I know—I'm sick about it, but I have to go. And it's not even where I wanted to go—I asked for Lucca. Anyhow, I'll try and talk them into coming back early." Though I was unwilling to give away my skepticism, I knew my wan smile was unconvincing. Max tilted his head to the piazza, a disappointed look in his eyes, but after a deep sigh, he took my arms and pulled me close again.

"I'll take you to Lucca one day. And as for your going away"—a slow, dangerous smile curved his lips—"I'll just have to get my fill of you tonight."

These words spoken by any other boy would have been offensive and crude in any other time and place, but from him, they were electrifyingly arousing.

He let his hands fall to my wrists and led me to a quiet spot on a bench facing the valley next to the boisterous piazza. "Let's sit here a while. I don't want to share you with anyone." Far away twinkling lights marked tiny villages on the other side of the vale as fireflies floated silently among the tall grasses. Max stroked the hair away from my neck and let his lips barely graze over my skin. "You're so beautiful, Sofia." His hand swept gently over my face; the tenderness tempered by the roughened feel of callouses from manual labor excited me.

My head felt light and wobbly, unsure how to respond to such praises. I leaned in and kissed him instead of speaking. No Italian class I had ever attended could have prepared me for such a conversation. Two teens swept away into our own world on the crest of a wave—I had never come close to such physical longing.

"Kiss me again," he whispered when our kiss was done. "Enough to last me until Friday. I'll imagine you with me, sitting here, your breath on my skin, and it must do until you return."

A smile formed on my lips. "Your words are intoxicating, you know?" I stroked his hair, then outlined his lips. "They're making my head spin."

"I hope making your head spin is a good thing." He tugged me onto his lap. "Because you might fall over onto me."

We laughed together, and when he laughed it was

like an auditory hug.

I let my head rest on his strong shoulder. As I watched the lights in the sky work their magic, I realized being away from him for even a moment was unbearable.

Chapter Six

Saint Joseph's Hospice, Italy, Present Day

"Sofia."

I heard my name spoken softly behind me, prompting me to jerk my gaze from the view outside Max's hospice room window. "Hi, there." My voice was subdued, even exaggeratedly so. His stare was fixed on me. In three strides, I was at his bedside.

"How long?" he murmured.

I puckered my lips as I mulled over the question. "Do you mean how long have you been sleeping or how long have I been here?"

He screwed up his mouth a little. "Both."

I checked my watch. "I've been here a touch over two hours, and you've been napping for an hour and forty minutes."

"If I nap again, wake me up." He cleared his throat noisily. "I want to be awake while you're here…as much as I can be."

I picked up his hand and folded my fingers around his. "Whatever you say." We were quiet for a long time. Then, I tilted my chin toward the window, and said, "You have quite a view." I immediately wondered if I spoke callously, considering he was in his hospice room and not a hotel or something. I shook my head. "I was admiring the countryside…taking it in while you were asleep." I looked down to hide a burning face. "I, uh…I went through Pescaglia on my way up here. It's surprising how things have changed…yet they're still so much the same. It made me think of us…when I first came here in '76. Remember?"

He squeezed my hand. It surprised me how much strength he still had in his fingers. "Yes," he said softly. "I've been thinking about us, too. I haven't been able to think much about anything else since I came back. Did I tell you I was staying at my mother's old house in Pescaglia?"

A sudden wave of nostalgia hit me, and I smiled picturing us making out on the thick wall overlooking the valley. "No, you didn't," I replied.

He nodded. "I stayed there for a while—before I got worse. Before they brought me to Lucca. I would sit in the field behind the house. My caregiver brought an old lounger he found up in the attic out to the field. I would listen to the sounds. I listened as I'd never heard them before. The birds in the trees, the rustling in the grasses. I would look for hours…at the clouds. At the mountains across the valley. They lay in a great line like the spine of the land." He paused as he recalled, his eyes dreamy and faraway. "It was as if long ago they were a great beast, only to lie down one day and never get up." His gaze found mine again. "Like me right now, my darling."

Gulping, I responded lightly, "Since when have you become so poetic?" I laughed nervously. *How am I ever going to make it through this?* "I mean…it's not enough you bring back images of you as a gangly teen, with the devil's own grin. Now you're sweeping me off my feet again with poetry?"

"Ah, you are onto me." He smiled, and for a split second, he reminded me of the Max I knew decades ago.

"You did make me love you, you know. Then again…I did always fall for those dark, dangerous, brooding types. Why, for me it was like…well it was like Mr. Darcy had come to life—in teen form, mind you."

"I was as far from a Mr. Darcy as you could get." Max chuckled softly. "But we did have our moments."

I nodded. "Yes, we did."

"Teen love." Max licked his parched lips. His eyes were faraway again. Like he was living in another time when he spoke about us. "I did love you," he whispered.

"I know you did." The air thickened with emotion. It washed around me like a whirlpool. *Change the subject.* "Did you see Simona when you were in Pescaglia?" I picked up the sponge and cup and refreshed his lips with cool water.

His eyes glazed over. "One day, I'll climb the mountains again. One day, we'll look down on these tall pines like they're matchsticks."

I was losing him again. Alberto was right about the lucid moments. It was like they came in waves, like tides on the shore.

"We'll climb them together, Max. You and me." I imagined it. The land at our feet becoming rockier with every step, the incline getting more burdensome ever so slowly.

His eyelids fluttered closed.

Then he'll see what God sees. He'll like that.

It was then my vision swayed, like seaweed

drifting back and forth. I closed my eyes, too, and held on to the edge of the bed afraid I would end up falling over.

Don't be so weak! Cold sweat clung to the fringes of my hair, plastering it to my forehead as if I had been immersed. Maybe, I was drowning. Maybe, as the water closed over my head, I would continue to relive the times with Max, newsreel style.

Chapter Seven

Pescaglia, 1976

"I'm so glad you're back!" squealed Vanessa, as she flung her arms around my neck in a hug. "How was Viareggio? You were gone for so long."

"Oh my gosh—I feel the same," I said, hugging back. It was Friday afternoon, and we had returned from our trip to the coast. Vanessa waited for me on my aunt Carla's patio. "It was nice, but I prefer the quiet up here. It's so tranquil compared to Viareggio."

Vanessa rolled her eyes. "Why don't you tell the truth—you missed him. You're glad you're back because you missed him."

"Of course, I did," I admitted. A silent pause and then, "I don't know what I'm going to do when I have to go home."

"Don't think about it now. It's a long way off," Vanessa assured me as we sat under the cool shade of the grapevines. "Listen…I have to tell you, Massimo has been showing all the signs he is 'cooked' for you."

I furrowed my brow. "Cooked for me?"

"Yes, cooked. Done. In love. Hooked."

"Okay, I get it," I said looking around to make sure nobody overheard. "Why? What did he say?"

"It's not so much what he said, but how he's been acting. Drawing little hearts in the dust on car hoods, sighing, and generally acting like he's cooked." Vanessa plucked a sour grape from the vine and put it to her lips.

"Shh, keep your voice down. I can't let my parents know Max and I are…together."

" 'Together' is right." She took a microscopic bite from the grape and grimaced. "You've never had a boyfriend before, have you?"

"Well…no. Max is the first."

"Have you guys…you know…done it yet?" Vanessa's gaze weighed me, watching my reaction.

I recoiled at the notion she would have even considered I had lost my virginity. "Oh my God, no!" My response seemed to overstate my sentiments on the topic, even to myself. I watched the grape leaves swaying in the breeze as I deliberated asking Vanessa the same question. "You?"

"With Sergio? Not that. Not yet." She curled up a corner of her mouth and shrugged. "But we've done other stuff. How about you and Max?"

"Kissing…and some touching but not much else. I mean…we practically just met."

"Anyway, Massimo wanted me to tell you his brother is lending him his car tomorrow. He wants to know if you can get away for a while—go for a drive in the mountains so he can show you around. I don't know what you need to do but maybe tell your mom? Give her warning?"

"Are you going, too?"

"No. Sergio and I are going on a picnic with his little sister. He has his own car," she said proudly.

"Oh. Maybe we can double date one day?"

"Of course, but in the meantime, make

arrangements for tomorrow. Massimo said you would be gone most of the afternoon."

****

That evening, it was all I could do to stop myself from screaming *hurry up* to my aunt at dinner. The trays of food came slower and slower as the wine flowed into the glasses.

"Okay, *Zia* Carla, *Zio* Mario, Mom, Daddy—I'm going to hang out with my friends. I'll see you later."

"Whoa, hang on there." My father held up a hand to halt me. "Who are these friends of yours you're disappearing to every night we've been here. I know almost everyone in Pescaglia." He looked at my aunt and uncle for insight. "Can they be kids from families I would know?"

Mario shrugged. "Probably. They hang around in the piazza in the evening, have ice cream, talk. Don't worry, nobody will steal her away."

"What?" He put both hands in the air, the ash from his cigarette falling softly to the ground. "I'm simply making sure she's—"

"Come on, Tony." Carla shook her head and smirked. "She's fine. Let her enjoy herself."

Mom's gaze was a bit more cautious. "You behave, now," she warned, wagging a finger.

I spent the evening cutting up with Max and about a dozen other kids from Pescaglia outside of the gelato bar in the piazza. I barely kept up with the speed of the quips and anecdotes, but I did find another reason to fall for Massimo—he was inherently funny.

Donna Summer moaned on the jukebox as they exchanged stories about their previous summers in the small town.

"Do you remember the Austrian tourist, a couple of years ago?" Sergio sat on the edge of the retaining wall next to Vanessa, roaring with laughter at the memory. "You've got to hear this, Sofia—you'll die laughing. He went to buy cheese up at Damiani's farm and…"

"Come on, Sergio. Stop laughing and tell the story." Vanessa giggled.

"I'll tell it, he's on the verge of peeing himself." Massimo smiled as he shook his head. "Anyway, it was three years ago, before my father's accident. This Austrian tourist, pink-faced with a blond buzz cut, came to the farm to buy cheese. Someone in the town must have told him about us—my father used to make it himself…anyway, this guy let himself into the corral, not thinking anything of it, like he owns the place." Max pulled the Marlboro's from his shirt pocket, stuck one in his teeth, and lit the end, taking a long drag for effect, then put his arm around my neck.

"As a sideline, we had a bull we used to keep to stud." He pulled me closer and gave me a wet kiss on the cheek, looking directly at me. "He was a lot like me in the stud department, very much in demand."

"Oh, you're such a conceited asshole." Vanessa laughed.

"That's my boy," shouted Sergio.

All the boys laughed, while some of the girls snickered and rolled their eyes.

"Anyway, finish the story," I said, doing some eye-rolling of my own.

"So he lets himself in, and the bull sees him. He's wandering around the corral, clueless about the bull. Next thing, I hear these shrieks, like little girl shrieks, coming from the—"

"Sofia!" A booming voice cut through from the left of the group. It was my father's.

I shot up, pushing Max's arm from my shoulder. An awkward silence hung in the air, as the three of us exchanged tense looks.

"Who's your friend?" he asked me, but his eyes were sternly on Max.

I gulped. *This is what happens when you get sloppy.* "My friends are," I began pointing them out. "...Sara, Katia, Vanessa, Sergio, and this is Massimo." He was standing next to me. Max extended his hand to my father, who took it half-heartedly.

"You're Maria and Salvo's boy."

"Yes, sir. Nice to meet you."

My father nodded and broke the handshake. "You, too." Dad turned to me, stone-faced. "Time to come home, Sofia," then stood and waited.

"But it's early—"

"Now." I knew by his tone there would be no quarter on this one.

"I'll see you all later," I mumbled, stepping out of the circle with my eyes downcast and my face certainly turning a crimson red. The horrible sensation I would burst into tears right there and embarrass myself in front of the entire Pescaglia teen contingent nipped at my insides.

Unwilling to reveal my anger to the others, I turned and walked briskly back down to the house, with my father close behind.

"I can't believe what you did, Daddy." My voice emerged in hiccups as I stomped down the incline to the familiar patio. "You embarrassed me in front of everyone."

"Hey, what's going on?" Mom was outside, shaking the crumbs off a tablecloth. "Why are you two fighting?"

"Your daughter was sitting in the middle of the piazza, letting some boy grope her."

"What? You what?" Mom's face twisted to a grimace.

"Oh, come on, Daddy." My eyes darted from my dad to my mom and back again. "Massimo had his arm around me. That's all. He had his arm over my shoulders." Then with a huffing breath, "I'm going to be sixteen in a few months."

With fists curled, I led the way into the house and plopped down hard at the kitchen table, my parents in tow.

"Who is the boy?" Aunt Carla's voice floated down from the bedrooms, but within moments she was with the other adults in the kitchen.

"Oh my God, this is so embarrassing." I covered my face with my hands.

"His name is Massimo," answered my father. "Do you know him?"

"Hmm, well I—"

"Please!" I shouted.

An uneasy silence fell over the room, then they began.

Dire warnings followed about the perils of the local boys, my virtue, and how easily I would be duped.

"Sofia, dearest, you are a sweet girl, but you come from a very different place."

"The boys here are sly—"

"You must be wary—"

"They are only words—"

"Okay, I get it," I barked. "I understand. We're just hanging out. Having a little fun."

"Make sure you're not having too much fun." My father furrowed his brow. "Stay away from him. I don't want you to get hurt. I don't want my baby getting hurt."

"He won't, Daddy. I know he won't."

"Oh, by the way," he said sternly. "Don't make any plans for next week. We are going to Florence. You might even learn a thing or two."

Away from him, again. All I could do was close my eyes and wish I were older. I wished everyone would leave us alone. Being in love and having no control over my own life was enough to make me want to scream at the top of my lungs.

****

When the dust settled from the disaster in the piazza, I had to scramble to think of a plan to be able to piece together some time for myself and Max, and the answer came in the form of my cousin, Simona. Since Simona was older, she had other interests and had grown beyond the piazza life of the rest of the youth in the village. But she did have her own Vespa, her own way out of town.

"Simona." I caught up with her later in her bedroom as she was applying fresh red nail polish to her toes. "I need to ask you something in the strictest confidence. There is a boy in the village—"

"Massimo?"

My mouth hung open. "You know?"

"Of course. And so does everyone else in town. It's an Italian village—everyone knows everybody else's business. Probably wondering how long he's going to hold on to you."

"How terrible." I grimaced.

"It happens around here—a lot. Girls come here on vacation and go home with a broken heart. The boys know how to talk to foreigners. They sweet talk."

"Well, it's not like that for us." My tone was defensive.

"I'm sure it isn't," said Simona, finishing off her little toe. The bedroom fell silent and was suddenly stifling.

"Well…" I started again. "I was wondering if you could cover for me tomorrow afternoon. Max is borrowing his brother's car. Taking me to a lookout in the mountains."

"Aw. Sure, I'll do it. Anything for love…and my little cousin. It might be best if you meet him somewhere. I can take you wherever you decide to meet."

I thanked her profusely and hugged her immensely, hoping what she said about boys and sweet talk was a truth only for others.

****

At two the next afternoon, Simona and I rode the short distance to the bend in the road, facing away from Pescaglia, and met Max there. He was waiting in his brother's Fiat 500, listening to an Italian love song playing on the car radio, slow and romantic.

"Thank you, Simona," I said as I dismounted. "I'll meet you back here at five."

Simona nodded her reply and turned to Max with a half smile. "*Ciao*, Massimo. Please, don't be an asshole. She's American—not used to the likes of you." Then to me, "Don't do anything stupid." She kicked the bike into gear, turned, and roared down the hillside toward Lucca.

Max got out of the car and walked over to me. He grasped hold of my hand and his lips touched my forehead, which aligned perfectly in height with his mouth.

"Are you ready, *amore mio?*"

Amore mio...he said, amore mio. "My love." "Absolutely," I responded. Our fingers linked, and he led me to the car, helping me in.

"Here, listen to this new song on the radio. It's by *Le Orme*—amazing." He sang along, off-key as he grasped my hand and brought it to his mouth, me still reeling at his openness and ease.

Twenty minutes into the drive, he turned the car into a side road, then veered onto a dirt path, which squeezed the 500 with overgrown shrubbery and tall trees on either side. To my delight, the clearing up ahead produced a stunning view of the greenest valley.

"Oh my God," I exclaimed as my eyes scanned the vista. "How did you find this place? The view is incredible." I looked over at him. He had moved his seat back and had reached over, pressing the release on mine, so I had more legroom.

My heart jumped in my throat. *This is it. This is where it's going to happen.*

"It's about fifty meters from a popular trekking trail up to the mountain. My brother comes here with his fiancée...you know...to be alone." Max stroked my hair gently as he spoke, then found my lips and traced them with his thumb. "Sofie," he said, his voice had a robust quality, "I've fallen in love with you."

As I considered I was probably about to lose my

virginity, sensations so foreign to me, up until I had met Max, took over my system. I trembled with excitement. My breathing deepened. "Oh, Max, I love you, too." His hand slid to the nape of my neck.

"You're so beautiful." In an instant, we were holding each other, his hands in my hair, pressing my face close to his heart. Feeling almost wanton, I sensed the emotions simmering inside me and let myself savor his luscious kisses. I was home—in his strong woodchopper's arms.

Max swept me up and kissed my skin as he lifted me effortlessly over to his side of the Fiat. I was lost in the headiness of the moment, my arms around him, my fingers knotted in his hair. We were all hands and kisses and impulse.

Slowly, we opened our eyes, still close enough to feel the warmth of each other's breath on our mouths, still filled with the tender emotions of joy and delight, of our newly forged love. Max turned and slowly set me back down onto my seat, not taking his dark eyes off me, still holding me close.

"Sofie, reach into my back pocket."

A smile crept across my lips. *He's so sweet. He has some little thing for me.*

My hand glided gently down his back. I slid my fingers into his jeans back pocket and tucked into the pocket fold, I touched a smooth wrapper. My fingers skimmed over it. It had a soft, circular something inside it. A rush of indecision and embarrassment swept over me.

Gingerly, I pulled the condom from his pocket and looked beyond his face to the small black and purple packet I held up. Blood rushed to my cheeks.

This is it, do I or don't I.

"Sofie...I love you. I want to show you how much I love you." He linked fingers with my other hand and kissed the edge of my jaw up to my ear.

"I love you, too." I looked at the condom, then looked back at him, deliberating. His eyes were weighing my every word, every movement as The Moody Blues ethereal "Knights in White Satin" floated from the car radio, filling the spaces between us. "I've never done it before. I've never, you know..."

"I figured you didn't. I don't want to pressure you if you don't want to."

"But I do want to. I want to...with you." I was nervous. A thousand questions descended on me. What would it feel like? Was I being bad if I did it? I was narrowly fifteen, after all. What would my friends think? Tracey, my best friend, had lost her virginity when she was fourteen, and then the boy broke up with her.

"I want to be the closest two people can be, *mio amore*." He kissed me and stroked my hair as I still held the condom. "Trust me."

My thoughts were a muddle, a confused jumble of sexually heightened raw emotions, deeply rooted parental warnings, and indoctrinated catholic guilt. What was I supposed to do? I loved him, and he said he loved me. I was deeply aroused, there was no doubt, and I wanted to make love to him so badly. Not just have sex, but make love, as I always thought I would for the first time. With the boy I loved.

I trusted him because he never gave me a reason not to. But I had only known him for two weeks. I lived in New Jersey, and he lived here. If I said yes and lost it to him, what would happen in two weeks when I had to go home? Did I care?

Do it. You love him and want him. Just do it.

One of my hands moved of their own accord. I watched it as though in slow motion. It reached for the other end of the condom wrapper, and with a sharp tug, the little package opened.

"My love," Max whispered in my ear. "You won't regret it." He moved lithely onto my car seat, moving on top of me but taking care not to crush me. He caressed my neck with his lips as I looked up and out the window. Overhead, a plane glided silently high up in the blue sky, a stream of puffy white smoke trailing behind.

"Won't I?" Abruptly, the words blurted out, as unexpectedly as my fingers had torn open the condom wrapper mere moments ago. The years I spent listening to Sister Mary Martin's warnings in her religion classes in parochial school had all come tumbling back to haunt me.

"Max, I don't know if I can."

There was a brief look of frustration on his face. He paused, his eyes changing from desire to disappointment, and then, as fluidly as he moved toward me, he slid back onto the driver's seat.

My head rested on his arm, as I lay there, waiting anxiously, scrutinizing his every move, watching for his reaction. Eventually, he pulled me over toward him, so my head lay on his heart. I listened to it, as it beat out his disappointment. "Toss it away." He kissed my hairline. "Throw the thing away."

I turned the condom over in my fingers, gazing at it as though I was about to throw away a trophy, an invitation to a "members-only" society reserved for those who had abandoned themselves to love and lust. Then I looked up at Max and never felt more love for him. As I tossed the unused condom out the car window into the overgrown shrubbery, I thought maybe, just maybe, I may reconsider my decision before I left.

We spent the rest of the afternoon in the car overlooking the valley, talking, kissing, touching, and whispering words of undying love. I told him I had to go away again, but I hoped the absence would go by quickly, so I could spend the rest of my time with him. When it was time to go, we made plans to meet again later, as we did every evening in the piazza. I tried not to dwell that when I returned from Florence, we would only have a few days left.

Chapter Eight

A couple of days after our afternoon in the mountains, my parents and I left for Florence for nearly a week. The entire time I was there, all I thought about was Max, how his words made me feel like a woman. Then I thought about what Simona said about him and Vanessa's question. I trusted him. How could anyone lie so well?

Any other boy I had been with was so awkward and immature, like the ones at the high school dances, who were even too afraid to ask girls to dance. They were such pussies, so stupidly childish—I doubted I could ever be interested in anyone other than Max ever again. He had spoiled me. He wasn't a boy or an adolescent—he was years beyond them. He had a job, commitments, and responsibilities to his family. He was a mature young man in the way he spoke to me, touched me, and treated me, and I could not be more attracted to him.

Five days in Florence were a dragging blur of art galleries, museums, gardens, palaces, and restaurants all melded into one big event. I missed Max so much it hurt. The only distinguishing marker was the morning we were to return to Pescaglia.

I understood, of course—Mom and Daddy wanted to show me the "cradle of the Renaissance" as they put it, but I couldn't appreciate it because the way I saw it, it was five days away from an already too short a time with Max.

As my father drove the twisting roads back to the village, I wondered what Max had been doing while I was gone. My mind wandered as endless rows of vineyards and olive trees rushed by the car window.

****

The butterflies in my belly were alive and well, as I anxiously waited in the piazza that evening, anticipating seeing him swagger over to me and scoop me up in a hug.

"Don't worry," said Vanessa reassuringly. "He'll be here. He's been working a lot in Camaiore while you've been away."

I pushed down my anticipation, so I wouldn't look foolish. Then, at nearly ten, when I had almost given up hope, he approached from the main road, dressed in jeans and a polo shirt, his hair carelessly blowing in the breeze, a cigarette between his fingers. When Max saw me, he gestured and walked over in a way he would have if he had seen me five hours ago, not five days ago. I got up and went to him.

"*Ciao*, Sofie." His voice was calm and even, as he took my hand and gave me a peck on the lips. "How was Florence?"

I abandoned all vigilance and wrapped my arms around his neck, breathing in his heavenly scent, wanting to make up for time lost. "It was everything I heard it would be—amazing. But I couldn't stop thinking about you."

"What did you miss most about me?" he asked, gently grasping the back of my arms. "Tell me." He cocked his head anticipating my answer.

"I missed being near you, your voice, your laugh." I looked shyly down at my sandals. "Everything about you."

"Why are you looking at your feet?" He cupped my chin to face him. "Tell me."

I struggled to figure out the words. "What shall I say?" Though I said it with a smile, the answer was almost flat, anticlimactic. Yes, I loved him, yes, I missed him, yes, he moved me in ways I'd never dreamed I could be moved deep inside my core. When he touched me, I felt exhilarated, beautiful, womanly. Yet despite it all, I had no idea why, right now, I wasn't ready to give myself to him all the way. "Isn't that enough?"

Max's face conveyed mild surprise. He breathed out noisily. "I guess it will have to be."

It was almost imperceptible, a fleeting look in his eyes, and then it was gone, but I detected it. Again, a momentary look of disappointment and frustration.

Vanessa and Sergio were sitting on the retaining wall, arm in arm, whispering, and snuggling. "Hey," Vanessa called out. We both turned at once. "Want to come to the movies with us tomorrow night? They're showing *Jaws*."

I took a deep breath. "I'll try to get away, but—"

"Can't you just tell your parents you're going? You need a little bit of courage, Sofie." Max's tone was blunt. He let go of my hands and searched in his pocket for his cigarettes. Once lit, he strolled over to Sergio's car and leaned on the trunk. His behavior seemed cold.

"I'll try."

"Great! Done," declared Vanessa and resumed snuggling herself into Sergio's neck.

I walked gingerly over to where Max was sitting, as he stared up at the stars, placing myself between him and the sky, so he couldn't help but look at me. "I'm sorry, Max," I said, searching his eyes for a sign of redemption.

"What for?" he asked teasingly. "Telling the truth? Give me your hands." He gazed at them, caressing them. "You have the most beautiful hands. Delicate. Soft." He kissed my palms and then guided them around his waist, bringing me closer to him as he sat on the edge of Sergio's car. "Sit beside me."

I complied. My head rested just under his chin.

"I work tomorrow in Camaiore again, but I'll be back in plenty of time for the movie."

I looked at the inky heavens, reassured by his words. "I can't wait." I sighed, then reached up to stroke his hair, clean and smooth and dark as the night sky.

****

Richard Dreyfuss, Roy Scheider, and Robert Shaw had barely launched the boat into the wide-open sea when Max took my shoulder, pulled me close, and kissed me. The four of us were seated at the back of the theatre, away from prying eyes, so the kisses kept coming, one more passionate than the last.

At one point, Max slipped his hand down my shirt and into my Dici bra, cupping my breast in his hand. I discreetly pushed his hand away, hissing at him to stop. Just then, up on the screen, Roy Scheider fired the final shot into the scuba tank, and the great white shark exploded into a million pieces. The theatre jumped, but the thrill was lost on me.

Was I being a prude? Or did it not seem the

appropriate thing to do, put a hand down my top when surrounded by dozens of shrieking Italians?

Once out of the theatre, we walked to Sergio's car. "I should be getting home," I said. "My parents said not too late."

"Oh, come on, Sofia—it's early yet. Let's go for a *granita*," begged Vanessa.

"There's a place around the corner—we can walk," added Sergio.

Max held my hand loosely, smoking his cigarette, his gaze focused on the cobblestones as he walked. I thought a moment about how I sounded like a broken record.

"I guess it'll be okay," I replied, hoping Max would welcome my rebellious moment.

After our lemon *granita* was done, we piled into the car and headed home, much later than expected.

When the car rounded the corner into Pescaglia and then up to the wall above my relative's house, my parents were waiting outside. They looked like they had been waiting a while, with eyes ready to throw daggers our way.

Daddy didn't wait for me to step out of the car. "Where the hell were you?" His voice echoed off the walls in the piazza as he approached the car.

"Shh! Not so loud," cautioned Mom. "Do you want everyone to know our business?"

"I don't care." He waved the notion away, then focused on Max, who was stoically exiting the car. "What do you think you're doing with my daughter?"

"Oh my God, Daddy," I wailed. "We only went to the movies and then for ice cream. Why can't you just let me—"

"It's all right, Sofia, never mind," said Max calmly, raising his hands in surrender. He turned on his heel and walked away up the incline, toward his house at the top of the darkened village.

"Daddy, it's barely past midnight!" I cried.

"Be quiet," snapped my father.

"I think we'll go now," said Vanessa, her eyes darting from me to my parents and then back to me. "Are you going to be okay?"

My head bobbed up and down. "I'll be fine." All the while my father was nattering in the background, and my mother was agreeing with him. "I'll see you tomorrow." I watched, mortified, as my friends hastily entered the car and drove up into the village.

In a flash, I descended the stairs and sprung into my relatives' house as if shot into it by a giant bow. I ran upstairs to my room, inconsolable, and wondered if Juliet Capulet suffered this way when her parents forbade her to see Romeo.

I didn't see Max the next day, or the next. Though I was hardly ever by myself, I had never been so alone.

Chapter Nine

Two days passed.

Max knew I would be going back home on Saturday. This fact troubled me most of all. What had I done to make him stay away? I should have admonished my father for being such a manipulator. Did I say something wrong? Or maybe I didn't say enough?

Everyone was in the piazza. Vanessa, Sergio, Katia, Claudio, everyone but Max.

Simona's often sharp remarks made no secret of her annoyance with Max. "Forget him. He's being an asshole. Just like all the other guys in this godforsaken country of assholes."

Seeing my pain, Simona offered some hope. "Listen, I know for sure he'll be back tomorrow night. It's the festival of Santa Maria here in the village—a big deal. He wouldn't miss it. You can talk to him then about why he's being such a piece of crap."

****

Pescaglia was bustling with activity the next day in preparation for the procession of the Madonna in the Moonlight. It was a big *festa* celebrating the town's patron saint—Saint Mary. There would be a communal feast, a band, and dancing after a nighttime procession of the Madonna through the streets of Pescaglia. Large tables were set up in the piazza to accommodate everyone in the village.

But all was lost on me. Inside, I was desperately sad.

In a last attempt to make Max fall madly in love with me again, I applied some makeup and chose my nicest peasant top, paired with my tightest bell-bottom jeans to attend the feast.

The mass was a long drawn out affair, in a packed little church built to hold no more than about a hundred people but was bursting at the seams with villagers and visitors from nearby communities.

At the end of the service, when the men hoisted the carrier posts on their shoulders and started the procession, I crossed the church threshold and scanned the courtyard for Max. There he was, achingly beautiful, watching the statue gliding past.

Doing my best to look reverent, I walked behind the statue and caught his eye as the crowd moved slowly beyond the church steps.

His wink and nod made my heart pound with a familiar longing. I wanted him to defy my father, to take me away and make me his. I knew now I would do this for Max. Having tasted a morsel of life without him, I didn't much like the flavor.

He sidled up beside me as I fell back from my relatives. "How are you?" he asked in a cordial tone, his gaze focused straight ahead.

"Not great." The response was brisker than I would have liked. "Where have you been? Did my father frighten you that much? I thought you would have come."

"I've been working—in Camaiore." He crushed a cigarette under his leather loafers and peered down at me. "My brother-in-law has a new contract—I can't just leave him."

"You're working into the night in Camaiore? I waited for you until eleven."

"I know. I'm sorry. I'm tired by then. All I want is to get cleaned up and go to bed."

There was a pause as I considered his reasoning. My heart wanted to believe, but I knew he was lying to me. He commandeered his friend's Vespa to get to me at one point, but he couldn't muster up enough energy to be with me in my last days in Pescaglia?

He had turned a corner, somewhere, somehow, and I was determined to find out why.

"Max, do you realize I only have tonight and tomorrow here and then I go home? I have to go back. That's all we have."

He nodded slowly, pacing his steps so they mirrored mine. "I work during the day, but I will come later. I'll be here tomorrow night. I promise."

He stayed until the end of the procession and then disappeared for the rest of the night. The remainder of the evening was spent with my family. The feast of Saint Mary was a national holiday in Italy. He was most certainly not working on a national feast day.

Brokenhearted, I managed to sit beside Vanessa after the feast—if I didn't talk to someone about it, I would burst into tears. Dark desolation, and the realization I had lost him, etched itself into my brain.

"Are you having a good time?" Vanessa took my hand and squeezed it. An unspoken understanding was shared between the two of us.

I tried to lie and say "yes" but couldn't. "Max said he would come tomorrow—to say goodbye." It took everything I had to admit what I was thinking. "Listen, Vanessa, if I speak the words, if I express my suspicion, then it might be real. He's avoiding me."

Vanessa breathed in, and tugged at her hair, looking like she was debating a thought. "Look…I have to tell you. My sister…she said she thinks he's met someone—in Camaiore. She's not sure but his brother seems to think so. You know…because I asked why he was being such a jerk. Massimo is being pretty tight-lipped about it."

The world fell out from under my feet. The small string of hope I clung to severed, and it was a long fall for me into the abyss of teen despair. Was this true? How could this have happened? His actions, his words; he said he loved me, and now he was with another girl? No, I couldn't believe it. I wouldn't.

"Did they see him with her?" I demanded.

"No, but—I mean, it's pretty obvious, don't you think?"

I listened to the music coming from the small band in the piazza and thought about Vanessa's words. I watched people talk and laugh. I watched as they danced, ate, and drank. The world went on, people breathed, joked, and loved, but my world was crumbling in ruins. It was as though I had left my body and was standing beside myself, watching it happen.

This was my heart breaking. Now I knew what all the love songs were about. This was what it felt like to ache for someone, to hurt with no wounds on your body to show for the pain.

****

I didn't sleep that night—I kept visualizing Max with someone else. He was laughing with her, holding her hand, stroking her hair. The images blistered my senses. Though I wanted to push the thoughts far away, they kept coming back, haunting me in my mind's eye.

The day after, I packed, spent time with my relatives, then sought out Vanessa, who had no kind things to say about Max. She expressed an affinity to my sentiments of rejection and disillusionment when it came to boys, though she and Sergio were perfectly happy. I knew she was being supportive, but I was positively lime green with envy.

After dinner, I ventured up to the piazza, in my mind now a sacred shrine to mine and Max's short, impassioned relationship. A teen relationship fraught with snatched opportunities, immense passion, mystery, and unanswered questions.

I made a pact with myself not to cry, no matter what. To be stern and as emotionally detached as he, if he would be that way—if not, then I would have to improvise my reactions.

My friends all knew it was my last night there, so they congregated gregariously, joking, and talking about coming to America to visit. They had treated me with a last *granita al limone* when Max emerged from the archway into the town square. He wore jeans, a light navy sweater, and leather loafers, looking fine as ever.

Max had the same confident, self-assured swagger that irritated the hell out of me yet was so irresistible I couldn't look away. Spotting me with a sideways glance, he walked over and sat next to me on the retaining wall. I remained composed, though all I wanted to do was wrap him in my arms and tell him I still loved him.

I looked his way, and our eyes met. His had a sad,

distant quality. Was he melancholy for me? Knowing what he had done to me? I wished I knew what he was feeling; what he was thinking underneath his overconfident exterior.

"*Ciao*, Sofia," he said, then he licked his lips and took a drag from his cigarette. "How are things?"

I moved my hand over his as it rested on the ancient stones on the wall. It was warm and familiar. I missed the feel of his skin. "I've been better." I swallowed hard and clenched my teeth because a lump began forming at the back of my throat, and if I didn't keep it in check, I would make a fool of myself in front of him and the rest of my friends. It was the last thing I wanted—to allow him the satisfaction of knowing how deeply I was still in love with him. "I leave tomorrow morning…early. For Rome."

He nodded, his gaze falling to the ground. *Of course, you can't face me, can you?*

"It's why I'm here tonight," he answered with staid calmness.

I fell silent, squeezed my lips together, and looked at the same spot on the ground, having a million things to say to him, but unable to say anything.

Vanessa and Sergio walked over arm in arm, recounting some event they shared. All I heard was buzzing in my ears, the drone of ascending reality that these few minutes would be the last I would ever share with him. I wasn't at all ready to let him go—to go back and let him go on to the next girl. How could I board a plane, fly back to Hoboken, and pretend to live my life as I did before? Everything had changed, in a matter of weeks.

"Look." Max took a deep breath and squeezed my

hand. "I'm sorry things didn't work out. But…maybe it's for the best…you know. You in America, me here…"

A grimace tried to creep over my face. "Things didn't work out," I slowly repeated. How cliché—*maybe it's for the best? Whose best?*

He nodded, then forced a smile. "Come on. I'll walk you back to your aunt's place." He turned, waiting for me, but didn't take my hand.

"I'm going to say goodbye to Vanessa and everyone else first. Wait for me at the arch." I watched as he tossed his cigarette to the ground, crushed it, and headed to the archway.

My eyes stung as soon as I turned to my friend. "Well, I guess this is it." I reached for her and hugged her for a long time.

Vanessa clung to me. "I wish you could stay longer." Then in a hushed voice, so no one else could hear, "I'm so sorry he hurt you. I should have told him to go screw himself when he asked me to introduce you."

I pulled away. "Don't be sorry," I said, smiling at her through misty eyes. "I'm glad it happened. But God, it's going to hurt." I sniffed and wiped my cheeks with the backs of my hands. "And I'm going to miss you the most. Thanks for everything. Promise we'll write."

"I'll write the first letter," she assured.

I turned to Sergio and held up my index finger in stern warning. "Be kind to her, or you'll hear from me." I hugged him, waved, and blew a kiss to the rest of my friends, then turned to the archway where Max waited, his arms crossed.

When I approached, he pushed himself off the ancient bricks and walked with me, matching his steps to mine. "So what time do you leave tomorrow?" His tone was obligatory.

"At seven a.m. We're catching a train from Lucca to Rome, then staying there overnight." *This is all very polite. Max and me conversing calmly about my travel plans, while my insides are being ripped out.*

We headed toward the end of the street to the stairs leading down to my aunt's house. I wanted to touch him so badly; the lips that kissed me so passionately, the arms which had held me so close I could hardly breathe; but his hands were in his pockets, so I couldn't even accidentally bump hands and lock fingers with him.

We stopped at the bend, each standing uncomfortably in the silence, broken intermittently by the song of crickets. Conversation was effortless with him before. Now, I didn't even know him, like it was a chore for him to be with me. How could I put all these emotions into words, without giving up my pride to him?

There was a long awkward silence, neither of us willing to speak before the other. Then, he began the inevitable last goodbye. "So like I said—I'm sorry, Sofia." He faced me square on, his gaze meeting mine. "I'm going to wish you a good trip home now and—"

"Wait," I interrupted, as my hands instinctively reached for his arms. "You can't end it like this without telling me why. You can't do this to me, make me fall in love with you and…and then take it all away."

Max broke eye contact and stared beyond me, angling his head to see past me. "Believe it or not, I've been thinking about us. You know I didn't want to fall in love with you."

My heart jumped with the faintest of hopes. I let my expression soften as the words spilled out of my mouth. "I know. Oh my God, Max…I didn't even know these feelings were possible. Those first days were—"

"I know, but now you are going home," he interrupted. "Across an ocean and it will all be over. I've known since the first time we met you would be here a few short weeks but…"

I tried to rally with a shaky grin but didn't succeed. "Is this why you've been like this? Is this why you haven't talked to me? Why you've ignored me?" I grabbed his arms, but my fingers didn't go halfway around them. "People have been saying—"

"Listen, whatever it is they are saying, it doesn't matter."

"Yes, it does," I protested. "Look, never mind all that—what's important is this does not have to end. We can write, talk on the phone—"

"But it will never be the same, Sofie. I won't…" He looked frustrated, and he paused as if trying to organize his thoughts. "The times you went away, especially the last time…I realized it couldn't be the same. I won't be able to see your face or…or know you're just on the other side of the piazza. Sofie, I can't do it."

Panic rose inside me as the impending doom of finality hit me square in the face. Somewhere in the distance, an owl hooted, and then a cool gust of wind came up from the valley and brushed up against us like a gloomy prophecy.

"But…but I don't want to say goodbye." My voice

was small, insignificant.

Max shook his head and looked at the ground. A faint laugh followed a slight smile, then, "It was a thing—just a thing," he said.

At this, my heart plummeted. "Just a thing?" I blinked. My mouth was wide open in disbelief, yet I pressed on. "You told me you loved me. Now you're turning your back on me. Letting me go and not even going to try to communicate with me?" My voice tried hard not to break as my thoughts and senses were busy working through this first shattered heart.

"I did love you," he said, looking me in the eye, trying to prove he wasn't lying. "But things change."

Which would win, my pride or my love for him? My judgment or my need for him?

I put my hands on his chest and let my arms slide around his neck. I held him, with no dignity left, stripped down to a need to believe this last hug would suddenly turn things around and make him come to his senses. Make him say "Oh, yes…You were right all along. I really do love you." Or maybe "Please don't go—it'll kill me if you go." I waited to hear the words, but they never came.

"Hey, come on." Max looked down at me. He took my arms from his neck and placed them at my side.

We stood, awkwardly silent, an arm's length apart. Something was happening between us. It was an exchange of, for lack of a better word, awareness, understanding. I closed my eyes, and then I knew in my heart, it was time. It was done.

Don't do it. Don't you cry. Walk away and don't let him see you cry.

Of all the things I had done in my life up until this

moment, this was the most confusing, most heart wrenching, and most important. But he must not see me cry. Crying I would save for later. Now was the time to walk away.

Determinedly, I backed away from him, my eyes still locked on his. I waited for him to say something. Anything.

"I should be going then." His tone was chilly, businesslike.

I took a deep breath of the cooling night air and held it in my lungs. "Me too. With pleasure," I said, my head held high. Without hesitation, I turned on my heel and walked to the corner away from his sight line.

Once past, I put a hand to my mouth to keep the sobs in until I reached the patio of my aunt's house. Once there, I allowed myself the luxury of bleeding the wound, crying the tears, until there was nothing left inside of me to cry anymore.

I was a child, yes, but it was true that sensitivities experienced in youth are the most powerful, the most inflexible.

The flight home could not have been more melancholy—this was the definitive break. You couldn't get more apart than living on another continent. I mean, there wasn't even hope of the occasional chance meeting at the library or the movies or the mall.

My gaze went beyond the window and through fat, salty tears. A stratum of clouds spread beneath me. I had no idea where I was, but I knew all I wanted to do was to go home.

The tears came and went for the next few months. There was still an extraordinary void in my heart like a piece had been wrenched away from it. But slowly the sharp edge of pain became dull. In retrospect, I cried over the hurt—the real hurt in my body, the ache of emptiness. But I was also angry because I believed I had no control over my life after Max.

Over the next year, my love for Max became less entrenched, less in the foreground, though still present. I still found myself thinking of him every day. Sleep made things better—when I slept, I didn't miss him, didn't feel any pain. I longed for sleep because sometimes, I would dream of him.

Sometimes talking about him with my Hoboken friends brought him closer, sometimes I was thankful the cutting edge of pain dampened, and still other times, I was glad to feel it—at least I knew what I experienced in Italy the summer of '76 was real.

As much as I tried to forget him, I gave him control of my state of mind, and I would spend my life trying to get it back. Deep down I wondered if I would weigh every relationship, compare it, contrast it to mine and Max's.

Chapter Ten

Saint Joseph's Hospice, Present Day

Though thinking back on all the shit he put me through when we were kids resulted in me wanting to slap him silly. I still had to keep the reason I was there at the top of my mind. All that crap happened a long time ago. *Stay cool.*

He held my hand for a long time. So I stayed. Not daring to leave, I remained with Max into the wee hours.

But when he didn't rouse at all, and I thought my back was going to break on the uncomfortable hospital chair, I had to give in. I figured if anything happened, I was close enough to be back at the hospice within minutes. Jet-lagged and exhausted, I tucked the blankets around him and quietly stepped out of the room. I left my cell phone and hotel number with the duty nurse and went back to the inn. I needed to get some sleep. The ancient winding streets back to Hotel Barberi were deserted, the windows dark. The desolation increased my melancholy, which clung to me like a cloak. And I was powerless to let it fall to the floor.

There were no phone calls during the night. They say no news is good news, or at least my mom always said, so I figured that was good news. I was back at the hospice and in Max's room by nine. I had just come from the pantry with ice chips when his eyes quivered opened.

"Good morning, handsome," I cooed casually. "Sleep well?"

"Sofia?" His face bore confusion. "W—when did you get here?"

Must be the morphine. "Uhm, this morning? Got here about twenty minutes ago." I circled around the bed and kissed his forehead. "They were doing your vitals, so I went to grab you some ice. But I arrived late yesterday. We talked a little, then you nodded off and on." I pulled the chair closer and sat next to him, so we were both facing the window. "I stayed for a while, hoping you'd wake up, but you had other plans. Went back to the hotel and slept."

"I'm sorry." He held up an open hand. "Yes…I…I remember now."

"Don't be sorry." My hand slid into his. "I stayed with you, read to you." I smiled teasingly. "Then you started talking in your sleep."

Max's eyes narrowed playfully. "What did I say?"

"You whispered something about a walk in the piazza, and then you mentioned Camillo's—"

"Please tell me I didn't." His voice was little more than a murmur, but he spoke with a smile on his lips.

"Uh, yeah, you did." I laughed softly. "You sparked some memories. When you mentioned the piazza, I had an avalanche of them come back to me—our early days in Pescaglia."

He squeezed my hand. "It was a good thing then? For you to remember?"

"I'll say bittersweet." I looked down at the floor,

laughing softly. "Had to keep from smacking you as you slept."

"Bittersweet," he repeated. "Yes." He turned his face to the window. "Is it the spring?"

"Yes. Gorgeous day. Warm and sunny." I sat closer. "Long Island was still cool, cloudy."

We remained silent for a long moment, pretending to ponder the weather, then I asked the question I had been dreading. "Max, what happened?" I leaned in and spoke softly. "How—how long have you been sick?"

He took in a shallow breath and expelled it. "Last year." He winced. "I had pain in my belly and back. I was losing weight, not eating. Around October, I went to my doctor in Toulouse. I thought I had an ulcer." His mouth was parched, so I reached for the ice chips. "No, the water and sponge." I grabbed the water. He lapped up the few drops I touched to his lips, then continued. "My doctor ran tests. I got the news."

I shook my head slowly. "Is that when your brother came?"

He nodded.

"Did you get treatment?"

"Yes, of course. Eni took care of everything. They sent me to a special clinic in Switzerland. They tried radiation therapy, chemotherapy, immunotherapy, even…what do they call it…hol-hol—"

"Holistic therapy?"

"Yes." His breathing was labored now. "Nothing helped. So I resigned, came back here."

"I remember you mentioned that yesterday…I'm so sorry, Max."

"Stayed as long as I could in Pescaglia before the hospital in Lucca. My mother's old house—do you remember—" Suddenly, his words were halted by a series of frighteningly intense coughs.

"Oh, God!" Panic rose in my throat. I tapped his back and turned him onto his side, eventually lessening the raging attack into ragged, shallow gasps. Soon, nothing but his thin breaths and the hum of machines filled the room. "Maybe you should take it easy."

"I'm better now." He set his head back down on the pillow and looked at the ceiling. "In conclusion, now I am here. Terminal. Hospice. Comfort care only."

His words splintered inside me.

"In the end, it isn't dying that scares me. If I don't wake up in the morning, I will know nothing of it." Max's words now came in a whisper.

"I don't know what to do or say to make it better." I shook my head and pressed his hand against my cheek. "Tell me what to do. Tell me what to say."

He squeezed his eyes shut, then slowly moved his head so he was facing me again. After a long pause, he opened his eyes, and they held a sweet warmth that was elusive earlier. "Enough. Enough about all this. Tell me about you. Talk to me about us."

Terrified, I swallowed and shrugged. "What do you want to know?" I leaned in. "Do you want me to tell you how you spoiled me for any other man? Instead of 'see Rome and die,' it's a 'kiss Massimo and die' type of deal?" I laughed, but I felt stupid. He tried to laugh too, though he looked like he was suffering while doing it.

"Oh, I'm sorry." I clapped a hand over my mouth. "Does that hurt?"

"Everything hurts anyway." He squirmed the minutest amount. "Come now, let me hear your voice.

Talk to me about us."

Confused, I screwed up my mouth a little. "Like…us now?"

"Maybe later. Talk to me about us—you. Before Florence." Max moved his fingers, so they encircled mine.

I understood what he wanted. What he needed. "Well, looking back, I think maybe I was testing myself. I wanted to prove to my adult self I was over you."

"Be honest. Were you?"

"I think so—the teen you. I wasn't prepared for what I found, though, when I came back in '83. I believe, in a way, I was looking for revenge. Maybe deep down, it's what made me apply to my university's studies abroad program, knowing one of the places of study would be in Tuscany. I think I was hoping to run into you—show you I was doing extremely well without you—congratulating myself, convinced I had done a brilliant job of not caring."

"But your hard exterior fell away at the carnival that night, didn't it?" His sly smile was lighthearted. This was the old Max back again.

"Don't flatter yourself, Mr. Damiani." I narrowed my eyes, not having any of it. "I was okay. It took a while, but I started dating. Had plenty of friends. My mind was on other things. High school flew by, then university…Next thing I knew I was preparing my M.B.A. applications…but I was lonely. Even now, looking at my twenty-something self—a void needed to be filled. I wanted to feel what I had experienced with you again. I dated others, but…none of the guys I was with were you."

Chapter Eleven

Florence, Italy, April 1983

I once heard it said, returning to a place is the best way to measure how far you've come. I was twenty-two and officially a post-feminist woman of the eighties. I'd had mature, sexual relationships with several men in college and wanted a life of my own.

I was an adult.

Yet it truly surprised me how much coming back triggered memories of the last time I was there. Before I left Hoboken, I resolved no such thing would happen, yet here I was. All these thoughts churned in the back of my mind as the train persevered through Northern Italy from Paris. I found myself wondering what he was doing now, how he looked. He was probably married, with a kid or two, balding and getting paunchy.

Shit! What is wrong with you? Stop!

The instant I realized my thoughts were on Max, I shook them from my head and considered instead all I had to do once I got to Florence. It was the last leg of a three-month dream university term—my last undergrad semester spent at the University of Syracuse Florence Studies Abroad Program. A three-fold intensive oral language study, starting with one month in Munich, then another in Paris, and the last in Florence—this would be my final month.

As I listened to Stevie Nicks on my Walkman, the train pulled into the Santa Maria Novella station, its brakes screeching painfully to a halt. I pulled down my carry-on bag from the train luggage rack above me—the other larger suitcase, which had served me well as an ottoman on the journey from Paris, would be a bit more daunting. For now, I moved it along with my foot to the exit.

As I unloaded both bags, I instantly felt at home. I knew the language here best. This last part of the three-month course would be a breeze.

Once off the train, I veered left to the side exit, where a lineup of taxis waited against the curb. I rummaged in my purse, searching for the address to my rental apartment, and pulled out a notebook, flipping to a page marked with an elastic. "Okay…here it is." Then looking up, I moved toward the next cab in line. "Hi. Are you available?" Hall and Oates was blasting out of the car radio.

"*Ciao, signorina*. Let me get your bags." The driver scrambled out of the Volkswagen, grabbed my luggage, and loaded it in the trunk.

"24 *Via Fra Domenico*, please."

As I watched the familiar grand lady that was *Firenze* glide by the cab window, I thought about what I would do once I was settled in. The brochure said the university campus was close to the city center, within walking distance of everything, which suited me just fine.

The cab pulled up to the place that would be my home for the next month. Eagerly, I exited the cab as the driver grabbed my suitcases. I looked up at the building—nice enough.

Lumbering up the steps to the entrance, trying to balance my bags was no small feat, but I managed. I buzzed for the superintendent. Within minutes a portly lady, with high black hair and Cadillac red lipstick, opened the glass door.

"*Buona sera*. My name is Sofia Romano—I'm a student at the university...renting here for the month."

"*Buona sera*." She hesitated, looking me up and down. "I'm warning you now: no parties, no drugs."

I raised my brows. "Uh, definitely okay with me. My father sent the month's rent and security deposit already, I believe?"

The lady's expression softened. "Yes." She opened the door wider and waved me in. "All right, come with me."

She led me through a rustic courtyard; grass, paving stones, and pebbles covered the ground in patches. A bicycle leaned up against an old washbasin, while oleander trees in giant terra-cotta pots and miniature fountains adorned the walls.

"Wait here," the lady ordered, disappearing into an office. My mouth curved into a pleased smile as I looked up. The apartments surrounded a positively medieval courtyard, an open-air oasis right in the middle of the complex.

Soon enough, the woman was back. "By the way, I'm Sonia Rossi—I take care of the place." She shuffled to the stairs, which opened to the courtyard. The tiled staircase was edged by a rustic banister that looked like it had been painted over about a million times.

"You're on the third floor." She looked at my bags. "Sorry, we don't have a lift," and started up the stairs.

I deliberated, then decided it would be easier to

make another trip, leaving the large bag at the bottom step.

"I'm usually always here if you need me," Mrs. Rossi added, peering at me over her shoulder.

Once on the third floor, she approached one of two doors—the one on the left. She took a key out of her apron pocket and thrust it into the lock. It opened to a cozy furnished apartment. Red couches splashed color into an ancient space, with whitewashed walls, exposed wooden beams overhead, and burnt sienna terra-cotta tile everywhere.

"That's your kitchen and eating area," she said, indicating the space off the main living, which housed a small kitchen table set against the wall of the galley kitchen. Mrs. Rossi pointed to doors directly across from the small foyer. "There is the bathroom, and in there, your bedroom."

I opened the bathroom door, which revealed a small sink, toilet, bidet, and shower. Next, I peeked into the bedroom. In the middle, was an antique wrought iron double bed, flanked by a couple of creamy white antique night tables. Against the wall stood an armoire, and next to it a small desk. It was positively charming.

My smile widened in approval. "I love it," I said dreamily, setting my small bag down.

"Good," replied Mrs. Rossi, matter-of-factly. "Here are your keys." She held up two. "This one is for the front door; this, to your apartment. Now you'd better go get your other suitcase before someone helps themselves to it."

****

Once I settled in the apartment, I called home. "Hi, Daddy? I'm here! I'm in Florence!" I shouted into the phone—a strange hybrid of the ones back home.

"Hey, baby girl!" Shuffling sounds. "Rita, it's Sofia." Then he shouted back into the phone, "Sofia! We miss you so much, sweetheart. Where are you now?"

"Florence. The landlady brought me up, like…minutes ago, and oh my God, the apartment is beautiful…it's—"

"Sofia! It's Mommy," she hollered. "Are you okay? Are you eating?"

"Of course, I'm eating. Mom, listen…the apartment is awesome. I'm going to take pictures of it and send them to you."

"Okay, baby. We're so proud of you, Sofie, I can't even tell you. Study hard. Make us even more proud. Everyone here says 'hi.' "

"Thanks, Mom. Look, I'd better go, this is going to be a harsh long-distance charge…"

"Wait, Sofia, don't forget what I told you. One weekend you need to visit your Aunt Carla and Uncle Mario up in Pescaglia. Promise you will, they're expecting you to call them. They know you're there."

Shit. I knew she wouldn't forget to ask me. "I will. I'll call them. Maybe I'll get it over with next weekend."

"Never mind 'get it over with,' they're family—"

"All right…yes, Mom. I'm looking forward to seeing them. I'll go."

"That's better. Look I'm giving you to Daddy again. Now, don't go out on your own, lock your door, and don't trust anyone, you hear me? I love you."

"Promise. And I love you, too." Sound advice, Mom; don't trust anyone.

****

The people in my intensive Italian Practicum were nice. They were mature students, as were many of my counterparts in Paris and Munich. The first week raced by, and on Friday, I was back on a train bound for Lucca, which would soon be pulling into the station where my aunt and uncle were to collect me for the weekend.

With a slight screech of rubber, they pulled up to the curb in front of the station. "Sofia! Over here."

I waved and smiled enthusiastically, needing a warm hug more than I wanted to admit, from the next best thing to my mom.

"*Ciao, Zia, Zio*—Aw, it's so good to see you."

"Look how you've grown into a beautiful young woman. Why…a mere seven years ago you were a skinny little girl," cooed my aunt. "My goodness, you are all your mother when she was this age."

"How is your European adventure so far?" Uncle Mario grabbed my overnight bag and walked around to the trunk. "And all your different language courses?"

"Saying 'incredible' wouldn't do it justice. And the experience will be a great addition to my resume, especially for a position with an international bank. I've learned so much, but mostly I think I made the absolute right decision going into business."

"How wonderful." Aunt Carla hugged me again and led me to the car. "Your mother tells me you are awaiting news from a couple of universities—oh, my goodness, she is so excited for you."

"Tell us more about it," urged my uncle as he put my bags in the trunk.

I tried not to gush too much. "Well, I'll be happy

with anything, but I'm hoping for the M.B.A. program at Harvard. Then, hopefully, I'll be able to live in Manhattan one day."

"Very exciting. Come, let's get you to Pescaglia," ordered my uncle as he put the car in first gear, pressed down the clutch, and turned the ignition key. "You still remember the old village from last time you were here, eh?"

"I sure do." The urge to cringe was overwhelming.

"Simona is working today, but she will be back in later tonight. She's a buyer for Benetton now, you know, loves it—oh, and I happened to mention to Vanessa that you were coming. So excited to see you again," my aunt gushed.

Simona, my cousin. Vanessa, my best friend when last I was here. I suspected in my bones Max's specter wasn't too far behind. I sensed an unwelcome blush creep into my cheeks.

"Stop, can't you see you're overwhelming her," said my uncle.

"Oh, poor thing," said Aunt Carla, shaking her head. "Forgive me." Then firmly to my uncle, "Hurry up, Mario. She needs some nice home cooking."

****

"You look amazing!" Simona gasped. "And you've filled out—look at you…you're not a gawky, skinny teenager anymore. You've got boobs!"

I laughed at her forthrightness. "And you at Benetton…what the hell!"

We chatted about old friends and old times over dinner, about school and business, about who was still in the village that I may remember. All the while, both of us avoided the elephant in the room—the tender topic of what became of Massimo Damiani.

"Come, Sofia," ordered Simona after we washed the dishes. "Let's go upstairs and change—incidentally, we're going out tonight. There's a Luna Park in Camaiore this weekend."

"Luna Park?" I grimaced. "Not sure what…"

"You know, games, rides, roller coasters…"

"Oh, you mean a carnival."

"Whatever you Americans call it. It's a distraction. I'm pretty sure Vanessa and everyone else will be there too. It's one of the first signs of spring."

"Okay, Luna Park it is."

I wanted to look casual yet stylish, so I chose my acid-washed denim mini and my off-the-shoulder khaki green sweatshirt, with a neon orange mesh accent top—all wardrobe staples.

Simona drove us down to Camaiore, a relatively large town, where the carnival was abuzz. We found a spot not too far from the midway and walked leisurely to the town square, chatting all the way about my European conversational learning adventures and about Simona's job as an accessories buyer for one of Italy's leading retailers. All the while, I retained my pride and resisted the gnawing temptation of asking her about Max and whatever became of him.

We weren't on the carnival grounds for long when Simona grabbed my elbow. "Oh my God, I don't believe it. Look straight in front of us, over by the shooting game. Do you recognize that guy?"

I didn't have to look. I knew by Simona's tone who it was. I followed her gaze, and that was when my heart nearly jumped out of my chest. It was Max.

I did manage to maintain a casual air, but inside my

stomach was clenched tight as a spring. "Maybe we should turn around, Simona."

"If you want...oh, wait I think he's seen us."

If it was at all possible, he was even more attractive than before. His face had character, and he had filled out of whatever teen gawkiness he may have had with thicker arms and broader shoulders. I also believe he had grown taller.

"Gag me," I whispered. *Breathe, breathe*, I repeated, boldly preparing to meet his gaze.

"Come on," said Simona. "Grow a pair...it'll be fun."

He stood in a semicircle of friends, talking and laughing and smoking. Beside Max was a little boy, tightly holding his hand.

As we got closer, he did a double take, catching Simona and me in his peripheral vision. I imagined the sparks in his brain, desperately trying to connect the dots and instead causing a short circuit.

Almost comedically, his hand stopped at his lips, with the cigarette not quite in his mouth. There was a spark of some indefinable emotion in his eyes for a split second, and then a smile overtook his features. He raised his chin in my direction.

"*Ciao*, Simona, Sofia. Come on over." He flicked the cigarette away and picked up the boy. "I want you to meet my son, Michael."

He looked like a miniature version of Max. Simultaneously, I experienced an incredible sense of relief and an enormous pang of disappointment. My fate was sealed. I was safe; he had a son and, I assumed, a wife.

I gently took the boy's hand. "Hi there, Michael.

Nice to meet you."

Max smiled at Simona but nervously kept his gaze away from me.

"So when did you come back?" Simona asked Max.

"I've been back a little over a week." He turned and gazed lovingly at his son, who was pointing at the carousel and hanging on to Max's jacket. "It's so good to see this little guy after so long away."

"Where have you been?" My voice cracked, though I tried to be cool.

"Libya." His eyes didn't meet mine.

"Why Libya?"

"I operate a track loader—at a refinery. My cycle usually lasts three months, then I'm home for a month."

"Quite a long time to be away from your son," I commented. Max gave me a side-glance and a smile.

"Don't I know it. And what brings you back to Italy?" His eyes were warming.

"University. I'm studying languages."

"So you're here then? Studying here?"

"For the next three weeks." I smiled politely. "I'm in Florence at Syracuse."

"Ah...I see. Are you staying at your cousin's here or in Florence?"

"In Florence, visiting Pescaglia until Sunday."

Simona's glance darted from me to Max as we conversed. "Look, I hate to break up this tender reunion"—Simona indicated with a head motion—"but Max, I think your wife is trying to get your attention." An icy glare from a slim blonde woman met Max's from the other side of the piazza.

"I should be going." Max put his son down, still

holding onto his hand, and turned toward the woman. "I have to get him back to her."

"Of course—*Arrivederci*," I said cordially. *I guess this is it, my friend. Fate has written our last chapter.*

I watched him, he and his son, hand in hand, stepping away. Then he halted and turned, speaking directly to me. "I'm bringing Michael up to Pescaglia to visit my brother tomorrow. Are you going to be around after dinner, say eight?"

There was measured silence from both me and Simona. Arguments raged inside me about the cons of doing this. If I said no, he would think me weak…think he was still able to rattle me. I spoke confidently, "We could probably be in the bar for an espresso, I think."

Simona nodded. "I think it can be arranged." She pulled in her lips to keep from smiling.

From the other corner of the piazza came a familiar squeal. "Oh my God!" It was Vanessa. "Sofia! Look, it's Sofia." Sergio was trailing behind her as she rushed over. "Give me a hug. When did you get in?" Vanessa's gaze caught the entire scene, as everyone in the group exchanged handshakes, hugs, and inquiries.

"Look at this." Sergio smiled, his arms outstretched. "It's like the summer of '76 all over again."

"Not quite," I whispered. The only one who heard me was Max.

"Let's go to Mommy," said Michael, pulling on his father's hand.

"Yes, we're going." Max smiled down at his son. Then to the group, "I'll see you all tomorrow…in Pescaglia."

We watched as Max walked away with his son

pulling him toward his wife. Then it seemed, all eyes ended up on me.

"Never mind, it's okay. I'm okay." I breathed in a calming breath and hugged Vanessa and Sergio once more. "Come on"—I motioned to the roller coaster—"let's go."

Chapter Twelve

"We saw Massimo at Luna Park last night. His son is adorable," I announced the next morning at breakfast as I grabbed a croissant.

My attention was engrossed in splitting the pastry and slathering it with marmalade, trying my hardest to appear unaffected.

"Hmph." My aunt Carla's brows drew downward in a frown. "There's always been trouble in that family. He *had* to marry the girl…went off and got her pregnant."

Simona winked at me as she raised her espresso cup to her mouth. "Like it's the first time that's happened around here," she mumbled.

"Never mind," her father retorted. "Eat your breakfast."

My mouth twisted slightly, surprised at my aunt's comment, then decided to speak my mind. After all, my emotions were completely neutral, and I was not above giving credit where credit was due, even though he did rip my heart out. "Well, I don't know much about the whole thing, but I do know from the last time I was here he wasn't in school because he had to work to support his family, and now he's working in Libya."

"Sofia, my dear, you focus on your schoolwork." Uncle Mario took the last sip of coffee from his tiny cup and pulled a pack of cigarettes from his shirt pocket.

****

It was the town where time stood still—exactly the thought that ran through my mind when Simona and I ventured up to the bar for an espresso after dinner.

The lamp in the square was the same. The bench near the retaining wall still stood like an old sentinel in the village. The old men in the bar were fewer now, but life in the village went on as it had for centuries before.

We sat with our friends who were still there, the young people who hadn't moved away to find work in an ever-shrinking agrarian industry in the area. Those who were still there remembered me. They asked about life in the United States again, about New York City. And I obliged and smiled and answered their questions again. I swore they were all welcome to visit when I made my first million and had a penthouse apartment in Manhattan. And I learned my old friend Vanessa and her sweetheart, Sergio, were now engaged and planning their summer wedding.

At eight thirty, fashionably late, Max stepped into the bar.

A chorus of, "What the hell, who is this…a ghost?" and "Look at what the wind blew in," and "Jesus, how long has it been?" greeted Max as he strode over to where we sat.

"Hello," was all I could bring myself to say. My mind couldn't let go of the past.

"Where's your son?" asked Simona.

"His mother had other plans for him today," he answered with a smirk. "She insisted on bringing him to Lucca to shop for shoes, but I know she's going to come back with a few new pairs of her own. She always seems to need a new pair when I come home with a fat paycheck at the end of my cycle. I had dinner with my mother and brother, then I thought I'd stop in here and grab an espresso."

There were hearty salutations and questions about Libya as Max grabbed a chair from the next table and positioned the backrest so he could rest his elbows on the back of it. When he talked, the entire place listened to him. He was funny and charming and relaxed.

"What are the people like in Libya, Massimo?" asked the barman.

"They're hardworking, more so than Italians."

"It must be hellish there in the summer," offered the barman.

"It's hotter than Hades in July," quipped Max. "And ten times smellier."

"What do you like best about working there?" asked one of the old men.

"I can eat as much and whatever I want. The commissary is second to none."

"And the worst?"

Max paused at this, considering his response. "When I first started, a couple of years back, I would come home on leave and my son wouldn't recognize me."

I could never admit it to myself at the time, but I hated his wife that very moment. They shared a child. They made a person together, something I figured he and I never would. She would always have a piece of Max, the bond eternal, that I would never have.

"It must have been difficult," said Vanessa.

"When I'm there for those three months, work is all I do. It's a twelve-hour day, six days a week." He nodded somberly and looked directly at me. "It's difficult when time robs you of things you would rather be doing, yet you know you have responsibilities you must live up to." For an instant, a trace of melancholy stole into his expression.

My heart suddenly swelled with a sensation I thought had long since abated. I decided to quell it straight away. "Well, I think we'd better go, Simona. It's getting late." I got up, and the table exploded into protest.

"Why," complained Vanessa. "It's so early. It's barely ten."

"I'll come back to see you before I go home. I promise."

"Tell me where you live," said Vanessa, clinging to Sergio. "We'll come out and visit you one day."

I found a pen in my satchel and scratched the address on the back of a receipt. "Here. Come any time. But now I have to go."

Simona shrugged and followed my lead. "Good night everyone."

"I have to go too," said Max, rising from his chair. "I need to get myself home."

A chorus of "good nights" filled the air, suspended in the bar along with the thick cigarette smoke.

"I'll walk you girls to the end of the road," Max said casually.

I took in a huffing breath as Simona peered at both of us quizzically. There was an awkward silence as the three of us walked to the retaining wall before the curve descending to my aunt's home.

We stopped there, and I realized we were standing in the very spot where seven years earlier, Max and I had said our last goodbyes. And where I had felt the raw, numbing pain of my first broken heart.

"Uh...I guess I'll say good night, Max," Simona announced. "I'm going to head to the house." There was an awkward pause, then she turned to me and asked with a grimace, "Is everything okay, Sofia?" The memory of our last goodbye was probably as plain as day on my face.

"Don't worry, Simona," Max reassured her. "Everything's fine. I just want to talk to Sofia." He turned and looked at me with pleading eyes. "If she doesn't mind."

I crossed my arms over my chest and cast my gaze to the ground, kicking at the loose pebbles underfoot. "If you feel the need to clear your conscience, I may take you up on it."

Max surveyed me as he took out his cigarettes. "Don't look at your shoes when you say pointed things like that," he said, with the utmost seriousness.

Smiling surreptitiously, I shook my head. "You're an idiot." My eyes were now steadfastly on his and cool as marble.

"Absolutely." He chuckled as he pulled a cigarette out of the pack with his teeth. Everything about him, even that small gesture, spoke to my attraction for him. I wanted to scream in frustration, yet the need to have him again rose from deep inside me, a warm sensation, which I quickly quelled under a mask of feigned annoyance.

Simona shrugged again and raised her hands. "Whatever. Look...you two should think about where this might end up. Because it's plain to see, things aren't over." She turned around, pulled her collar up around her neck, and disappeared down the steps, her voice echoing in the misty night air. The skies had threatened rain all day, and it had begun to drizzle. "Good night, Max."

"Good night." He called out his salutation, then refocused on me as he smoked his cigarette.

We both stood silent for a long moment, neither attempting to begin. Then after drawing a long breath, I spoke.

"Your little boy is very sweet."

"Thanks. I like to think he takes after his father." A disarming smile took over his face.

"It kind of warmed my heart to see you two together at Luna Park." My tone was amiable, but I couldn't let him off easy. "Almost makes me believe you have a heart in there somewhere."

"Okay." He nodded as his smile turned into a sour grin. "Okay, I guess I deserved that."

"You wanted to talk?" I asked.

"Let's go for a ride." He motioned up to the sky indicating the drizzle. "My car's in the piazza." He pointed to adjacent steps leading up to the retaining wall beside the bench—it was deserted now as it was a chilly, early spring evening.

I followed his lead. For all I knew, he wanted to make amends for the immature way he ended things seven years ago. He seemed to have grown up, developed a sense of responsibility. Marriage and a child, I supposed, would do as much to a person.

Nevertheless, I couldn't deny the chemistry between us. It was still electric. Yet my need to challenge him was stronger than my sense of emotional survival. It was my day to finally have the last word in a relationship that had ended on his terms…terms that so long ago, he had offered no explanations, no reasons, only abandonment. Despite the danger that may lay ahead, I wanted to go. I would be strong, but I would finally have my say and force myself to be done with him. I had given up my pride to him before—never again.

I got so worked up thinking about what I would say to him, I inadvertently blurted out, "Okay, but if you think I'm going to fuck you tonight, you'd better think again." Triumph flooded through me when he winced at my words.

"Whoa!" He threw his hands up. "That came out of nowhere."

I hid my smile from him.

"From 'your little boy is very sweet' to 'I'm not going to fuck you'…that has to be the fastest shutdown ever—under twenty seconds I'd say."

He had disarmed me. I laughed despite myself but managed to rein in my giggle with a sniff and a toss of my head. "I wanted to make it clear, so it's out there on the table, that's all."

"Okay, my lady. Unnecessary, but understood." We reached the car, and Max opened the passenger door. It began raining harder as he made his way around and got himself in.

"Somewhere quiet so we can talk?" he asked as he closed the door.

I agreed. He pushed on the clutch and moved the shift into gear, steering his Fiat 500 smoothly out of the piazza, the bar lights now dim.

"So tell me about what you're doing now. You're in university, right?"

"Yes. Syracuse in the States—and here actually. I mentioned at the carnival I'm studying languages abroad."

"And you're doing this for…" His voice trailed as he drove the car nimbly through the narrow streets of Pescaglia.

"Future job opportunities. I want to go into business, specifically international banking." As much as I knew it was petty, I couldn't help but rub his nose in the fact that I was a major catch. "I studied commerce in university and realized I was a natural, so much so I'm determined to get my M.B.A."

"Incredible. I'm proud of you. I always knew you had a good head on your shoulders." We reached the outskirts of the town, where he turned the car onto the main road leading out of the village.

I marveled at his last statement. Then turned to the window and stuck out my chin stubbornly. "I had a good head on my shoulders but not good enough for you."

The silence in the little car was thick enough to cut. I looked over at him again. "Look, Max, I know you're not taking me out for a ride to see how dark it gets around here. Is there something you want to say to me?"

Momentarily speechless at my forthrightness, he swallowed and finally spoke. "I wanted to talk to you about us. You know—about us before. I want to say…I'm sorry. That I was shortsighted. And I acted like an asshole toward the end."

He didn't drive much farther, slowing to a clearing at the crossroads out of the town proper. Once parked, he turned off the ignition, jacked up the sleeves of his sweater to his elbows, then looked over at me. His expression was without the usual mask of bravado, his eyes dark and soulful, gentle, and contemplative. "I want to properly apologize. I know I hurt you."

In mere seconds, he managed to shatter the hard shell I had built up so carefully. My eyes veered from his face down to his shoulders, then forearms. All of him threatened to weaken me.

In a snap, my eyes found his again. "I accept your apology." I made certain my tone was cool.

He seemed taken aback at my attitude. Like I wasn't supposed to forgive him. Then he forced a smile and a tense nod of acknowledgment.

"That's it?" I asked.

"I can't believe I'm saying this, but I'd give anything to go back." He spoke like his words were on an expelled breath he had been holding in for years. "But I can't."

Oh fuck, was my immediate thought.

"What the hell are you talking about, Max? Going back?" I chose to snap at him. "I don't understand. We haven't seen each other in years. I haven't heard from you in seven years. Where is all this coming from?"

"I have to explain to you now that you're here. I overthought. I thought, 'What are you doing—you're going to fall for her, and she lives in America, and I'm a woodchopper in a shitty village, supporting the village's lowest caste.' I don't know…maybe, I didn't think enough."

His voice was small, managing no more than a hoarse whisper as he now focused on the darkness outside. "You were too high above me, and I was afraid to admit to myself how I felt about you. I was certain you would end up hurting me. I was sure you would ignore me once you got back to America."

Now it was my time to wince. "You're so full of crap. You're not thinking I'll accept this garbage as truth, are you? If you felt that way, why…? Oh my God—I can't believe you just said that. You threw it all away because of your male pride. All these years and now…"

"I was a fool. The biggest fool—a stupid unthinking idiot. I'm embarrassed to admit it."

"Well, you should be embarrassed! And I'm the idiot because I'm still sitting here with you. Now take me home."

"Wait, try to put it in the context of that time—I was young. My brain was between a pair of balls. My feelings confused me—"

"I don't know whether to laugh or cry." I combed a trembling hand through my hair. "You're married, Max, you have a child. That's the essential point."

He breathed out hard. "She got pregnant a while after you left. She got pregnant, and I married her. We're separated now. Have been for months."

I arched a brow. "I see." The iciness in my voice betrayed my hidden jealousy. Just thinking of him with another woman made my stomach squirm uncomfortably. "So you were with her while we were together. You were sleeping with her because I wouldn't fuck you? Is that the way it was?"

"Look, I met her while we were together," he explained, his tone apologetic. "I met her while I was working with my brother-in-law in Camaiore. That's when I distanced myself from you. As I said, I was an idiot."

"Were you sleeping with her while we were together?"

"No." The word hung in the air like a bloated speech bubble.

We sat in his Fiat for a long time, staring into the darkness as the steady rhythm of rain pelted down on the windshield. I couldn't help but feel a sense of loss all over again, my wounds now reopened after Max's revelations. Thoughts of what could have been and what never was chased themselves around in my mind until his voice broke the silence.

"I don't expect your forgiveness, Sofie. I understand now, I owed you an explanation. And I want to apologize."

"It doesn't matter anymore. This is ancient history." I sighed heavily, covering my eyes with a hand. "Oh my God, I think I need to smoke a joint." I blurted out the declaration scarcely aware of my own voice.

"You don't smoke weed, do you? I hear it's not good for you."

"Hey! It's 1983! And after hearing all this—it would be the best thing for me right now."

"Why do you smoke it?"

I gazed up at the roof of the Fiat. "Because it makes me high. I could rise above all this and feel good."

He reached for my hand and held it in his. It was the first time I had felt his touch in seven years. My heartbeat skyrocketed. "I don't need it. You do that to me." His voice was honest, candid. "You make me high."

I couldn't believe this was happening. With eyes

closed, I forced myself to relive the pain of our last encounter years ago. And all the suffering I experienced afterward. I gulped hard, clamping back a sob as hot tears found their way down my cheeks. "I forgive you, Max. Okay? Now you have closure. I forgive you. Take me home. You have to take me home." Beyond any doubt, this wouldn't spare my heart. I gathered up all the strength I had and tore my hand away from his. "Please."

Nodding somberly, he placed his hands on the steering wheel.

Try to rise above your anger. Try to rise above. Look at him, for chrissakes. "Look." Mixed emotions surged through me. "Maybe one day, we'll get it right…but not now."

Instinctively, he pushed the clutch pedal, engaged the brake, and turned the key. The wrenching, gnawing feeling in my stomach, the feelings of love, frustration, rage, and desire, all jostled for the prime spot in my heart, all at once as we drove.

The spaces between us filled with unspoken sadness and regret, filling faster until it nearly suffocated me the closer we got to Pescaglia. I knew this overlapping of paths would be our last.

We moved in silence, the short distance back to the village and into the narrow medieval streets, now engulfed in a drizzly fog. When he pulled up to the edge of the retaining wall and the path to my relatives' house, he drew up the parking brake and glanced over at me.

"It was nice seeing you again, Max. I mean it. I hope everything works out for you." Deciding it might be best not to tempt my resolve, I didn't wait for a response. I opened the door of the Fiat and walked straight into the rain.

Max's hard exterior melted away a little, I thought, as I made my way down to the house. It was a good thing it was raining—at least it would meld with my tears, and I wouldn't have to explain why I was crying.

As I lay in bed, I thought about how men are unreasonable in their contradictory demands on women—and they say women can't make up their minds—how perfectly remiss the statement was. Still, his remorse and regret were clear, and so as much for my own sake as his, I would try to find it in my heart to forgive him.

****

"Do you have everything?" asked my aunt, as Uncle Mario drove to the Lucca train station the next afternoon, in a relentless rain, which had not stopped since the night before. Though the events from last evening still had me rattled, I hid it well.

"I do. Thanks for driving me." I hugged them affectionately before boarding. "And tell Simona to call me."

"I will, dear. Now listen," Auntie Carla reminded me, her hand on my shoulder for motherly emphasis. "If you need anything let us know…money, food, whatever. You're my niece and like my own daughter, I worry about you."

"Okay, I promise." I smiled warmly. "See you in a couple of weeks? I'll come back before I go." I gave them a wave as I entered the station, juggling my overnight bag as I took cover from the rain.

The train rolled slowly along the tracks before clearing the train station, then once it hit the countryside, it moved along swiftly, the driving downpour splashing mercilessly against the window in my packed compartment. I looked out to the gray clouds lying like twisted blankets in the sky.

Why couldn't the sun be shining—the rain just makes everything worse, I mused as I listened to my mixed tape on my Walkman. John Cougar was blaring in my ears.

"John Cougar knows a thing or two about 'hurting so good,' that's for sure," I murmured in the crowded compartment. The old woman beside me ignored me.

I now understood why Max decided to cool it off…but it was the cold way he did it, which always stuck with me. *Don't let him get to you.* Then, *Why with him? Why not with some guy back home? At least he would have been easier to corner, to demand an explanation from, instead of having to wait years after the fact, for an account of his rationale.*

With a multitude of tracks, Santa Maria Novella Station opened for the train like an unfolding fan. Soon we slowed and pulled up to the platform.

Following the flow of passengers, I alighted. No cab for me today. I walked stoically in the downpour, eyes on the pavement all the way to my apartment.

People around me rushed like mad to take cover under any shelter, but not me. I didn't care that I was soaked to the bone; in fact, I wanted to be soaked. I wanted the rain to wash away all the crap I had harbored inside me for seven years.

I reached my building and let myself into the courtyard. As I passed by the oleanders, I thought of an article I had to read for school tomorrow. Somewhere in the distance, church bells pealed—the call to Sunday mass. Unhurriedly, I climbed the stairs, though the rain was hitting me sideways. I was in no rush to be alone in my apartment, already knowing it would give me too much time to think.

My shoes clicked on the marble and echoed in the courtyard. I reached the first-floor landing, then circled the pillar to the second-floor staircase, around the pillar again, and finally to the third and final floor.

My gaze shifted from the steps to my apartment door.

And there he stood, in sideways rain, dripping wet and shaking. His clothes clung to his body, and his hair stuck to the sides of his face. My stomach lurched. The sudden surge of longing frightened me.

"Max." I gulped. "What are you doing here?"

"I love you, Sofie." His eyes pleaded his anguish. "I've always loved you." He said it like he had to say it, or he would burst into a million pieces.

My mind tried to process the revelation. The singular rebuttal that came to me was, "How did you find me?"

"I called Vanessa. I made her tell me where you lived."

I strode by him, chin up, pulled the key out of my back pocket, and stuck it in the door. "I'm going to kill her." I shook my head decisively. "No. You have to go."

"I won't let you leave again." His voice ricocheted in the *portico*.

"You're joking. Max, you're married. You have a son." I flung the door open and stomped into the apartment, my nostrils flaring. "What do you think is going to come of this?" I demanded as I flung my bag into a corner.

"I'm separated…and I've never stopped loving you." He took a step toward me, his hand reaching for me.

I recoiled. "Don't you dare touch me." My eyes narrowed, and my hand shot up to halt him. He obeyed, stopping in midstep halfway into my apartment. "Do you have any idea what you did to me?"

"I'm so sorry—"

"I fell in love with you. I was an innocent girl, and you made me fall in love with you. It took me years to get over you—"

"Please, listen to me—"

"No! Please…shut up! I've had enough of being civil! You had your say last night. Now you listen to me, you son of a bitch." My lips curled in anger. "When we met, it was like I was born to know you…I was born to fall in love with you. You made me fall in love with you. Everything you said and did to me drew me in. And then you ripped it away." I gulped hard to control the tears, but they found their way down my cheeks just the same.

"For the longest time after I went home, you were all I could think of, your face in my sleep. Your voice came back to me in my thoughts. For the longest time, I wrote your name on my notebooks, on the sand, in the snow. Your name next to mine, like it would make it all come true."

Tears swelled in his eyes, too. "I'm so sorry. I should have asked you to stay, gone with you…anything but let you go. Soon after you left, I realized I had made a mistake."

He stretched out his hand to touch me again, but I

stepped back. "Well, you know, Max, I grew up from the girl you fooled to a woman who knows better." I wanted to hurt him and run to him at the same time.

"I'm sorry, Sofie. I was horrible—I know it now." He came closer. "I love you. Please."

His tears were breaking my control.

"Don't, Max—no, we can't." My hands covered my face. "I can't complicate things. I have graduate school and plans. I—"

"I don't care." In a confused fog, I heard him take the final steps toward me. Then his arms encircled me.

In an instant, my common sense, logic, and resolve gave way. Everything inside me worked to push reason aside. For a long time, we stood there, him holding me, quietly, patiently waiting. Though Max was soaked, his hands were warm on my back.

Then I did it. I gave in.

Slowly I brought my arms around him and held him, feeling his uneven breathing. And I understood it…I felt safe like I was home. I was again consumed by the impossibly irresistible sensation that I was important, that I was someone's center, that I was desperately needed. It filled me up.

His hands gently stroked my hair, as he whispered over and over he was sorry.

"Look at me," he said, as he pushed the wet hair off my face and lifted my chin. "It's all my fault. Everything. I was an idiot. I let you go."

"But that's just it, Max…you didn't let me go. You…pushed me away. Like nothing mattered to you." I looked away, but I sensed his eyes on me.

"Yes, yes, to everything." His voice was resolute but remorseful. "My God, Sofie, you must believe me.

I've been asleep for seven years, a hollow shell of a man. You've brought me back to life, back from a pretend life."

"For you...what about me?" I wanted to resist, yet I had no desire to back away. "How can you do this to me again, you bastard?" A warning voice whispered in my head—everything inside me told me to throw him out of my apartment.

He stroked my cheek so gently and tenderly with his powerful hand, never taking his eyes from mine. "I agree," he murmured. "I'm a bastard. And I don't deserve you. I'm asking for forgiveness. And I'm asking for a second chance."

I turned so my eyes locked onto his, and I knew I had lost.

There was a long pause, then Max spoke. "It's strange how Fate works." His voice was a whisper, his lips barely a breath away from mine. "Did you ever imagine you would be at the carnival, here in Tuscany, at that right moment, when I was home? Sofie, there is something more here. Something is pushing us together."

I drank him in. The sound of his voice, the scent of his skin...it wrapped around me like a warm blanket. "I don't know about fate, Max." My chin moved toward his. "But I do know I can't say no to you. Not anymore."

As we kissed, my eyes closed, but I saw everything, as though I was hovering above, watching as I floated.

"Let me love you, Sofie," he murmured.

There was no need to delay the inevitable. I wanted to take everything from him I was too innocent and too inexperienced to take seven years ago.

"This doesn't make any sense, but it's the most natural thing in the world...you and me." I brushed my lips against his chin and held him closer.

His gaze came down to study my face. "Are you saying you want me to stay?"

"Yes." I placed the palm of my hand in a prayerlike fashion on the side of his face. "Make love to me, Max."

We linked our fingers and without breaking eye contact, he kicked my apartment door closed. Then we moved together, edging closer to the bedroom. Never taking his eyes from mine, he swept me up into his arms as a masterful Rhett Butler ever did to a reluctant Scarlett and carried me to my bed. Gently, he eased me down. We peeled off our wet clothes, and then he kissed me again, moving his mouth over mine, his fingers lost in my soaking wet hair.

"God, Sofie," he whispered.

I felt the anticipation growing in my belly, the warmth of his closeness against me. We moved together and with every caress, every brush of his body against mine, every kiss, my desire unfurled like petals opening to the sun.

"Tell me you love me, Max."

He slowed his moves.

"This is so much more than love." His voice was husky. "It's my religion." He caressed my naked back, my waist, my hips. I burrowed my face against his skin, and our breathing aligned...two souls, one breath, one heart.

If I was his religion, then he was my altar. This was home to me. I was home in his flesh. Everything I imagined it would be, we made come true that afternoon. My world was filled with Max again.

Chapter Thirteen

Saint Joseph's Hospice, Present Day

As I spoke to him about our time together in Florence, the nurse came to replenish his morphine IV—he slept immediately afterward, which gave us precious little time to speak. It was always the same between Max and me…never enough time.

Then a deep gurgling cough startled me out of my chair and back to his side.

I massaged his frail back, his paper-thin skin against bone, as I tried in vain to settle down his rattling breaths. He winced horribly, as the pain of the disease took over his gaunt face.

"Okay, take it easy now. Breathe easy." I turned him over onto his side, so he wouldn't choke on his bile lest he vomited. As I stroked his emaciated shoulders, I remembered how broad and strong they were. How he was able to lift me as though he were scooping up a rag doll.

I hated myself at that moment. The memory of our lovemaking fresh in my mind now clashed with the thin figure on the bed before me and prompted pangs of shame. *What's wrong with me…the man is close to breathing his last, and I'm thinking about that.*

Yet somehow, I found thinking of our past therapeutic, cleansing in a way. Daydreaming helped me to cope. Gazing out the window and thinking of us the way we were, made being here easier. It took my mind off the incessant hum of machinery in the hospice room.

"There now, better?" I asked, my voice sounding more chipper than I had intended.

"Yes." Another cough and sputter. "Thank you, my angel."

I held him until he relaxed and continued to massage his back until his breathing settled.

"You missed your calling, Sofie," he said softly. "You should have been a nurse."

"You're too kind." I kept rubbing his back, thinking distraction would help ease some of the pain. "I was daydreaming while you were sleeping of when I was here for school in '83. Do you remember?" A smile unwittingly crept across my lips.

"Do I remember?" He chuckled softly. "I think your bedroom in that apartment has only recently stopped smoldering."

I shook my head and laughed and thought what a fool I was making of myself—a middle-aged woman, giggling like a schoolgirl. "Those were such good times. Do you remember the place in Piazza Frescobaldi where we used to go? What was it called, Camillo's? With the table at the back. I think half the time the server was hesitant to approach us. We were so…into each other."

"Hmm, I'm surprised they didn't throw us out."

Rubbing his back settled him, so I gently turned him over, then scooped up the water and sponge and touched the moist tip to his lips. He licked the drops of water gratefully.

There was a long pause, then something occurred to me. "Does it bother you, Max? Me mentioning all this?"

"No, I've thought about it often. About everything. New York, too. I loved you," Max said matter-of-factly. "With my whole heart, body, and soul. Those first two weeks were pure heaven. The best fourteen days of my life." He took in a shallow breath. "Before it all went to hell."

Upon hearing this, I stiffened and put the cup away.

"Before life interfered," he added.

I quirked my head. "Says you." My smile was conciliatory. "Enough about that now. I won't have you coughing again. I'm going to grab a cold cloth for your forehead." I stood and walked to get the basin, filled with cool water. A soft white cloth was draped over the side.

"No, we should talk. It's one of the reasons I...I had them call you." Max closed his eyes, his every word now betraying the effort spent in speaking even the simplest of phrases.

"You're tiring yourself out." I squeezed the cloth and gently placed the cool compress on his forehead. My brow furrowed, partly in frustration, partly in pity.

"I promise, I'll stop when I'm tired," he said, determined to have me relive this with him. "I remember it. I'm thinking of you right now, as you were then. I remember how your sandals made that slapping sound against your feet as you walked on the Ponte Trinità, the way you wore your hair, even your scent. It was delicious. Come closer," he whispered.

I obliged. As I turned the cloth over on his head, I

moved near enough so he could smell my hair. "Just as I remember it, Sofie." His eyes closed.

"You were everything I remembered, and more. Everything that made me fall in love with the skinny, uppity, virginal American girl in '76 was reaffirmed twenty-fold as soon as I saw you at the carnival.

"But you weren't a child anymore. You were a self-assured, poised woman, able to express herself and her wants confidently. It made you even more irresistible to me...if that was even possible. When I saw you, my entire core jumped. Like the ghost of a lost love come back to life, you were there when I least expected it, and you took your place within me again. It was all I could do to keep from scooping you up and burying my face in your hair...like a drug, you settled into my brain and veins and heart and wouldn't let go."

Though he was whispering, his breathing was labored, and I became concerned. "Max, maybe you should stop. I don't want you—"

He shook his head weakly, so I stopped talking. I moved closer as his voice was so faint.

"When we spoke the night after, in Pescaglia, I wanted to explain my immature behavior, my stupidity in abandoning you years before without an explanation. To try to set things right between us and tell you the truth. I had the chance to set things right, and I blew it again.

"Then, when you agreed to meet me one last time, I thought you would tell me to go fuck myself. But you came, and you talked with me and revealed your hurt...and it nearly tore me up inside. I was a vile excuse for a man to have made you suffer so...an arrogant, horny teenager." He tried to draw a breath and instead mustered a spasm of coughing.

"Max, don't—"

"No, let me finish. That night, all I thought of was you. I couldn't let you go again. I set out in the morning for Florence after begging Vanessa for your address. I was fully ready to accept your refusal to even listen to me and send me away. I was willing to gamble my pride and my dignity to reaffirm my feelings for you. If you sent me away, I would've gone back to the one bright spot, my son. But I couldn't let you go—not without telling you how I felt.

"Then an unimaginable perfect miracle happened…you took my hand and made love to me. Incredible, perfect love. Like everything inside you had been bottled up for years and was suddenly set free. Making love to you…holding you, possessing you—it was perfection in its physical state. I couldn't get close enough to you. I wanted to become you, to live in you, with one soul and one mind and one skin. Everything flesh and blood could ever aspire to be, to attain, to experience, to embody through the metaphysical and physical in this world, you and I experienced that afternoon and beyond."

He winced his pain, paused, and breathed shallowly, then continued.

"At the time, I could not be more certain of anything, than my love for you, Sofie. You were everything. No cause, no country, no one was more important than you to me."

Chapter Fourteen

Florence, 1983

Max held me, exhausted and soaked with sweat. Eventually, our breathing evened. Everything would change now.

"You saved me today." He took my hand from his chest, brought it to his lips. "If it's possible, I love you even more now than before."

I glanced up at him with eyes still half closed, my hair a tousled mess. "Making love with you was everything I ever imagined it would be, and more."

He kissed the top of my head as his hand cupped my shoulder, then suddenly he blurted, "Sofie, come back to me."

His words were candid and matter-of-fact and reverberated around the bedroom until they had no place else to go until they finally settled into my brain. It sounded so easy, saying it like that.

"Yeah, sure," I joked. "Right away. Let me just make it happen right now."

He sighed. "You think I'm joking? I'm serious."

I lifted my head from his chest and looked straight at him. "Max, I'm going to say it straight out…I love you, and I always have deep down, but do you know what you're asking?" My hand moved to his face. I took his cheek in the palm of my hand.

"Yes. I refuse to waste another minute." His tone was determined. "The right thing would have been for me to stop you from leaving the last time you were here. I should have pulled you away and made you stay."

His newfound conviction made my head spin. Making love to him, professing our love for each other, this climax to a long-buried storyline in our lives…still, the question went unanswered.

"That was then, this is now. What are we going to do? You work in Libya," I said, propping myself up on my elbow. "This is so sudden."

"So what? Does life have a timeline? Tell me you'll stay, and I will too. This last one will be my final cycle in Libya." He reached for his cigarettes in his pants pocket.

Though my heart raced to hear his words, I was afraid his decision was a hasty one. "It's so fast, Max. I mean, this could all be some…some wild infatuation, that'll burn itself out in a few weeks."

He smiled assuredly and put the unlit cigarette and lighter on the bedside table. "Listen, I suppressed this yearning for you for so long it was scarcely a smoldering ember, nearly buried and choked by years of duty and obligation." He gathered me up in his arms. "But the ember came alive again the minute I set eyes on you at the carnival. And within moments, I knew it was something different altogether. When we spoke, Sofie, you were so strong. So independent. You've grown into a beautiful, confident woman."

I smiled suspiciously. "Now, you're playing with me."

"No, I promise you, it's true." He held my chin

with his thumb and forefinger. "You intrigued me, defied me, made me question myself."

Yes, I felt the connection too; there was a bond between us, and it had been there from the beginning. Bent but never broken.

"Make love to me again, my sweet darling," he whispered, as his lips slid down the side of my neck. "I can't get enough of you, now that I have you."

He had me. "Oh, Jesus, Max, you're like a drug to me...the more I get, the more I want."

Max's words were everything I wanted to hear from a man—what any woman wants to hear.

Our loving whispers and murmurs electrified the bedroom. The time passed, and the room filled with the shadows of late afternoon.

When we finished, the sheets tangled around us, Max spoke again, a huskiness still lingering in his voice. "Sofie, I don't know about you, but I will never forget this afternoon as long as I live." He looked over at me and smiled a wicked, charming, devilish smile.

I laughed softly at his remark but soon broke into an uncontrollable peal of giggles. This set Max off, and soon we were both laughing at the childish purity of his remark.

"I have something to say too, my inexhaustible Max." I giggled. "I'm starving. And after this afternoon, I believe you owe me dinner."

He laced fingers with me and brought my hand to his mouth, kissing it lovingly. "I owe you a year's worth."

The unrelenting rain of the afternoon had given way to a cool, clear evening, with the occasional puddle on the cobbled ancient side streets of the old city, the last evidence of the storm earlier in the day.

I felt an unrelenting ache to be close to Max, and we both found it extremely difficult to keep our hands off each other in the car on our way to the restaurant.

Once we found a parking spot, we exited the Fiat, linked fingers, and strolled lazily across the Santa Trinità Bridge. Piazza Frescobaldi was seething with life at this time of day. People filled the streets, shopping at their local butchers and grocers for their evening meal. It was a society very much accustomed to slow, real food and savoring life's every bite to the fullest.

"I've never seen Florence like this—from the point of view of someone smitten and cooked in love," said Max as he wrapped his arm over my shoulder.

"I think the skies opened up just for us, Max," I mused. "The difference between my mood this morning and the way I feel now is comparable to gray, cold rain and the red sky at tonight's dusk."

Max turned to meet my eyes. "You have acquired quite a way with the Italian language since you were a little girl of fifteen."

"I have an affinity to languages. I learn fast."

"Three languages in three months? I'd say yes," quipped Max.

"I'm serious," I said confidently. "And I studied Spanish during my undergrad. So it's really four. But only languages will not be enough. If I'm going to carve out a career in business, I'll need an M.B.A to compete with the best candidates. And the best place for that is Harvard. It's the top-ranked university to study business and management."

"Harvard." Now it was Max's time to ponder. "So

you have more school then, after this year."

"If I want to make a Wall Street career a go of it, I'm going to have to."

"How long?"

"Two years."

"Two years," he repeated.

I swallowed. He was digesting the implications of my plans. "Let's not worry about it now. Today is all about love and being together. Where are we eating anyway? Making wild, passionate love always makes me hungry."

"You drive me mad when you talk dirty," he joked, as his hand slid down from my shoulder and found my waist, pulling my body closer to his. "Ah, here, this is the place, Trattoria Camillo. They serve the best truffle pasta in Florence."

He pulled me around and showed me a little hole in the wall restaurant, tucked between a butcher shop and an *enoteca*.

The topic of what was to become of us was avoided that evening. Over dinner and copious amounts of wine, no more than the lightest conversation and romantic murmurs were allowed. I shared the highlights of the seven years spent apart from him, gushing about New York City, mainly Manhattan, and how a school trip to the financial district had sealed my choice of careers.

"And you?" I asked, holding up my glass of Chianti.

"And me." Max sighed. "Let's leave me to another time. My life has been anything but eventful."

"Come on. Tell me…I want to know."

He set down his knife and fork and folded his arms

on the table. "After you left in '76, I was called to military service. Shortly afterward, I got married. While I was serving my last month, my father died, so they let me go home for compassionate reasons. My brother-in-law found me this well-paying job in Libya through his oil and gas distributor. It was supposed to be temporary until we all got back on our feet. I needed to support my mother and younger brother, and my wife, then Michael...temporary became permanent. My plans for school had to be postponed...or should I say abandoned." He poured me another glass of Frescobaldi Reserve. "As I said, my life has been anything but eventful."

I felt a pang of pity for him. During our earliest days together, he spoke of going to school and becoming an engineer. Max never got to realize his dream, which made me appreciate how fortunate I was to have supportive parents who would sacrifice anything, so I could have everything.

The evening sped by too fast, a few hours spent talking and catching up seemed like seconds. The slow, lazy stroll back to the Fiat was purposely unhurried. We stopped on the Santa Trinità Bridge and gazed out over the Arno River, a testament to centuries of culture and history, which made Florence one of the most romantic cities in the world.

"I think this is my favorite bridge," I said, looking out onto the lazy water.

Max grasped my hips as I stared out on to the horizon. "Turn around so I can kiss you." He spun me about, so we were face to face and tightened his grip. The touch of his lips was a delicious sensation, an understood tenderness resonated inside me. We turned to see the setting sun to the west.

"This sounds so cliché, but I wish today could go on forever." My forehead rested against his chin as we watched the last pink sliver of the sun sink into the Arno. "Do you have to go tonight?"

Max exhaled noisily, then nodded. "I'm sorry, but I promise, I'll be back soon. You must attend class tomorrow anyway, yes?"

"I must," I answered, with a hint of a frown.

"Tomorrow night then?"

"All right," I agreed.

Max drove back to my apartment uncharacteristically slow. The day was ending, and we were unwilling to allow it to end without a last admission of love. Lingering at my front door, we kissed again, me standing on tiptoe, he ultimately taking hold of my waist and lifting me up to close the distance.

"Tell me you love me one more time," I demanded. "I can't hear it enough from you."

"There is nothing I am more sure of than what I feel in my heart for you. I love you more than my very breath…I swear I breathe only to to keep my heart beating so I can love you more."

My knees were water. "Oh, Max—what you said there…say it all the time to me."

Mere hours ago, I had prided myself a strong woman of the eighties, yet I had managed to morph into a lovestruck puddle of goo in the span of one afternoon.

A last kiss closed the day for Max and me. It was a day filled with promises, love, and fulfilled desires.

It didn't matter that tomorrow may bring reality around, along with inconveniently conflicting emotions.

It was bliss.

Chapter Fifteen

Monday came and went. As much as I tried, I simply could not focus on the lecture. My mind kept turning to memories of Max pure and clear, my daydreams almost as wild as our nights.

We made plans to meet at my apartment at eight on Tuesday—I was skipping classes on Wednesday. Enough said.

My Italian literature class had barely wrapped up when I gathered up my Petrarchan anthologies, notebooks, and sped off, while the rest of the class was still in the process of getting up from their seats.

And though it was a nagging presence in the back of my mind, I pushed away thoughts of what we would do less than three weeks from now when the time came for me to go home. I held on and hoped we would figure something out.

When the buzzer rang from downstairs, I sprang off the couch and pressed the answer button. "Hello?"

"Sofie, it's me."

"Come on up." I pressed the button to unlock the front door. I felt like I was at the top of a roller coaster before the thousand-foot plummet.

Before long there was a knock, and despite my best efforts to not appear too excited, I tore the door open and wrapped my arms around his neck. "My love."

His lips pressed against mine with passion, love,

and affection as his warm hands roamed up and down my back.

"You're so beautiful," he whispered.

"Shut up and kiss me," I whispered back.

"I—missed—you—so—much." Between each word, he planted kisses on my shoulders, neck, and face.

"I missed you, too." My eyes closed as I let my head rest against his chest, listening to his heartbeat.

Then I remembered. "What happened yesterday? Did you see Michael?" I looked up into his jet-black eyes, my brows furrowed with worry. The seeds of guilt were sinking in.

"I did," he said in a serious tone. "Dina has started talking about Michael and custody; I hope we can be civil since our separation agreement is mutual."

"Me too," I agreed. "But the one thing I regret about this is the effect it may have on your son. She cares about him, loves him." I walked to the fridge to get us a couple of chilling Stella Artois.

"Please," he said, raising his hands. He crossed the room to the couch and sat down. "I hope Dina keeps his best interest in mind when I tell her about us. The kid is going to get hurt if she doesn't."

I was unsure of how to comfort him. "Try to stay positive," I said weakly as I walked to him, handing him one of the bottles. "Maybe she'll be reasonable. It may not be so bad, and you're worrying for nothing."

"When it comes to my son...she knows he is everything to me. It's hard to be positive when she has the power to keep him from me." Max took the beer and gulped down a mouthful. "I'll do whatever I must to spare him any pain."

I settled down beside him on the couch. "Of course, Max. Please don't jump to conclusions, creating situations in your mind you may not have to deal with at all. You may have nothing to worry about."

His face softened as he reached for my hand. "Yes, you're right. I've been going crazy since last night. When I brought him back to his mother's, he asked me if I had to go away to work again." He stared at me. "I'm thankful it's not a shock for him, my having to leave all the time, but I imagine…down the road…I don't know how he's going to deal with it later."

I shook my head and reached over to run my hand through his hair. "I can't imagine. If there is anything I can do to help, you know I'll do it." Max had such love for his son. Pausing to look at the worry in his eyes, made me hurt for him.

We talked into the small hours. We spent a lot of time listening to each other, soaking in our excitement, basking in that push and pull, bathing in the sound of our voices. When we got tired of talking, we made out like teenagers. A balmy warmth radiated from the spot where his lips touched my neck, slowly spreading through the rest of me. From that moment on my clothes were a hindrance, but he solved the problem in under a minute.

Destiny and Fate owed us some fulfillment—our small fraction of time together. Our love bent but never broke.

****

We woke up late the next morning and very hungry. We found a restaurant that served American breakfasts and feasted on bacon, eggs, toast, juice, and espresso coffee with a cappuccino chaser.

"Have you decided where you're going to stay?" I asked apprehensively. "Now that you've formally separated."

Max nodded as he dabbed a napkin against his lips, savoring the last of his coffee. "I think the best thing is to stay with my sister and brother-in-law—she lives in Camaiore. My older brother moved abroad—work was more plentiful in Belgium. Moving to Pescaglia with Franco is too far from Michael. If I live with my sister, I can see my son more often."

"Good thinking," I said approvingly. He had a plan.

"Maybe we should talk about us now," he said, pushing his plate aside.

"We will," I answered. We played footsie under the table—I didn't want to talk about reality. I wanted to dream a little longer. "But not now. Let's talk later. Let's go see some Raphael. And some Donatello...and some da Vinci. We can talk after."

"Whatever you wish, my lady."

Max paid the bill, and we left. Holding hands, we walked into the street, cobbled by some long-forgotten workers centuries ago. "Max, you know...we're just a couple of people with troubles and worries, trying to make sense out of life, out of who knows how many millions who've walked on this street before us." I laughed inwardly as icy reality found me despite my best efforts to keep it at bay. "In a century, no one will know us. No one will care what we did or didn't do, right?"

"I don't know." Max motioned to turn left onto the Piazza dei Pitti—the Palace was a few steps ahead. "Let's go to Palazzo Pitti—I prefer it to the Uffizi. And in truth, what you said about no one knowing us or caring what we did or didn't do…I believe what we do now will affect everyone in our future." He angled his head so he could see my expression. "Why suddenly so introspective?"

I thought deeply about what he said, about what our future held. "I think I was hoping you would have given me a different answer." I caught sight of the Palace and brightened a little. "Never mind. Come on, let's go." I thrust my arm around him and led him to the entrance, with the sun peeking out and warming us to the afternoon.

We strolled through the magnificent rooms of the Pitti Palace, sumptuously decadent in their décor. Gold leaf, elaborate frescoes, and marble sculptures abounded alongside paintings by all the Renaissance masters, lining the walls leading from one room to the next and then the next. The ceilings were not spared the opulence, bearing scenes of life in the royal realm of the Duchy of Florence.

"I studied this, Max. Look up there—it's the Florentine symbol—the fleur-de-lis, but you probably already know that." I was mesmerized by the grand spectacle of art surrounding us, but Max seemed less interested. "All this is a display of wealth of the power held first by the Medici in Tuscany."

Max was behind me, nuzzling my ear as I now stood in front of a window overlooking the Boboli Garden.

"Look out there. Imagine the Hapsburgs and then the Savoia Dynasty looking out onto the same things, the same garden we're looking at now. Doesn't it do something to you?"

"You do something to me." He slid his hands down to my waist and spun me around, so we were face-to-face. "Kiss me." He stole one, not caring in the least we were drawing disapproving looks from other gallery patrons.

"Stop! You're not listening at all," I chided. "Let's go outside. I'm dying to walk under the pergola."

I took the lead, grabbing Max's hand, and found my way to the Boboli exit. It was a sumptuous green space in a busy city with neatly landscaped greenery accented by the occasional pond and water feature. We chattered and joked along white pebbled pathways winding amid citrus trees, around sculptures and statues in abundance. Cascading fountains, boasting cherubs, and gods were positioned strategically alongside tidily manicured shrubs and hedgerows.

Hidden behind a wall of ancient greenery, we found our purpose for the walk. We ventured under the *Cerchiata,* an avenue of trellises made of trees and vines bent to resemble an arbor tunnel. At the other end of the passageway, a marble bench sat directly across from a statue of Neptune spouting water, where we decided to sit awhile and drink in the beauty of the garden. It was a clear, sunny day, and though it wasn't yet summer, the sun was warm. Warm enough to make tourists in the garden take off their spring jackets.

"God, this is incredible," I declared. "Beautiful."

"Doesn't compare to you," he said, his gaze not straying from me.

I smiled and took his hand. "I'm glad we decided to postpone all the practical talk and focus on enjoying 'us.' It's long overdue, I think."

"You were right. The time to talk of these things

will come," he agreed. "With all the ugly practicality that goes with it. Let's take one more day in Utopia. I must go back tomorrow morning, though—to get some things to my sisters, straighten out a few details, but the day after, I'll come back, and we can figure it out then."

I was comforted. "Sounds fair to me." It was going to be all right. I needed to let things flow for a while. Let things grow naturally instead of always needing to be in control, trying to play it like a chess game, looking a thousand steps ahead, steering things in the direction I thought was best for everyone.

He had to breathe, too. "I have to go back to class tomorrow, anyway."

Max's eyes lit up and crinkled in the corners. "Then we must act fast," he said with boyish enthusiasm. "Let's get out of here."

"Are we going to the Uffizi now?" I asked, perplexed as he pulled on my hand.

"Ach! The Uffizi is overrated. Don't worry. It's been there since the 1700s and will be there for many years to come. I'm taking you to Lucca. I wager you've never been before, and I remember from '76, you wanted to go and never did get there."

"You're right," I affirmed as I trailed behind him, exiting the garden. "I never have and I—"

"Well, we are going today."

"Now? It's afternoon already."

"And you are in for a treat. It's scarcely a thirty-minute drive and a little-known gem in Tuscany." He gestured to the throngs of people already on the street opposite the palace. "All the boorish tourists flock like sheep here, to Florence—which is filled with pretentious, uppity Florentines. I want to show you

Lucca. It's a road less traveled—less crowded. And it offers a much better slice of Tuscan life than Florence."

As we approached the car, I huffed out a purposely yielding breath. "How can I argue with that. Take me."

With blasts of the horn and a few strategically placed cuss words, Max expertly worked his Fiat out of the Florence city center. We sped down the multilane *autostrada* to Lucca, a mere forty or so miles from Florence. Amid the speeding cars and motorcycles flying by us like mosquitoes were farms with neat rows of sunflowers and grapevines, lovingly placed on gently rolling hills.

Max maneuvered from the highway to the off-ramp and into midafternoon traffic, then pulled into a parking area close to the imposing city walls, ancient giant monuments left over from the Italian Renaissance era.

"It's more picturesque if we walk from here. You get the full effect if you walk through the gateway as they used to when Lucca was under siege ages ago."

"More like they stormed the city walls and overtook the sentinels and battered the gates. I don't think an opposing army would just walk through."

"You are full of insight, aren't you." He put his arm around my neck and pulled me closer.

Upon crossing the threshold into the city proper, there was much less automobile traffic.

"Doesn't anyone drive in Lucca?"

"They limit the number of cars inside the walls—maintains the charm of the old city."

"It's positively medieval in here. I mean it's modern in some respects, but the buildings, the streets, even the signs—so quaint. I love it."

Lucca endeared itself to me. I gazed in awe at its

ancient cobbled streets, handsome architecture, and shady promenades hidden behind the medieval walls. It made it ideal to explore on foot.

"Now isn't this better than some stuffy old gallery?" Max's head turned toward a shop we had passed. "Hey, look over here." He gestured at what looked like a sporting goods store. "I've always wanted to do this, and I've never had a chance. Let's rent some bicycles and take a ride on top of the city walls."

"On top of the walls?" I furrowed my brow.

"Yes—they are huge. The expanse is so broad there's a bike path…on top of the wall. It takes about half an hour or so to go all the way around. The whole city is surrounded by this massive wall."

"Wow. You know a lot about this place. You seem attached to it."

"It's my big city. Or the closest thing to a big city for me. It's no Manhattan, but it's mine." He broke into a smile. "Come on…let's go rent those bikes."

Once we got the bikes, we rode through enchanting streets, passed by artisan shops, and through the piazza, which displayed a huge bronze statue paying homage to Puccini. We traversed by the ancient cathedral and medieval bell tower and peddled up the gentle slope to the top of the wall. The path on top encircled the city.

Families strolled, couples snuggled on park benches, and businesspeople took in the light afternoon breeze while having their breaks, soaking in the view of the city and the surrounding countryside. I imagined myself running up here in the morning, a perfect place to jog, and marveled as we rode by a coffee shop and restaurant, all on the path. We spotted a man selling ice cream from a small shop alongside the route. Max approached him and held up two fingers. "*Granita al limone*," he said. My favorite.

The man produced two cups and scooped lemony crushed ice into each one.

The texture was coarse and flaky—like eating snow, which melted deliciously in the mouth. "Mmm, so good." I licked my lips.

"Come here, I want to show you something." Max got off his bike, kicked the stand, and gestured over the side of the wall. I parked my bicycle next to his and followed as I slurped on my granita. I looked down. The wall dropped about twenty feet into the old moat. As I closed my eyes, I let myself imagine how it would have been like during the Renaissance when these walls protected the city from invaders. It sounded archaic, antiquated, and went against every fiber of my being, but I could see Max being my protector.

"This is remarkable." I reached back and locked fingers with Max's. "Thank you for bringing me here. I've never seen anything like this. Thank you."

He inhaled deeply and kissed the back of my head, then slipped his hand around my waist and held on. "I would do anything for you—you and my son. I want you to meet him, get to know him."

"I'd like that, Max...very much." I thought a moment. "Does he know about us yet?"

"He's too young to understand."

"And what do you tell him if he asks why you're not at home?"

"I told him it is best for his mother and me to live apart for now. He's used to not seeing me for long stretches, but I could never get used to it. If anything, my work obligations in Libya the past five years have confirmed to me how much of his growth I missed. I don't intend to miss anymore."

I nodded and gave him a compassionate smile, but deep down in my heart, his words did not bode well for me. I pushed the conversation out of my mind.

"We should head back to the rental place," I suggested.

We started back on our bicycles, peddling at an easy pace, not wanting the afternoon to end.

We took the slope, down into the historic city center, and once the attendant had taken our bicycles, Max took my hands in his. "All this walking and biking has made me hungry. What do you say to an early dinner? They have some incredible restaurants here."

"Why not? What do you suggest…pizza?"

"You can get good pizza anywhere. Here, they serve authentic dishes from Garfagnana—a mountainous region a few kilometers north of Lucca—it's rustic, pastoral even."

Lucca's historic center was peppered with cafés and restaurants, offering an eclectic mix of delights, tempting visitors to relax over a glass or two of local wine and to people watch from one of its many piazzas.

Max and I lingered over a slow dinner into the evening. Tortellini stuffed with green vegetables, then thin slices of beef with capers and mountain herbs. For dessert, a soft and sweet cake, filled with raisins and dunked in a glass of sweet wine.

We drove back to my apartment—it may as well have been a flying carpet.

"Thank you for today, Max," I said as we entered. "It sounds so idiotic, but on the wall today, I felt like a Renaissance lady with my shining knight at my side."

"You're much stronger than you give yourself credit for." He caressed my back with the palm of his hand as I looked up. "You're rescuing me when it should be vice versa."

I angled my head quizzically. "What would you rescue me from, Max?"

"From foolish men who realize their mistakes too late." He ran a tender finger down my cheek. "And you? What would you rescue me from?"

"I would rescue you for one night," I replied, "from reality. And I would give you a happy ending."

Max smiled big as his eyes clung to mine. "You're mine now."

My body filled with a warm glow when he took my hands and lead me slowly into the bedroom. We floated there, oblivious to the constraints of time and space.

Our lovemaking was slower that night, deliberate and unhurried. Giving one another a world filled with dizzying patience and staggering urgency. Candlelight, soft and romantic, glowed against our moving bodies, as together, we found the measure that bound our silhouettes. It was as natural as breathing, as steady as a heartbeat. We trembled when it was over, our hair sticking to the side of our faces as though we were caught in a cloudburst.

"Never mind what I said about the other day," I whispered lazily before I drifted off. "Today was the perfect day."

Max left the next morning to go back to his son, and I was more in love with him than ever before.

I was contented, so much so my need to figure out our future was pushed aside in favor of enjoying the present.

I attended classes during the day while Max spent time with his son, but the evening was for us. We made love, ate, and drank at Camillo's Trattoria or wherever we found ourselves wandering to, after we had our fill of each other, and then made love again far into the night. Max would always leave early in the morning to be with Michael.

Then, on Sunday morning, my aunt called. "*Pronto*, Sofia—how is my expert Italian business tycoon?"

"*Ciao*," I said, a little off guard. "Great. Everything is good here. How is Pescaglia? And Simona?"

"All is well. I wanted to ask if you were coming by for sure before you leave for America? We would love to see you again."

The realization time was marching on hit me square in the face when put into that context. "I-I'd love to come by again," I stuttered but kept a cheery voice. "How about next weekend?"

"Perfect. Shall we come to get you?"

"No, that's too much trouble. I'll take the train. Maybe you can pick me up at the station next Saturday?"

"We're looking forward to it." There was a pause and then, "By the way, this is absolute nonsense and I know people are silly but…you and Massimo. Are you…together?"

Again, I was speechless. How did my aunt get wind of this?

"Why?"

"I don't want you to get distracted. Your mother and I have talked about what your parents want for you. Your future."

My future. My parents and my future. Blindsided, I was unsure of how to respond, not knowing what the ramifications were in terms of spilling the truth and risk her telling my folks. If she told, the inevitable result would be an all-hell-breaking-loose situation because they might think I would fall for him and consider staying in Italy instead of going to graduate school. I lied. "No, of course not. I saw him at Luna Park with Simona, but…that was it."

Silence. I imagined my aunt biting the side of her cheek, struggling to believe me. Finally, she answered, "I thought so, sweetheart. Forget I asked. It's silly."

But I was curious. "Why? What's wrong? Why do you ask?"

"There's talk up here…people know you're here, and—"

"Look, don't worry, okay? Everything is fine."

"I won't. Take care, Sofia. We'll talk soon."

Reality swallowed me up like quicksand. As I hung up the phone, a swell of panic rose in my throat. Less than two weeks left. What could possibly be accomplished in such a short time?

I paced to quell the anxiety, back and forth in my tiny apartment.

It's been that long already—shit! And we still have no idea what happens afterward. What happens afterward—you make it sound like a wake. But that's our reality. That's what's coming.

I racked my brain thinking about the here and now of our situation, instead of the fairy-tale I had been living these past days.

It was always days with us. Hours. Seconds. There was never enough time.

I breathed in to calm my anxiety. "Get your shower, calm down, and as soon as he comes through the door, say 'today we must figure things out for sure.' "

As I toweled down, I heard the buzzer squeal in the living room and nearly tripped over the towel, as I ran for the button.

"*Pronto*, Max?"

"Yes. Let me up."

"Come in." I pressed the button and knew I had approximately half a minute before he made it up the three flights of stairs, so I unlocked the door and ran for the bedroom.

"Sofie?" he called from the living room. "Where are you?"

"In the bedroom, dressing." I barely finished the sentence and slipped on my panties when he peeked his head in the door.

"Hmm." His eyes filled with appreciation as he scanned my legs. "Don't dress just yet." He crossed the floor, put his hands on my shoulders, and kissed me with a familiar passion. "You look like dessert." He leaned down to kiss me again, but I drew back.

"Max, wait." As I spoke, his eyes took on a look of confusion. "Why do we have to have sex as soon as you come over, whenever you come over…I mean, can we not have sex for once?"

Putting his hands to his sides, he backed away. "Well, it's not like we've been doing it forever, you know—it's barely been a week, but…you're right. Though I would call what we do making love, not just having sex." He walked into the living room. "I'll wait for you here."

Feeling a twinge of guilt, I looked at myself in the mirror critically. "Bitch," was all I could produce. *He has no idea what's swirling around in your head right now.*

I slipped on my jeans, topped them with a light sweater, and pulled a brush through my hair. A quick stroke of pink lipstick and some blush, and I was done.

When I entered the living room, Max was lying on the couch, watching an Italian variety show with Claudia Cardinale and Mick Jagger. He reminded me of a kid in time-out. "I'm sorry. I didn't mean to pounce on you." I stroked his hair.

He reached up and grasped my hand, gently bringing it to his mouth. "It's forgotten. And I can't keep my hands off you because I love you."

"I know." I sat beside him on the couch. "I love you, too. The reason I snapped is because time is slipping away. I'm confused. I don't know what to do. I've been thinking, and I'm not sure if…I don't think we can resolve all the things we need to in the time we have."

The words I'd been preparing all morning stuck in my throat. I didn't know how to begin, so I got up and walked to the window, pretending to admire the courtyard. "Look, Max…I have to say this. The reality is, I have a lot of time invested in my education—my career. And we've really been together no more than a handful of days." I turned to face him, but he had nearly made his way to me. "At this point, how can we be sure this relationship is strong enough to survive what's coming?"

"I think I have a plan for us, Sofie." He stepped closer, letting his hands slide up my arms to my shoulders, then back down to my wrists. "It would probably surprise you, but I've thought about us, too. About our future. I'll give you mine, and then you can give me yours."

I was reassured knowing this. "All right, you go ahead."

"Well, the way I see it…you should stay here…with me. We can find our own place; I'll find a job here instead of returning to work in Libya. If you want, you can stay in school, or…you could find work as an English translator or interpreter, or a teacher."

My breath caught in my lungs. "Oh my God, Max," I said, surprised. "I have to finish school. I may have an opportunity to attend Harvard…I thought you were going to say you would come home with me—to live in America."

Max's eyes held disbelief. "I can't do that. What about my son?"

"Bring him with you. Or send for him when we get settled."

He shook his head. "Dina will never let him go. She will delight in the fact she's got him instead of me."

"You can fight for custody, can't you?"

"It's hard enough for a man to be granted custody of his child…but to bring him an ocean away from his mother? They'd never give him to me."

An uncomfortable silence swelled between us. It mushroomed and expanded until I thought I would suffocate.

With measured words, I tried to quell the quiet, the uncertainty. "I don't want to argue with you, Max. All I want is to figure out where we're going—where this is all going." With tears forming in my eyes, I took his arms, wrapped them around me, and held him. I buried my face in the hollow between his neck and cheek. "Max—just hold me," I whispered in his ear.

He coaxed my face from his shoulder. "I promise you we'll figure something out. I won't let you go a second time."

Perhaps he realized the impending reality of what it now meant to be "us." He stroked my hair and caressed my face with his fingertips. "Promise me." His hands slipped down to my arms and tenderly brought me closer. "Promise me you will never forget this moment…everything we are. The way we are right now. No matter what happens, you will always remember this."

I reluctantly parted a few inches from him to look into his dark eyes. "Always. Forever." My head sank back down as I listened to his heartbeat.

It was a long while before Max stirred. Neither of us wanted the moment to end. We barely had two weeks left, and we were no closer to resolving the impasse than the day before.

Chapter Sixteen

The days passed, and we clung together like we were on a sinking ship.

On Thursday afternoon, I strode to my apartment after class, listening to my mixed tape, my headphones over my ears.

Max did not come that night. It gave me much time to think—too much time.

Alone, in bed, my mind drifted. Time, in my sense of it, was fragmented and pitched this way and that—some of it rushing by, the light of day, the darkness of the night, slipping through choppy intervals of time with him. In school, focused on reality, then at night, floating in a dream world of lovemaking.

I thought of when I was younger, my first time in Italy. How my life here and now would have been altered if things had been different back then.

If Max hadn't cooled things off, if we had continued our relationship, until I left…if, if, fucking if, would it have survived the distance of an ocean, and the time in between? Did Max have it in him to wait? Did I?

Maybe his leaving me seven years ago was the universe's way of ending an already doomed relationship. A relationship resulting from a random meeting between two people from different continents.

Was it what they call serendipity? Are "we" not

part of the puzzle of the universe, Max and me? I let it mull over in my mind. That and the ultimate question—what were we going to do come next week?

Endless deliberations kept me awake deep into the night until, in the wee hours, sleep finally found me.

It was like I had barely shut my eyes when the first thing next morning, the squeal of the phone in the living room jarred me awake. "That must be Max," I murmured groggily.

"*Pronto?*" I gripped the receiver with both hands, anticipating his voice.

"Hi, baby, it's Mom!"

I had to refocus. "Mom. Hi. Is everything okay?"

"Oh, yes, everything's wonderful—I hope you're sitting down!" The excitement in her voice was hard to miss.

"Why?" I could not have been more indifferent.

"A letter came for you…"

"Yes?"

"From Harvard…"

My dad in the background. "Tell her, Rita! Tell her!"

"Is it bulky or regular letter size?" I tried to sound eager. *Maybe I won't have to decide—maybe it'll be decided for me—maybe I won't be accepted to graduate school.*

"Bulky!" she squealed.

Then it's a "yes."

"Open it, Mom."

A momentary silence, then an admission of guilt. "Oh, hon, we already did," she chirped. "—you're in! They sent you an offer of admission from Harvard into the Master of Business Administration program. You're going to Boston in September. Harvard! Oh…Sofia, your dad and I are so proud of you, sweetheart."

I sensed she was tearful, doubtless bittersweetly so. If I had heard this news three weeks ago, I would have been thrilled. "Oh, wow—so cool, Mom."

"*Oh wow? That's so cool?* We thought this is what you wanted."

"I do, Mom. I'm just…overwhelmed." My words had no energy. "Shocked even."

"Is she happy?" My dad in the background again. "What did she say?"

"Yeah, she's happy."

"Here, give me that thing." Shuffling, then Dad. "Sofia? What's going on over there?"

I cleared my throat. "What do you mean, Daddy?"

"I mean, are we still on the same page, is what I mean. I gotta confess, honey, I'm hearing things from your uncle I don't like."

My stomach clenched. What was it going to be? Should I tell my dad about Max? What good would it do to tell them? Face my father's wrath now, over the phone, rather than later? It wasn't that I was afraid of my dad, it wasn't even about disappointing him, though I knew I would if I stayed in Italy.

"What's it going to be, Sofie?" he prompted, with added edginess. "Sofia? Why aren't you saying anything, sweetheart?"

I wanted to tell him everything, but my mouth refused to form the words.

"Okay, honey, if you can't speak, then let me do the talking. Your uncle called me with some…concerning news. Now you know your mother and I are not that sophisticated, but we understand.

Things are different now with you, young people. But we came here so you could get a good education and become something. This is the land of opportunity—we've always said that. If you work hard, you can be anything you want to be. We know the work you've put into your education, and you know the sacrifices we've made to put you through school and will continue to make for you."

My defenses and my reasons for doing as I pleased were slowly breaking down with every word my father uttered.

"Please, do not throw it all away on a whim." A pause. "For God's sake, say something, Sofia…you're scaring me."

I swallowed, then with a heavy heart, I gave him my answer. "You have nothing to worry about, Daddy. Everything is fine. Everything's on track."

"Oh, thank Christ, Sofia. I was worried maybe you were…never mind."

Though I couldn't see his face over the four-thousand-mile span between there and home, I sensed a massive weight of worry and apprehension had been lifted from his shoulders. "Now that I've heard it from you, I know I can rest easy. I love you, baby. Here's your mother."

Another phone switch and then Mom. "Okay, sweetheart, we won't keep you from your studies. I know it's early in the morning, and you're probably in a rush to get to school, so we're sending you big hugs and lots of kisses, and we'll see you soon. Congratulations, my darling girl."

My heart sank into my stomach. "Okay, Mom. Love you…and Dad, too."

As I hung up, I felt like a squeezing fist had taken hold of my heart. I was caught between two worlds. Max, my love for him and my desire to be with him on one side, and my commitment to my future career and my education on the other. The singular way to have both was for Max to come with me. The conversation had sealed our future.

Dragging myself through the day, on barely three hours of sleep, my mind was preoccupied with murky thoughts, new developments, and insurmountable complications.

Me and one of my friends from architecture were leaving the school after a particularly long day in micro-lectures. We were deep in discussion about our streams of study, exiting the small courtyard into the street…and there was Max. The sight of him took my breath away. I stopped midstep, in the middle of a sentence with architecture girl, Nella.

"Oh, thank God," I sputtered. "Max, I need to talk to you." I walked over to him, my voice growing edgier with every syllable. "You know you could have called me."

"Um. Okay, so I'll see you tomorrow. Maybe?" she said. I heard her words, but my eyes were on Max.

"Oh, sorry, Nella." I turned back to her. "Yes, see you tomorrow." My glare shot back to meet Max's.

"Sofia, I've been incredibly busy these two days."

"I didn't know how to reach you…I didn't know what—"

"Sorry, I should have gotten to a phone and called, but I swear I've been busy. Between working with my brother-in-law again to work off my living there, and Michael, I couldn't get away." He took a step toward me. "Forgive me?"

I looked into his pleading eyes as he held my face in his hands. I wanted to end my questions there, but my curiosity won. "How could you not get to a phone? I mean, it's so easy—go to a...a bar, I mean they all have them."

He pulled away completely, took a pack of cigarettes from his Levi's jacket pocket, and shook one out. "I explained," he said, placing the cigarette between his teeth. "I would have, but I was busy working...and I was with my son." His carriage turned crisp. "Christ, for a time you can do no wrong, then you reach a point where nothing you do is right."

"Pardon me?" I recoiled. "What the fuck is that supposed to mean? All I'm saying is, you could have let me know." Nervously, I pulled at the strap of my bag as my eyes strayed down to my feet.

"Oh, no...don't look at your shoes. Never mind that now." I saw a cigarette hit the ground, and his hand reach out to me. "I don't want to fight."

I lifted my gaze to meet his. "Let's walk."

Max looked puzzled. He slipped his hand into mine and lead me down the breezy cobbled sidewalk. "We're walking. Now you talk to me."

I shook my head. "I...right now, I..." The words stuck in my throat.

He shrugged. "Sofia, tell me." The breeze died, leaving his words hanging in the silence.

After drawing in a long breath, the words spilled out. "Okay. I-I need some security...I need to be confident you're going to keep an open mind...and you'll be there for me."

"Of course. What makes you think I'm going to

walk away from this?"

There was no other way to do it. "I have something to tell you." A wave of raw grief washed over me. "While you were gone, my parents called. I got a letter...I was admitted to Harvard. For this September. I'll be in Boston...for two years."

Max walked silently, his eyes focused straight ahead on the sidewalk in front of him. Though he didn't once let go of my hand or say anything or even blink, I sensed a change in him. I gave him time to digest the news before asking for his thoughts. If he was upset, I didn't blame him.

Our long stroll in crushing silence ended at the Ponte Santa Trinità. I leaned uneasily beside him on the stone, peering at the Ponte Vecchio just upriver on the Arno.

"You've decided you are going to do this for certain." Max turned and leaned his elbows on the wall so he was facing me.

"This has been my plan for...for a long time." My eyes couldn't meet his. I leaned over the parapet and stared down into the green waters of the river. The murky water and its consistency were evocative of how I felt inside: foggy and unclear. I was a dichotomy of jumbled sensations reacting to the events going on around me, instead of me having control over my own life.

Suddenly, Max exploded. "Goddammit, Sofia!" He punched the wall so hard with his fist, it drew blood. "No. No!"

"Stop it." I grabbed his hand to keep him from thudding it against the bridge wall. "Don't do that." Taking my scarf from around my neck, I wrapped up his raw hand to stop the bleeding.

I wished I could stop time from marching on, as easy as I had stopped the flow of blood. I yearned to go back to the beginning and relive the days when we were teenagers and go on forever. To re-experience the engulfing passion of a first love deluging the soul, ebbing and flowing like the rhythm we found in our lovemaking. We were at our best and most in love when we were possessing each other.

Max held his bleeding hand. His gaze drifted to the other side of the bridge.

"Why are you doing this? Are you punishing me?" In his eyes, I caught a reflection of something that ripped at my heart. Need. "Is this payback somehow?"

"No. I told you about this. Remember? Harvard…"

I took his hand and leaned over the parapet on the bridge. "Look…see the water?" I gestured to the rushing river. "It's obscure, unclear, like us—like our future. Right now, that's us."

"The future is unclear for everyone, not only for us."

"Yes, but a couple can work toward a common goal, a long-term commitment, or—"

"You know I'm committed to you."

"Then prove to me you are. Prove to me you understand that I must go back—that your love for me is all you say it is. And you'll be there for me."

Max looked taken aback again. "I don't know what you're thinking, but I've tried to make up for what I did. I told you, you've always been the one." His eyes, dark and deep, seared into me. "Why, suddenly, are you questioning me? You still don't trust me, do you? Are you testing me by telling me you're going away? Is it true?"

"That part is true."

"Another two years away from you...I can't even think...you aren't the only one who needs commitment," he interrupted. "I need some security, too. You know what I want, what I need. I need you here with me—me and Michael."

"I have another idea. Wait for me. When I'm done with school, you and Michael can come to New York."

Love and sorrow, the twins...I could almost feel the dark clouds looming in from above to obscure the sun.

Chapter Seventeen

Saint Joseph's Hospice, Present Day

Darkness surrounded her. Great trees with outstretched limbs caught her dress. She looked down, and saw she was dressed as Snow White, though a more womanly version than the kid's fable. Running blindly, she tried to cry for help, but fear strangled her screams, so much so she couldn't cry out at all.

Terror pushed her forward, twigs scratched her face, branches tugged at her clothes—there was no light to run to—there was always light before, but this time, none. Hhhhe, was all she could manage to squeak...again, Hhhhe, but no cries or screams left her mouth. "No...no...no...no!" she shouted repeatedly, yet her words were silent. Tears gushed, and fear overtook her until she could run no more. She fell in a heap on the dirt and disappeared into the ground, swallowed up by the black earth.

"Aaahhh!" I awoke with a start, disoriented for a split second. I had fallen asleep.

It was dark, save for a bedside table lamp. The day had slipped into my third night by Max's side. For the most part, he slept, a result of the powerful cocktail of pain killers they gave him to stave off the agony.

A basin of cool water and the cloth I had swathed over Max's head earlier in the day sat at the ready on the bedside table. I turned toward him, and he was still fast asleep, gurgling uneasy breaths as his chest heaved to take in more oxygen.

"Oh my God," I whispered, wiping sweat off my brow. "That was some scary shit." *Water,* I murmured. *I need water to get the bitter taste out of my mouth from the horrible dream.*

I tiptoed to the sink and let the water run before I filled the Styrofoam cup. I splashed the cool liquid on my face, then turned again to look at Max. As I gulped down the water, I heard a soft knock at the door then, without waiting for an answer, a blonde-haired, ponytailed nurse, holding an IV bag, made her way to Max's bedside.

As she hooked up the new IV bag, she started and gasped in a breath. "Oh, excuse me. I didn't realize you were in here. I'll replace his bag, check his vitals, and I'll be done."

The nurse's fussing woke Max, bringing on a coughing fit. She managed to settle him down, and when she left, Max's gaze was on me. "And here you are." His voice was raspy.

"Here I am." I walked to his bedside and sat beside him, taking his hand in mine.

"Aren't you tired?" he asked, squinting.

"I had a little nap. I'm fine."

"You are going to make yourself sick if you don't get some sleep. Go."

"No. Maybe in the morning, I'll go to my hotel and grab a shower." I smiled, hoping it was an encouraging one. "I came here to be with you."

A sly grin crept across his withered lips. "I'll try not to die while you're not here."

Even his cancer doesn't mask the dryness in his humor.

But the stark reality of his off-the-cuff remark struck a nerve in me. A nerve that was overtired and overcome with the events from the past days.

"Well—aren't you…" I wanted so much to retort with a glib remark, to pretend I was stronger than steel, more resilient to the things haunting mortality than the average person, but my façade had grown weak from the torrent of old feelings. They came rushing back to reclaim their place. These stubborn forces were a wall I couldn't get around or climb over. Perhaps, all I could do was to burst through.

As the lump in my throat tingled to a familiar breaking point, the memories became tears, spilling down my cheeks. Max was visibly taken aback.

"Sofie, no, please." In his weakness, he mustered up enough strength to reach my cheek and caress it weakly. "I'm so sorry, Sofie. I'm an insensitive shit."

My free hand wiped the memories away. "Yes, you are," seemed the most appropriate response. It took a minute in the darkness for me to find my stoicism and keep my emotions in check. "Okay…I'm good now."

"Are you? Maybe it was a selfish mistake to ask you here."

"No, Max, never think that. It was a shock at first, even to hear your name after all these years but…don't ever think this was a mistake."

He breathed in shallowly and turned his face away. After a long pause, he spoke in a voice barely above a whisper. "I want to tell you another reason I asked you here. Do you know at all, what it is?"

"I assumed it was so you wouldn't be alone."

"Death doesn't scare me. Neither does being alone in facing it." He turned his gaze back to me. "Dying without setting things right does, though. I want to make things right."

"Max, it doesn't matter. All that is done. It's finished. A million light-years from here would be the same as what happened to us twenty or thirty years ago. What's important is I am here for you now. Doesn't that say something?"

"You are here out of pity. Out of mercy for a dying man. Look at me. I'm a shadow of the man I was, a ghost." His voice was a quivering whisper. "Can it be you could have loved me? Would we have shared a life if things had gone differently? If I had done things differently when we were young? When I think of it…all my wealth…all the money in the world couldn't turn back time, couldn't make things right in the past. It breaks my heart to think our choices, our stupid, selfish choices, kept us from being together. I had you. And you slipped away."

I paused, collecting my emotions as they lay threadbare for both of us to see on the hospice room floor. "You're *not* going to make me cry again."

I gulped down the tears and waited before speaking again, focusing on the full moon outside the hospice window. "Look out there, Max. Look at the moon. Look at how the stars are placed around it like sequins on an inky quilt. They're there because that's the way it is. We don't question it. In the grand plan, they are the way they are—like us. Don't think about it anymore."

Max turned his head toward the window. The light from the rising moon caught his cheek, and at that moment, despite the disease, he looked twenty years younger. "It is beautiful."

We were silent for a long time, then he cleared his throat and turned back to me. "What I did, your choice...I knew...I could accept. You knew who and what I was made of, but when the time came, your mind was made up about me. It was made *for* you."

He was rambling. Max's breathing was becoming frighteningly shallow and his monitors beeping out of control.

"Okay, let's slow down." I rubbed his arms, trying to calm him. The monitors were beeping out of control. "Take a breath and stop talking. Listen, you're making the machines go crazy."

He coughed. "Water."

I sprang up to get the cup and stroked the sponge over his lips. "What you're saying is true, but it's not fair, Max. I did what I thought was best for me at the time. For both of us. And I know what you're thinking. But it was so long ago. Now stop getting agitated."

He licked the cool water from his lips. "Hindsight. Hindsight is everything. I-I'll be calm." There was a long pause, then he turned away from me. "Do you love your husband?"

I scrunched my forehead and smiled, implying *don't be ridiculous*. "Of course, I love him."

He thought a moment. "As you loved me?"

My smile disappeared. "It's none of your business, but in the spirit of being truthful I'll answer the question." I sat and chose my words carefully. "The love my husband and I share is deep and secure, and for the most part, up until a few weeks ago, rooted in mutual trust and loyalty."

"Sounds very exciting." Max laughed mockingly,

then coughed out a breath.

"I'm not taking your bait."

"You said up until a few weeks ago. What happened?"

"Nothing."

"What happened?"

"He had a lapse of judgment." I sniffed out a laugh. "Then a sudden attack of guilt and good sense."

"What an asshole."

"Don't go down that road, my friend," I cautioned, half jokingly.

"I wager that oaf couldn't satisfy you—probably never has."

"How could you say such a thing?"

"Because I know you. He's sucked all the life out of you."

"You can't make sweeping remarks like that. Maybe it's not all about passion."

"Of course, it is. Life is about passion, about yearning and wanting and living it—"

"Max, I could not have lived in a Petrarchan sonnet. I needed more."

"And you found this 'more' in your husband?"

A tentative pause, then, "Yes." I fell silent for a minute, then asked, "Why are you pressing me on this?"

"I want to know if the man you married has given you everything you needed. What you thought I couldn't give you."

"You think I settled, don't you?"

"I know you did." He let go of my hand.

"Max—"

"And you're lying," he interrupted.

A flush of red rose from my belly to my cheeks. He was right. "This is ridiculous—why are you rehashing this now?"

"Because maybe I want to know if you have regrets. That you regret not being with me. That your life isn't as perfect as you—as you thought it would be." More coughing followed his shout.

"My life is far from perfect."

"*We* could have been imperfect, I think. Lived imperfectly." He turned away. "Go, Sofia. I need to rest now. Go."

"I'm an idiot," I mumbled under my breath, but the anger was distinguishable. Then to Max, "I came here to support you. I left my family to—"

"I said go, then!" he shouted out. "Go back to—" Max coughed again, this time a fit so prolonged and so loud, it brought the nurse into the room, followed by Vittorio, his caseworker.

"Oh my, what is going on?" asked Vittorio. "I was in the room next door, Max, but your voice is hard to miss tonight, my friend."

"Tell her to get out," Max rasped out with surprising vigor through his retching. "Get out."

The nurse turned to me contritely as she worked on Max. "Maybe you should go."

I was stunned, unable to move, my hand over my mouth—he was throwing me out of his hospital room.

"It's probably his toxicity giving him hallucinations," Vittorio murmured, apologetically. "I have to get his doctor, but perhaps it is best if you return tomorrow. Unless you wish to speak with someone. How are *you* doing?"

"I'm fine. No thanks." I grabbed my handbag and

backed away, leaving a shouting, heaving Max to be tended to by a nurse young enough to be his granddaughter. I set my hand on the doorframe. "Please let me know if anything changes. You have my number?"

"We certainly will," replied Vittorio, still trying to calm an agitated Max.

Walking to the elevator, I shook my head in confused embarrassment. Awkwardness overwhelmed me. He was upset, yes, but it wasn't due to his illness or toxicity—I knew for sure it had nothing to do with toxicity. Max was mad as hell at me. He had challenged me…and my decisions.

With a shaking hand, I pressed the elevator button, then thought again and took the stairs. Once in the stairwell, I sat on the first step, covered my mouth, and sobbed, deep, guttural sobs. For a long time, I stayed there, rocking back and forth like a desperate child, hoping to God no one discovered me, a bawling idiot.

Regret.

Regret weighed on me as the world weighed on Atlas.

Regret happens when you take a love that is strong and mix it with ambition and fear, and you must decide what to do with it and like every decision ever made, the choices are based on a combination of the facts at hand and the personalities involved, and right now, Max had taken it all and mashed it up and handed it back to me so I could relive it.

The bastard.

When I was ready, I wiped my tear-stained face and made my way downstairs and out to the car, like a robot. I put the key in the ignition and drove back to my hotel, numb.

Emotionally drained, a suffocating void opened inside me. I couldn't stand the silence. With James gone from my side, the bed was a vast creaking emptiness. It gave me too much time to think, so I made calls.

I dialed the last number I had for Simona, which would have been the old house in Pescaglia. Simona's voice spoke on voicemail. I left a message along with my cell number. "Hey, Simona. Surprise, it's Sofia. Um...so I'm staying at the Hotel Barberi a half kilometer from the St. Joseph's Hospice near Pescaglia. I know you'll have a coronary when you hear this, but I'm here with Max." I took a deep breath. "He's terminal, and we don't expect he will make it to the end of the week. If you get this in the next few days, call me."

I hung up and dialed my home number on Long Island. Voicemail there, too. "Hi, guys...Cara, I just wanted to say I love you, baby. I miss you, so much. Can't wait to see you. Call me as soon as you get home, okay? No matter what time. I'll be waiting."

The aloneness at that very moment was crushing. What did I want? What was I going to do about James...and Cara? Was I happy, or was I pretending?

Cara. I thought of her as a baby, and now a woman. I thought about my postpartum and how it got to me, my mind flitting from strange assumption to strange conclusion—why did girl babies evoke our most intense tenderness? Then I thought, it must be because of the pain of love that awaits them. It would be there awaiting them, just as all their little eggs are already stored in their tiny ovaries.

Cool water on my face—that's what I need. I rose from the edge of the bed and went to the bathroom. I turned on the light. It was the unkind fluorescent type. When I looked at myself in the mirror, I saw me for who I was. Deeply etched lines in the corners of my eyes and around my mouth, a faint sheen of silver growing out of the blonde at my temples.

My mouth over the years had sunken into a downturned expression, my eyelids sagged, their folds needing to be rubbed back into place upon awakening. The appearance of a throat wattle, taut only when I lift my chin to apply my mascara in the morning. The powerful geography of an old face formed from years of laughter, frowns, scowls, and smiles.

I was on the bad side of middle age—hell, I was beyond middle age. When was the last time I met a hundred-and-twelve-year-old?

"I won't survive here if I don't talk to someone." My thoughts were unanswered words, uttered to myself in the quiet of the hotel room. I walked to the window and opened it wide, allowing the crisp air to enter my lungs.

Looking out in the dimness, I discovered the faint buds pushing out from the tender limbs of the shrubs below the hotel window. It was the start of a new cycle of life for nature. I searched within myself for a trace of childhood exhilaration at the sight of this new cycle, but I found none. Only a quickened awareness of time passing.

My feet moved as if under their own accord to the bed. I grabbed my phone and dialed Simona's number again. This time she picked up on the first ring.

"*Pronto?*" It was her, her voice distinctly different,

more worn, but hers.

"Simona...it's Sofia," I gushed, on the verge of tears.

"Sofie." She was breathless. "I just got home. So you're here...I listened to my messages, and I swear I was about to call you. Oh my God, Max...I'm so sorry, my darling. I'm so sorry, but...I can't believe you're here? What...what—"

"I know, I know," I interrupted. "*I'm* still finding it hard to believe I'm here, and I've been here for three days."

"You came back because...?"

"Because he asked me." My tone was matter-of-fact. My heart overflowing with emotions for which there were no descriptions, no names.

"And your family?"

"They'll be here probably the day after next."

There was a heavy sigh on the other end. "Come stay here with us. All of you come to Pescaglia. I'm away most of the week, at work in Milan, but Katia and I are usually here on weekends. You remember Katia, don't you? We are married now."

"How wonderful to hear, Simona...you and Katia?" I marveled. "Married and living in Pescaglia."

"Yes. Things do change. Anyway, please, come stay. There's plenty of room."

"No, it's okay. I need to be close to the hospice, and James and Cara will stay with me here, but I would love it if you could come. We could catch up."

"I'll have to rearrange a few things, but I'm sure I can be there."

The conversation with my cousin did me good. Simona offered to take over for me, keep watch over

Max if need be, an offer I gratefully accepted. The regular mundane chatter was a relief from the creaking depths of sadness I experienced at the hospice. A release from the emotions that I had to push down and keep from Max. I had to be strong, I had to support.

It helped for a time, but my brain had different intentions in store for me as I lay in bed, trying to find sleep. Images churned and twisted in a sickening vortex as I thought about Max and James. They had never met as parallel lines never would meet, but each had a separate place in my life, with me in the middle.

My mind involuntarily worked its way back to '83, back to the seeds of mistrust, which would forever shape my relationship with Max and eventually bring my and James' relationship to the brink of a potentially permanent schism.

Chapter Eighteen

Florence, 1983

Max came Thursday night, but it was late. Our conversation was tense, our peace, eggshell fragile.

"Going back and forth from here to Florence and then back the next morning is costing me. Gas is expensive," he asserted. "And now not knowing if I'm going back to Libya…it all depends on what you decide."

The pressure was mounting. We were sprawled on the couch, watching an old movie on the puny TV.

"And my sister's been up my ass lately, constantly breaking my balls about what I'm going to do…when I'm going to move out, am I going back to Libya or staying here, start looking for a job. Jesus Christ! Our own mother was never so demanding."

A deep sense of foreboding swept over me like I had just written my own obituary. It shouldn't be this hard already. It was too soon. It should be all roses and flowers for at least another year or two until we have our first fight over some silly, insignificant thing.

"And Dina?" I looked up to assess his reaction.

"I think my wife was happiest when I got the job in Libya. I was off making tons of money, supporting her and Michael, and she did whatever she wanted. I think she's worried I'll stay here." He hung his head back on the headrest. "I'm going to ask her if she would let me at least take Michael for a couple of weeks to America."

"Yeah…good idea. So you can visit, maybe even stay for a couple of months, in the summer."

****

Max dropped me off at school the next morning. I would see him in Pescaglia the day after—officially, my last weekend in Italy…unofficially, to be determined if, in fact, it would be. Would I hazard putting off leaving for a few weeks to get things settled here? I knew I had to make up my mind fast.

My studies at the university were ending. I was completing last-minute assignments Friday evening when the phone rang. I thought it was Max again, trying to allay my fears.

"Hello?" I said, my tone friendly.

"Hello. Is this Sofia Romano?" The woman's demeanor was composed, businesslike.

"Yes. Who is speaking?"

"This is Dina Damiani—Massimo's wife."

A wave of panic arced over me like a dark shadow. I stood silent, unsure of what to say. "Yes. Can I help you?" I winced at my feeble response.

"I want to speak with you about Massimo…and my son."

A crushing doom surrounded me. "I'm not sure if this is appropriate." My voice broke slightly with unease. "Does Max know you're calling me?"

"No, he has no idea. He would never approve of it." Her voice was calm, considering she was speaking to her ex's lover.

"What is it you want?"

"I wanted to let you know I bear no ill will toward you. I couldn't care less what Massimo does."

My first thought was *this is too easy—there's another shoe somewhere around here, and it's about to drop.* "Well, thank you. I wouldn't want to—"

"My sentiments, however, are not likely to be shared by my son. In fact, I think he would be rather devastated to learn his father is considering leaving him to go abroad with you."

Everything inside me sank to my knees. He had clearly discussed this with her. "I don't understand. What is it you're saying?"

"He asked me if I would consider letting my son accompany him on a trip in the future. Naturally, I know all about you and Massimo."

I swallowed to keep my voice from cracking. "Max tells me you've been contemplating separation for some time—several months before his last trip to Libya. Y-you have to know, I wouldn't have agreed to see him if you and he were still together."

I thought I heard a soft laugh and wondered if she was mocking me.

"We've had a special relationship, but it has run its course. In fact, I would say it ran out of steam a while ago. Our son and my husband's absence in Libya are what kept us together in name only for so long, I'm afraid."

"Why are you telling me this?"

"Because"—her voice was like warm honey on the other end of the line—"I feel like I know you. I want you to know the truth."

"How do you mean? What 'truth'?" I held my breath.

"Sofia, I've known about you from the beginning. Max and I would talk about you when we first met. About how uptight you were."

My mouth went dry. I suddenly felt ridiculed, stripped naked.

"It's all so vivid because we had just met. Poor Sofia—he didn't have the heart to tell you he had fallen in love with me."

Devastation sank its teeth into me at hearing this poison, but instinct told me I couldn't let her know she had gotten to me. "Is this why you called me," I responded coolly, "to tell me this?"

"No. The reason for my call is to tell you my son will never leave me for longer than a day or two, no matter what Massimo may think. He will remain here, with me, his mother, where he belongs. And as much as it will hurt him if his father chooses to abandon him to follow you to America…then that's Massimo's choice."

"And what do you want me to do?"

"The decent thing. If you know what that is." An unbearable pause stretched between Dina and me.

"Michael was conceived that last night you know, the night of the festival of the Virgin Mary. Isn't it ironic?" After her last searing remark, the line clicked dead, leaving the squirming earwig of her parting words in my brain.

I stood for a long time with the phone in my hand, listening to the dial tone. After a while it stopped, and then the operator's recorded voice came on telling me to hang up and try my call again. I obliged the operator. Then I thought, did that really happen? Did I experience an exchange with Max's wife, telling me their dirty little secret about how they ridiculed me and then fucked afterward?

I walked to my bedroom and lay down. I felt no need to cry. I only experienced emptiness, contempt. My mind was busy at work, though.

Should I confront him with this? Maybe Dina's bluffing...trying to derail us, destroy any chance of mine and Max's relationship from working out. Or she's lying? Then again, maybe she's not...

Chapter Nineteen

Saturday morning came. I packed a few things and headed to Santa Maria Novella Station. Carla and Mario would be waiting for me at the Lucca station, per instructions, like two weeks ago. *Two weeks ago. A mere two weeks ago I was the happiest I'd ever been, now…*

I reflected on the difference and the wonder of how events played out with Max. Time without him passed slowly, but with him, events sped up and consumed every spare moment, hurtling the aftereffects in lightning speed, gobbling up any void within. It was the only way I could explain it—the experiences here with him, our relationship, seemed to excel in speed.

Beautiful fire, burning hot and fierce for seconds but destined to fizzle out and die in a blinding burst.

I kept up a cheerful façade with my relatives, but underneath I was a mess. Simona arrived midafternoon from work, and for a while, things were lighter. After dinner was when everything spiraled downward to the inevitable.

When we were in the kitchen doing the dishes, my aunt asked, "Sofia, I'm curious. Have you heard from Massimo?"

Simona rolled her eyes, handing me a wet dish. "Oh my God, Mamma—will you please let it go. Why do you insist on harping on this issue? It's none of your concern."

"Your uncle in America made it my concern," snapped Aunt Carla, then she laser-focused on me. "He asked me to look after you while you were here. And I don't mean to pry, I'm just asking. What are your intentions? Are you planning on staying?"

"Whoa." Simona surveyed me, her eyes wide and her face a grimace. "Staying here? You're not seriously thinking of staying here? There are no jobs here. The economy is shit—people are trying to get out, and you want to stay?"

"Relax, Simona," I urged, passing the dry dish to my aunt who was placing them carefully back into the cupboard. "I need to get some air."

I walked out of the kitchen, grabbed my sweater from the coatrack, and marched out onto the patio. My uncle was busy tying up the new growth on the grapevines over the trellises. "Hey, where are you going?" he asked.

"For a walk. Be back soon."

Walk. Walking is good.

I walked the ancient stone streets to the top of the village, pulling my sweater around me, unsure if the chill in the mountain air or the cold words from my aunt and cousin had run a chilling finger down the length of my spine.

Every so often, I saw someone I recognized. I smiled cordially and inclined my head in acknowledgment.

Following the cobbled road, I walked uphill, passed the built-up portion of town, up beyond the cemetery road, and eventually out of town. It took all of thirty minutes to traverse the town from the bottom, where my uncle's house was, up to the top. A small hamlet compared to Hoboken.

I knew Max's old house was close by, a stone's throw from the road beyond the wild apple orchards and ancient chestnut trees. A rush of nostalgia lapped over me, as I thought of the last time I was up here—we were out behind his house, and his little brother spied on us making out. My innocence, trying to save myself for God knows who.

Moving closer to the clearing, I stopped, craning my head to see if his car was there. It wasn't. Maybe he was still with his son. I turned away preoccupied, took the steps toward the path, and kept going until I reached the lookout off the road on the hillside which jutted out overlooking the valley below.

The truth. I need to know the truth.

I hopped the fence, climbed down to the grassy spot, and walked carefully to the side of the steep precipice. My gaze swept over the landscape. I took in the incredible view spreading before me like a tapestry. The craggy mountains in the background, with snowcapped peaks, looked like an artist's giant stroke of a brush had painted them.

Affirming my insignificance against the majesty of nature surrounding me, I thought about the fact that I didn't matter much. Then I recalled one of mine and Max's conversations. *Every little thing we do affects this universe in ways we cannot possibly imagine at the time.*

Would it be worth it? Was I prepared to argue my case with myself for the rest of my life? The questions wouldn't stop.

Could it be that everything I wanted paled in

comparison to the love we shared? Was I fighting true feelings I had inside...to please everyone else? To fulfill a legacy my parents had made for me, goals I had made for myself many years ago in a world without Max?

This was it. The moment I had been waiting for where everything came together. The moment of lucidity where it all became clear and right and true because everything I had worked for was neatly laid out for me like a smorgasbord of pros and cons.

Max, whose love had consumed me, wrapped itself around me, lived inside me, and had captured my heart, body, and soul, wanted me here, but would it last, would it be worth the gamble? Would love be enough?

After Dina's phone call, thinking about what that meant...it was the only alternative. Then it all came crashing down around me.

Right there on the craggy hillside, I experienced a clarity in my mind I hadn't come across in days. Though I had an immeasurable ache in my heart, the knowledge that I had made up my mind made everything clearer, easier to bear.

It was time to get back. I scrambled up the low ridge, skipped over the fence, and stepped back on the path. Rounding the wall back down to the village, I trailed my fingers along the stones in the retaining wall, which held back the trellised hillside above me, ancient and moss-covered. I mused at how the wall was a testament to centuries of life around the village, though sitting silent and fixed to their place for years. I wondered how many other lovers had pondered their future before me along this very path.

As I came around the final bend, Max pulled up in

his Fiat, so incredible was the timing it gave me a start. A broad grin took over his face, as he pulled on the emergency brake, turned off the engine, and hastily came to my side.

"*Ciao*—look who's here," he said as he approached me and kissed me. "Were you looking for me?"

Gently, I pulled away from his embrace, unable to pretend. Even if I wanted to, I couldn't stay with him after knowing what I knew then. "In all honesty, no. I was walking, taking in the scenery, and mulling over everything, thinking."

Max held me at arm's length and tilted his head. "Should I ask what you've been thinking about?"

"What else can I think about?" I said softly. "You and I, of course. What will become of us…our future? What should I do? How do I choose?"

His face took on a worried look. He straightened up and walked to the edge of the retaining wall on the road, looking far into the distance. I noted his scabbed knuckles were white as he gripped the top bar on the age-old rusty barrier. After a long moment, without turning to face me, he simply asked, "And?"

"And…I've decided I'm going home. I can't pretend anymore that you and I are going to work this out. Next weekend, I'm going home as planned."

He turned, a startled, confused, crushed look took over his face.

"You're playing with me," he whispered.

"No." I backed away as he moved closer. "I can't stay here. I'm going home, and in September I'm moving to Boston."

"But what about us?"

"What about us, Max? We cannot work this out. I know we can't. Are you going to give up your son? I couldn't live with myself knowing I forced you to make that choice. And I'm not giving up Harvard."

"I told you, I would figure it out. But tell me why?" His voice broke. "Why so sudden?"

"I will tell you why." My tone was carefully neutral. "But before I do, I need to know one more thing for certain."

"Anything," he blurted out. He was on the brink of panic. "Anything if it will change your mind."

"No one can predict the future, but I believed you were totally invested in us. That you were in it for the long term. Because I was…in '76 *and* yesterday. I loved you so much, Max. I always have, more than you can ever know."

"Tell me what happened, Sofie." His voice was deep, serious.

"I know it's not going to work because without trust, without that base, the faith and belief and conviction that I can depend on you and rely on you—without that assurance from you…" I gulped at the words as Max listened to me. "I can't stay. I know you lied to me about Dina."

His hand reached for mine, and I let him take it, on his face, a combination of stunned shock and shame. His gaze fell to the ground.

We paused a moment, the silence thick as quicksand.

"I asked you that first night, Max. And you lied to me. You did sleep with her, and you were still with me." I waited for him to defend himself. I even shook his hand to elicit a response—any response, but it was clear none was forthcoming. "Massimo, say something."

"All right. I made a mistake," he admitted. "I was wrong. I was an arrogant piece of shit, and I was wrong. Come on, I was young—"

"Finally, you admit it?"

"She told me she was pregnant shortly after you left…" Max ran a hand through his hair. He pulled out a cigarette and placed it in his teeth, fumbling in his pocket for a lighter. "How did you—"

"How did I find out? Not important. And don't go thinking it was my uncle or Simona or Vanessa. They never said a word." Somehow my calmness made the statement more powerful, and his silence spoke more than all the words he had uttered since I had been there. "Listen, Max…it's not solely the mistrust. It's everything." I thought of Dina. "It's everything around us."

"So y-you are deciding for me?" He stammered in disbelief.

I turned from him and looked up at the windows in the village. Some already had hanging baskets of flowers, a sure sign of warmer weather. When I first came back, I was astonished at how pretty it was—a snapshot in time. The quaintness of how each building was different, borrowing this and that from another era, and how the maze of narrow winding streets was as complex as the heart. But now, all I felt were fingers around my heart, squeezing tight. I turned and walked. "I need to get out of here." With long strides, I marched down the lane, my gaze focused on the road leading out of town.

"Why don't we go back to my car?" Max's voice

trailed behind me.

"No. I need to walk." Tears stained my cheeks, uncaring of the passersby staring as I walked.

I strode downhill and out of town, all the while, Max following a short distance behind. I walked to the roundabout at the base of the village and farther toward the little Madonna sanctuary just beyond. There was a wooded area, with an old bench used for silent prayer and meditation.

The statue of the Madonna was tucked away in a protective cove among the overgrown shrubbery, with some long-forgotten dried flowers sitting at the base. Though I wasn't of a prayerful nature, at least not since leaving parochial school, I sat on the cement bench, closed my eyes, and begged for strength for what was coming.

It wasn't long before Max appeared through the clearing and pushed the shrubbery aside to enter. "Sofie," he said simply, appearing to want to say everything but unable to speak a word. He sheepishly took a seat beside me and waited. "Talk to me."

After a long pause, my hollow-sounding voice spoke. "The way I see it, I have these dreams. I have these amazing technicolor dreams I need to make into a reality for me…and for others, too. Your dreams are different…together…everything becomes muted and confused. We've morphed into other people. We have other lives, and we'll have to come to some terrible compromise instead of supporting each other as brilliant individuals with passion and drive, and we'll end up regretting it—resenting each other."

He was silent. I knew him. I knew with every word I spoke, he was turning inward. He would take so much, offer so many apologies, before his pride and need to preserve his dignity kicked in.

"I agree with you on all counts…unequivocally, except the one about the others. No one else should share our dreams." His voice was even, serious. "I can't turn back time to 1976. I can't change what happened, but I would like you to acknowledge that I love you with my heart and soul. I gave up seeing my son for you. And I still hadn't gotten a clear answer from you about Michael and me."

If only you knew the whole story. I knew in my heart I couldn't stay there. I thought of Michael and about how much Max loved him…and about what Dina said…if Max followed me to New York, it would tear their relationship apart. There was no other way.

"You shouldn't have to give up seeing your son for me…you have your answer now. We must face reality. I have no intention of living here. Not now, or ever." I dabbed at my eyes with my sleeve. "But it's not only that, Max…if you came to America, you would resent me for taking you away from Michael. You said yourself, you missed him so much when you were in Libya. You would end up hating me." I shook my head slowly from side to side as my heart swelled against my diaphragm so I could hardly breathe. "If it was just one thing, maybe, *maybe,* it could have worked…but the odds…well, the odds are all against us." It was unbelievable to me that it could unravel so fast, but it had.

He rose calmly and took his cigarettes out of his jacket pocket. "Well, that's it then. I asked for flexibility, for understanding. You can't give me either. I think you're making a mistake."

Classic Max, cool and distant when he's backed into a corner. He waited for me to say something—anything, but all I managed to do was to focus on the little Madonna in the shelter, to concentrate on it with every molecule of my mind so I wouldn't break down in sobs.

"I'm going to let you cool down, think things over." He walked toward the exit through the shrubbery, pushed a stray branch out of his way, and then turned to me. "I'll drive you home to Florence...tomorrow...we can go to Camillo's and—"

"No. No, you can't."

"Why not?"

"It has to end now. I'm serious."

Max's facial expression was skeptical. The look a person got when their bluff was called. He lit his cigarette and swaggered back to me. "Come on, how long are you going to punish me?" He put his hands on my shoulders in an almost patronizing fashion. "I'll see you tomorrow."

"No, Max." My voice grew firm. If I didn't stay strong, I wouldn't make it. "If you come to my apartment, I'll call the peace officer. I mean it, I will."

"Are you really going to throw us away? All that we are?" His eyes narrowed as he let his hands fall to his sides. He chuckled, but there was no humor in his mood. "I'll call you."

"So you do know how to make phone calls—when it suits you. Goodbye, Max."

He shook his head at my remark. "I'll call you tomorrow." He leaned down to kiss me, but I drew back, so he kissed my forehead instead. He turned, hesitated for a second, then walked through the trellis and out of the sanctuary.

The reality of it all settled on me like heavy cream as I sat in the secluded, silent refuge. It cast a stubborn cloudy layer on everything and refused to wash off.

So there was the logic, the rationale. Time to be pragmatic. As much as it hurt, it had to be this way.

How was I going to make it through next week, go to school, pretend nothing was wrong, when all the while, my soul was broken, and my heart lay shattered inside me in a million pieces?

Why did I let this happen again? I could hear my friends back home. *What did you do on your trip to Europe? Oh, I met new friends, went to school, lived on my own for three months, made incredible, wild love with the man who I thought was my soulmate, and then discovered our relationship was doomed. How was your summer?* Ugh!

The one other thing I was positive about was I was ashamed to face myself…to let myself fall into this all over again. But I had to go back now. Staying in this sanctuary forever was not an option.

I would say my goodbyes and leave for Florence tomorrow first thing—alone.

****

The phone was ringing again. It rang for the hundredth time that day.

I knew it wasn't my aunt and uncle. They had said their farewells at the train station. It wasn't my parents because I had called as soon as I got back from Pescaglia to let them know to pick me up as planned next weekend at Newark International. I had a mental picture of my mother turning a cartwheel when she got the news.

Putting a pillow over my ears didn't drown out the ringing, and when I took the phone off the hook, a very pissed off recorded operator voice strongly advised me to please hang up and try your call again…relentlessly.

From the opposite end of the couch, I stared at the phone, knowing full well who it was. It was him, and I knew he would try and talk me out of leaving. Though everything inside me told me not to pick up, I slowly crept over the pillows and grasped the receiver.

"*Pronto*," I said slowly.

"Sofie! It's me." I was right—it was Max. "I've been calling all day. Why did you leave so early yesterday?"

"I was done, Max. I'm done right now. Why are you calling me? I thought I made myself clear."

"You decided hastily. You've had time to think."

Breathe in and stay strong. "I've done my thinking, and my mind is made up. I'm leaving this Saturday." There was a subtle silence on the line.

"Let me come over…we can talk—"

"No. Don't try to come here. I swear, it's over. I'm leaving, Max. Goodbye." I angrily slammed the receiver down onto the cradle, and after a few seconds, plucked it up and placed it on the table. My insides felt beat up. I was all out of tears. Not long afterward the recorded operator came on the line.

Hoping the sound of rushing water would drown out the sound, I walked wearily to the bathroom and turned on the shower. I undressed and climbed under the warm water. I sat on the floor of the shower. For a long time, the stream from the showerhead flowed over me.

I dried off, curled up in bed, and eventually drifted

off to sleep.

****

The next days crawled by with me in a zombie-like state, completing assignments in a fog of sorrow and through bouts of tearfulness. Each night, my mom called to ensure I was still coming home. Each night, Max called, and I hung up as soon as I heard his voice. I hoped he would stop trying to contact me because I still didn't trust my resolve when it came to him.

It was my last Friday evening in Florence. I had already called Simona and said goodbye, and my school friends had gone home after sharing a bottle of wine and promising to stay connected.

The buzzer sounded on the wall, and my heart sank into my stomach—*Max?* I walked hesitantly over to answer it. "Yes?"

"Surprise, my friend!" It was Vanessa's voice—dear, sweet Vanessa.

I waited at the open door until she made it up the stairs, running all the way, and met her on the landing with open arms.

"Oh, Vanessa, you are a welcome sight. Thanks for coming." I grabbed her arm and steered her inside.

"My pleasure, Sofia, I left right after work because I couldn't let you leave without saying goodbye properly."

"I agree. Some wine?"

"No, espresso please."

"So tell me, how are the wedding plans coming?" I asked politely.

Vanessa sat at the kitchen and gushed about the venue, the chapel, the photographer, and of course, I happily listened as I fixed her a coffee. It warmed my heart to hear her so excited about her future with Sergio, but it also reminded me of the similar feelings I had for Max, which eclipsed everything.

Vanessa must have sensed my desolation as I handed her the tiny espresso cup. "Oh, listen to me go on. I'm so sorry, darling." She reached over and gave me a huge bear hug—at this point the best medicine for me. "I heard what happened, from my mother."

"Of course, I'm the talk of the town," I said, dripping sarcasm. We walked to the couch and sat down.

"Ach!" She waved the notion away. "Don't give those old busybodies another thought!"

I chuckled half-heartedly. "I'm going to miss you."

"Likewise, Sofia. So tell me where you two are at."

"*We* are nowhere. Max is where he is, and I am going home tomorrow—that's it, plain and simple."

She placed her hand over mine. "I'm so sorry it didn't work out."

"Sounds familiar," I murmured. There was a pause, and then I had to ask, "Tell me, Vanessa, did you know Max was already sleeping with Dina while he was seeing me...you know, last time?"

"Of course I did."

My mouth twisted into a grimace. "Why didn't you tell me?"

"Honestly, I thought you knew. Or at least made the connection for yourself. It's not exactly something that casually comes up in conversation. Besides, I thought at the least, he would have come clean about it all. But how did you find out?"

"That's not important." I sat back and rested my head on the upholstery. "I still can't believe he lied to me…again—like, three weeks ago about it. I was so naïve." A deep sigh escaped me. "Maybe I was blinded by how much I loved him—then and now. But it's ancient history. There are so many other issues that…well, they can't be resolved. We're in different places. There's just too much that's gone on, too many different commitments…too much life already between us."

Vanessa shrugged.

The phone rang. "Excuse me one second. It's probably my mother." I reached over and picked up the phone. "Hello," I answered casually.

"Sofie…please, please don't hang up. Just listen." Max's voice was desperate.

I looked at Vanessa and mouthed, *Max*. "I asked you not to—"

"I know, but…hear me out. Think for one moment. Try to think of us. Think of how we were before—of you getting on a plane tomorrow. I can't be-because I love you too much to admit to myself that I may have messed everything up again."

"Max. Stop. It's not only about us. My parents have sacrificed everything for me to do this. I-I mean it's not easy to—"

"Listen…stay there. I'll come get you right now. It'll be you and me…we'll go away…you're gone, disappeared."

"I can't." I was growing tired of being strong. "I have to go home. What will my parents do when I don't get off the plane tomorrow? And what about Michael? Aren't you forgetting him? You won't see him anymore. Don't tell me you're prepared to give him up."

"I'll figure something out."

I put my hand on my forehead and closed my eyes. "No, Max. You need to think beyond now. Please, make it easy on yourself and don't call me anymore. The answer is no."

There was a rattling, shaky sigh on the other end of the line. My stomach was in knots, and I thought I was going to be sick. My heart was breaking, and I knew he sensed it.

"Okay, Max, I-I have to go now. I'm sorry, but I c-can't..."

We stayed on the phone for a long time, crying, not wanting to let go because we knew it meant each would return to the lives we lived three weeks earlier.

"I'm going to hang up now, Max. I'm so sorry, but it has to be this way."

There was no response, simply a click, and then the dead sound of disconnection. I hung up and gulped hard. My eyes bordered with tears.

Vanessa was at my side in an instant, draping a comforting arm around me like an angel's wing. "I'm so sorry," she said, rooting around in her purse and pulling out a tissue. "I wish it could have worked out for you." She sat with me and let me cry it out, then, "Is there no other way?"

"If there is, I can't see it." I thought about my response, but the answer was the same. "Is all this a good basis for a relationship, especially a long-distance one?"

"When you put it that way, I see your point." She bit her lip and tried one more question. "What if the shoe was on the other foot?"

I shook my head, confident. "Never going to

happen, so the point is moot, my good friend."

She nodded, scrutinizing me with a half-empathetic, half-cautious look. "Are you going to be all right?"

The response eluded me. Yet I knew exactly how it would be because I'd been through it already. Some days, I felt everything at once. Other days, nothing at all. And I wouldn't know what's worse, drowning beneath the waves or dying from the thirst.

I nodded. "I'll be fine. I'll just have to get over him—all over again."

I had made the choice this time—for us both. I wished him well.

I would always face forward, move onward. It hurt, but it was my decision, and I thought I did the right thing. Yet it wasn't until seventeen years later that I would question it.

Chapter Twenty

Saint Joseph's Hospice, Present Day

"Good morning." The charge nurse behind the fourth-floor desk seemed to have a perpetual smile, which I supposed was one of the requirements of working at a hospice—to have a sunny disposition.

"Good morning," I replied. "How was he last night—after I left?"

"He eventually settled down. I've seen him agitated before, though yesterday he was particularly loud." She raised her brows in emphasis.

"Can I go in?"

"Of course."

"Thank you." I proceeded gingerly to Max's room and knocked softly on the doorframe.

"Hello," I called in and peered into the room. His face was turned toward the window. It was a breezy morning. The trees on the hills opposite the hospice swayed gently back and forth at the wind's disposal, like the fans of invisible courtiers. "Good morning," I tried again.

He turned his face slightly toward me. "Ah. You did come back." His face turned laboriously back to the swaying trees. "I wasn't sure you would."

"You remembered." I raised a cheeky brow. "Of course, I came back. I'm here for you, no matter how much of an asshole you are."

He smiled wanly. "I'm sorry. I didn't mean to snap yesterday."

"Snap? You threw me out." I chuckled despite myself, as I straightened out his blankets. "Don't you dare do that again."

"I won't." He breathed heavily as he tried to maneuver a more comfortable spot.

"Can I help?" I offered.

"No." He wheezed noisily. "Every position is uncomfortable today. I'm so tired of lying down."

He was the most alert I had seen him since I'd been there. "Did you get your medicine? Shall I call the nurse?"

"No. She was just here. The effect must be wearing thin. Maybe I'm getting accustomed to it." He winced when he finished speaking.

I thought distracting him would help. "You know, it's lovely outside. There's a balcony down the hall—a very pretty view, maybe I can ask the nurse to help get you in a gurney or something, and we can enjoy some sunshine?" I glanced at the tubes he was hooked up to and doubted I would be successful.

"I'd like that," he whispered.

"I'll be right back." I walked to the nurse's station, where she was busy keying in nursing things on her computer.

"Excuse me?"

She looked up from her monitor and smiled.

"I wonder if it would be possible to take Mr. Damiani out on the balcony for a little fresh air?"

The nurse bit her lip and grimaced. "I'm sorry, but I'm not able to authorize it. It's too risky to move him at this time—his condition is so delicate."

"He's dying anyway…I mean I hate to be blunt but…"

"I understand, but I cannot allow it. He is too weak."

I drew in my lips and conceded. "Thanks anyway." I walked back to Max's room and sat down at his bedside.

"Sorry, handsome, the nurse says no can do." He ignored my sorry attempt at levity.

"No matter, I think the morphine is starting to kick in." His speech was slower. I watched as his eyelids closed and wondered how long he had left. This agonizing thought fed the anxiety growing in my gut.

I waited, anticipating he would open his eyes again, and when he didn't, I blurted out, "Hey—my husband and daughter are arriving tomorrow. I spoke with them last night, very late, and they're excited. They've never been here. My husband thought it would be good for me if…if they visited Tuscany while I'm here with you." My voice became gentle, almost contemplative when he opened his eyes. "I'm wondering if you would like to meet Cara. Only if it's okay with you, though."

Max took a shallow breath. "If you think it is, then it is."

"Good. Good." I exhaled, relieved at his answer. "So do you want me to do anything for you that maybe you didn't get…uh, didn't get a chance to do? You know, call family, friends?"

"You said something about your husband yesterday, about trust, loyalty." He drew in a heavy breath. "But your eyes said something different."

The question stunned me. "Why would you say that? There's nothing wrong with our marriage. Everything's fine."

"I don't believe you. You've got your eyes firmly planted on your shoes."

To my horror, I realized my gaze was on my feet. An unwanted grin crept across my mouth, as I weighed the absurdness and the accuracy of his last sentence. Then I became serious again. "All right, I'll tell you. I caught him in a lie."

"What did he lie about?" He seemed to be more awake now and rather enjoying the conversation.

"I found texts on his phone that shouldn't have been there."

"From another woman?"

"Yes."

"Did he sleep with her?"

"No."

"Got caught before he could do it?"

"Maybe. He said he had no intention of sleeping with her, but…the jury's still out on that one."

"What an idiot." Max chuckled weakly. "How ironic. The perfect Mr. Jones O'Halloran is human after all."

"James." I was becoming irritated. "And this is none of your business. Like I said before, I wouldn't walk down that road if I were you."

"Nobody's perfect, Sofie."

I considered it and then pushed the thought out of my mind, continuing with my checklist for Max. "Your family—do you want me to call them?"

"I made my peace with my family already, I told you."

I nodded. "What about advance directives, like a will?"

"Done. My brother is the executor."

"Of course. Is there anything else I can do? What about a priest?" I cleared my throat for the next one. I leaned in closer to Max and spoke gently. "Funeral arrangements…I'd like to support your spirituality."

"I don't have any spirituality, but the funeral is arranged. The last thing I wanted was to burden you…or anyone."

My eyes stung. I picked up a pamphlet from the lobby of the hospice about caring for someone you love who is approaching end of life. I hesitated to ask the next question. "I want you to talk to me about what has meaning for you. I want to pray with you if you'd like and arrange visits by anyone you want…maybe your son—"

"No." His reply was curt and decisive.

"But why? I can—"

"No."

I questioned whether to speak my mind, but reckoned if I didn't do so now, I would regret it forever. I spoke softly. "Max, I-I have to tell you…when you admitted to me that you and your son hadn't spoken in years…I felt…I felt responsible. Like I—"

"What happened between my son and me is not your fault. We were okay for a long time afterward. It was me. My work…the company…too busy." His eyes were closing again. "You remember?"

A wave of relief overtook me. "I do remember your work." My thoughts connected to that part of our lives. "Fate liked to screw with us, didn't she, Max?"

"This she did." His eyes fluttered like trembling

butterflies on his sunken sockets. He slept. He didn't stir for a long moment.

I waited, thinking of Mary Magdalene again.

Finally, he opened his eyes. How long would I have this time? Minutes? Seconds? I continued the conversation where he nodded off.

"Um…how about things…do you want me to bring any special or meaningful objects here, from your mother's house, to keep close at hand?"

Max was pensive. "No—everything I need, I have right here." He weakly squeezed my fingers. I brought his frail hand to my mouth and kissed it. It brought a smile to his face. "I'm looking forward to meeting your daughter. If she's half the woman her mother is, she's twice every woman I've ever known."

Immediately, I underwent a visceral reaction to his statement. My eyes clouded and spilled over. The tears fell on my crisp cotton shirt. I turned my head from him, so he couldn't see me.

Max had graced me with two compliments—the obvious one about myself, but he also anticipated Cara's strength of character and disposition. I thought of Cara, her dark eyes and her caustic humor, and my tears quickly turned to a smile. "Tell me, Max, what are the happiest times we've shared together?"

A sly smile came to his lips. "When I came to your apartment in Florence. The first time we made love. I looked like a wet dog coming in from the rain, and you seduced me."

"It was a mutual seduction if I remember correctly."

Max licked his dry lips, so I swiftly picked up the water cup.

"Yes, it was nice," I said as I touched the moist sponge to his lips. "There, that's better." I watched his reaction to the next question. "And the saddest times?"

"There were so many, my love. I don't know how we are still here, able to speak to each other."

"Yes." My thoughts roved. "I think considering everything, we were pretty cordial there."

"Are you thinking about Florence? You didn't see me when I hung up the phone." Now, he turned his head away.

"I'm sorry, but there was no other way—your son…Harvard…I-I felt I had no recourse."

"There's always recourse. Right here, right now…this? This is when there's no recourse."

I nodded in agreement. "You are a wise man, Massimo Damiani, but I suppose with tremendous highs there are bound to be devastating lows." He nodded slightly and coughed, a deep ribcage rattling cough.

"Whoa…okay, steady." I patted his back with soothing motions. "Do you want to keep talking, or do you want to stop? I can read to you if you like."

Max breathed heavily, shook his head, and winced, squeezing my hand anew. "No reading. I get to ask a question now. What do you think are the defining moments of all the days we spent together? You know, the most important?"

"All the days we spent together?" I mused. "You know really when you think about it…there weren't many, relatively speaking."

"We had thirty-seven days," he said with staid calmness.

"Thirty-seven? You've counted how many days we

had together?" I smiled warmly, on the cusp of blushing.

"I did. In truth, it was more or less thirty-seven, some were half, some entire days into nights, some merely a few hours. Everything that was us…thirty-seven days—out of forty years." His gaze found mine. "I think we shared more love in those few days than most people share in a lifetime."

I leaned down and kissed him on the cheek, closing my eyes and remembered.

"Your lips are still soft," he said after I lifted my face from his. "But you still haven't answered my question. What are you most proud of? What will you remember as our best moments?"

I thought about it. "I think our best moments were when we were together in New York. We were both mature, focused, driven. We worked like mad during the day, and then…that last night."

Max's eyes closed as he allowed a sly smile to take over his features.

"Are you thinking about it?" I asked, almost embarrassed by his grin.

"Mmhmm," he said simply. "I certainly am."

"Well, Max Damiani, I hope you're satisfied. I haven't blushed in years, yet you've managed to make me feel like a schoolgirl today."

"I certainly am," he repeated, his eyes closed. Then, he put his head to one side and let out a horrendous, burbled coughing fit, the severity of which frightened me into going to the door and shouting for the nurse.

"Please! Can you help us! It sounds like he's drowning." Within minutes the cough had lessened, and

Max was asleep, exhausted from our conversation, the morphine overtaking the cough.

The young charge nurse was gone, and instead Alberto from a few days ago was back. He came around the desk and in a few long strides was at Max's room in seconds.

Alberto scanned the machines, placed the diaphragm of the stethoscope to Max's chest, and then his back, and listened, after which he looked up at me. I had backed up to the wall to let him work. "I'll page the doctor, but as I look at his vitals, I believe his body is beginning to shut down. We took out the feeding tube before you came, but the doctor may suggest stopping the IV, too."

His speech was steady and calming as he took the stethoscope ear tips out. "He doesn't need it at this point. The body doesn't need anything when it is dying. The fluids are not being absorbed, so they gather in his lungs and throat, thereby causing difficulty when he tries to breathe. I'm sure it's why he's been coughing so much. I'm going to page the on-call physician, but in the meantime, I'll ramp up his oxygen—it'll make him more comfortable. I'll be right back." He adjusted the dial on the oxygen tank as he spoke.

"Okay." My voice was small and purposefully unimportant. "Is it all right to still give him water with the little sponge?"

"Yes." Alberto nodded with an unconscious smile. "Now if you'll excuse me." He bustled out the door, disappearing into the hall.

I watched him leave the room, then helplessly looked back at Max, his breathing labored and sporadic. *It's starting.*

With great effort, I willed my feet to move back to his bedside, unsure of what to do or say next. All I could do was to offer comfort. My hand reached out to his and wrapped it tightly with the reassurance he wasn't alone.

"I'm here, Max," I whispered in his ear. "Try to hang on a little longer." His hands were cold. I grabbed an extra blanket from the foot of his bed and gently pulled it over his body, up to his neck. "I mean it, Max, goddammit, you hang on."

Seconds turned to minutes and the minutes to nearly a half hour before the physician strode into the room, with the nurse in tow, and bid me a good evening.

"Good evening?" I glanced at my watch, and only then did I realize it was well past six o'clock.

"I'm Doctor Ranieri, the on-call palliative care physician. Are you next of kin?"

"Nice to meet you, Doctor. I suppose I am." I looked back down at Max. "He hasn't moved or roused in the last hour, but his breathing sounds horrible."

"It's perfectly normal at this stage." He barely turned his attention to me, focusing instead on the IV tube and monitors by Max's bedside. Then to the nurse, "We're going to remove fluids but maintain the pain management. I'm going to leave a scrip for fentanyl if the morphine produces some ill effects."

"I've been thinking…take away fluids?" I furrowed my brow at the thought. "Isn't that cruel? I mean…how can that help?"

"Though it may seem cruel, nature's process of what we call a 'dry' death is usually more comfortable. Dehydration causes natural endorphins to be released into the brain which produces natural pain relief and euphoria. IV fluids prevent the natural comforting process. And contrary to what you may think, IV fluids do not relieve dryness of the mouth as well as moist swabbing does." He gestured to the cup and the little sponge. "I've seen the discomfort that continued use of IV's trigger, and believe me, it is better for the patient if we stop it. It may cause fluid in the lungs which causes difficulty breathing. It produces saliva…a dying person cannot swallow, so their respirations sound like blowing air through a straw into a glass of water. Our team will do everything we possibly can for him, his comfort, and for the family to have the best experience possible during this time." Though the doctor's tone was patient, it sounded to me like he had recited this speech many times.

"I understand. Thank you." I watched as the nurse detached the clear plastic bag and took away the saline solution, which kept Max hydrated, leaving a much smaller bag containing what I figured was the morphine feed.

We were alone again, with no more than the rhythmic beeping of the monitors and the steady hiss of the oxygen machine to keep us company.

An unpleasant, loud gurgle came from my stomach, so I checked my purse for something to eat and found a granola bar from some long-forgotten lunch back home in New York. I looked at it, unwrapped it, and took the nourishment, not tasting much of the oatmeal apple crisp. After swallowing the last bite, I walked to the sink and let the water run until it was cold, then cupped my hands under the tap and drank. The beeping and hissing persisted as I returned to my place beside Max's bed and reclaimed his hand.

My vision focused on the brilliant red dusk playing over the horizon, the budding trees in the foreground, looking sullen and darker now. I thought how wonderfully fitting it would be if Max could see it, experience the colors, the beauty of the sky at twilight. But he was asleep.

"Hold on, Max." I placed his hand against my cheek as I had done so many times before. In the quiet, I wondered what death would be like. Would there be a light at the end of a dark tunnel, holding the answers to all the questions in the world, holding the warming comfort of unconditional love all human beings craved, or was there darkness, blackness, nothing?

Alive. I'm alive. What bliss life is, imagined from the standpoint of a stone or the black water of the sea. I feel and love and hurt. Stones and water don't die, but they don't feel or love or hurt. Our molecules will light a candle to the consciousness of the universe after we are dead, yet the universe hates death.

I recalled reading somewhere that people who came back from a near-death experience or having a sense of being dead claimed to see family members long past. Others declare they had a feeling one's "soul" had left the body and embarked on a voyage toward a bright light, a departure to another reality where love and bliss are all-enveloping. Heaven maybe?

Alternatively, I also read scientists attributed this to biological functions present during death like tunnel vision or euphoria from pain killers or the firing of the brain synapses right before death. In any event, I thought if it was real, then there is life after death. If not, it was the body's way of coming to terms with this inevitable part of life.

Chapter Twenty-One

Abruptly, I opened my eyes and realized I had fallen asleep in Max's room. My head lay heavy on my arm, and the other hand still grasped Max's. In the distance, I heard a familiar sound I knew was significant. My arm ached, and my hand was asleep, but I had to hurry and reach for it. My cell phone rang in my purse.

After searching for it, I found it at the bottom of my bag. "Hello?" I said blearily.

"Hello, Sof, it's me." James' voice floated from the iPhone.

"Hey. Hello." I spoke in a hushed tone. Rubbing the sleep from my eyes, I got up and walked outside the room, leaning on the wall. "What time is it there?" I focused, unsuccessfully, on my wristwatch.

"It's just after 5:30 p.m., and we're about to board our flight."

"Sounds good. What time do you arrive in Pisa tomorrow?"

"We should be there at around 11:30 a.m. your time."

"Okay. Is Cara excited? Let me talk to her." I heard shuffling sounds as James passed her the phone.

"Hi, Mom." Hearing her voice made me realize how much I missed her.

"Hi, baby! I can't wait to see you and give you a

big hug. I know it's only been a few days, but I miss you so much. Are you excited?"

"Yeah, so excited, and I miss you, too."

"Okay. Now you have a safe flight, and call me as soon as you touch down over here, okay? Remind Dad, 'cuz he'll forget."

Cara giggled. "Yup! Um, how's your friend?"

"Max is not doing well, honey. He is very sick, and probably…will pass away very soon."

"Oh…that's so sad. Are you doing okay, Mom? You're so brave to do this. I don't know if I could do it."

"Me brave? Nuh-uh. I mean, you have to be brave because you must. He has breathing tubes and monitors hooked up to his chest for his heartbeat, an IV with pain medication, and he's very thin but…I can take it. It's about him, not me."

"You're kind of like my hero right now."

"Cara, you're stronger than you think you are."

"I don't know. Maybe. Okay, Mom, Dad wants to talk to you. Love you and see you soon."

"I love you." More shuffling.

"Hey."

"Hi, James, listen, call me when you land—" I swallowed, and after a moment's pause, "I appreciate this, James, you know, right? Despite everything else."

He remained silent. I pictured him relieved, thinking there may be hope for us yet. "Sure, I do. I love you, Sofia. I love you so much. Listen, we'll talk when we get there, you promise? We gotta go, they're starting to board over here, but we'll talk when we get there. Okay?"

The tension in his tone was obvious. There was a

great deal of emotion behind the words he was speaking. And then I did something new. I did a premortem. Instead of waiting for a disaster to unfold and then stress about the relationship postmortem in the days to come, I thought of where my usual responses took us at times like these.

"I love you, too," I said sincerely. "Yeah, we'll talk. And oh, call when you know the train schedule, so I'll know when to come to get you at the station."

"Yes, I know. Don't worry."

We said our goodbyes, and I set the phone back in my purse. I ran my tongue over my parched lips—they felt like sandpaper.

I went back into the room to get a cup of water and found Max with his eyes half-open, focused on the doorframe.

"Hey," I whispered. In two strides I reached the bedside and sat on the edge. Gently, I tucked a stray wisp of hair away from his eyes. "I didn't realize you were awake."

Max blinked up at me. "I thought…" His breath was a shadow. "I thought you left."

"No, I'm here." I shook my head. "It was just a phone call. I didn't want to disturb you, so I went out into the hall."

Max nodded weakly. "Sofie…" There was a long pause. Then he spoke as though it took everything he had to utter the words. "When I said I wasn't afraid of death…I lied. I'm afraid."

My eyes went glossy, so I held my breath. *If you let go of your self-control now, you won't be able to stop.*

Never would I have guessed he would have admitted it to me. The ending of life is expected. We all live in this mortal plane, but the thing I hated most was how it exposed all our weaknesses and left us naked for everyone to see.

Death teased us. It was being longer and more painful than it needed to be. "Don't be afraid." I shook my head, not taking my gaze from his. "I won't leave you alone. I promise." Scooping up his hand, I held it between mine. His eyes slowly closed.

There, in the quiet, my stomach went queasy. My mind had time to rove. I thought of the possible consequences of my actions in the next twenty-four hours.

Exhausted and drained, I craved a good night's sleep but didn't dare leave Max alone. Staring out of the hospital window into the darkness, fireflies danced their tribute to the night, and crickets sang their nocturnal songs. Healthy people slept comfortably in their beds, and I mused about how they would wake tomorrow morning to the normal trivialities of their day as I sat and agonized about the result of tonight's telephone conversation.

I thought of Max and me in Manhattan in 2000. Then of my husband and my daughter and about whether our family would survive into next week.

Chapter Twenty-Two

New York City, 2000

It was early spring. A new millennium with the chill of a cold winter still hanging on pierced the morning air. Y2K was over. Airplanes never dropped from the sky at the stroke of midnight, and everything had settled into a proper normal rhythm on Wall Street—as normal as it ever could be.

My day started as usual. I arrived early and sat in on the longwinded morning debrief meeting. One of only two women senior analysts in the room, which had reached an all-time level of boredom about thirteen minutes ago.

Meanwhile, I had four urgent calls to return. Every one of them needed to be returned by ten thirty. Aidan, a junior analyst across the boardroom table, noticed the agony in my eyes. My whole insides were about to shout, "Oh, God…shut up. Let's go!"

Every time I made eye contact with Aidan it reflected my own urgent need for freedom. Each time the chairman was about to conclude, he announced, "And another thing…" *Please, somebody, get a couple of number two pencils to stick in my eyes.*

Just when I thought I couldn't take another investment caveat story from the Old Man, a rather stressed looking Basil Cormier, head of International

Investments, stuck his head in the room.

"Pssst! Sofia." His tone was hushed, yet urgent, wiggling his finger for me to come to the door. I glanced at Aidan, shrugged, excused myself, gathered my notes, and joined Basil outside.

"I've been trying to track you down." He was breathless like he'd been running. I squeezed my lips together as I visualized Basil scurrying all the way here from his office. "Why aren't you at your desk? I thought you were home, but there was no answer, so I called your department and asked Valentine, and he said you might be in here...what are you doing here anyway?"

"Uhm...morning debrief? Don't you guys in Global Investments have—"

"Never mind that now," he interrupted. "I have an assignment for you. Walk with me." He turned on his heel and strode down the hall.

"Absolutely." I followed as if propelled. "So what's this assignment all about? Has it been in the papers?"

"Maybe. Have you ever heard of Eni S.p.A.?"

"Uh, maybe? Eni Spa?"

"Not spa, S.p.A." We rounded the corner to the elevator, and Basil pressed the up button.

"Oh, yes—it's Italian for a corporation."

"Exactly. It's a joint-stock company. An Italian multinational oil and gas corporation. Anyway, they are in negotiations with the Russian government beginning next week, and they require people...investors in our firm skilled in French, English, and Italian."

"That's me! Sounds right up my alley...but why me?" The elevator pinged, and the doors glided open.

We entered.

"From what I gathered from the liaison officer you were handpicked for this." Basil pressed "Level 3." "His assistant searched our database for, and I quote, the 'best fit.' You were it."

"I'm flattered. And intrigued. What's the deal about?"

"It's about oil, France, Italy, Russia, and a pipeline."

The elevator came to a smooth stop, and the doors opened. We veered left toward Basil's office.

"Interesting. I'm going to have to research. So when do I meet this liaison?"

"Right now—he's sitting in my office." Basil put his hand on the doorknob and pushed the door open, allowing me to enter first. Two people sat with their backs to the door in the plush leather chairs across from Basil's desk. A man sat in one and a woman on the other. The woman was perched on the edge of her chair with a daybook and a pen in her hand. The man had his elbow on the armrest, his hand casually resting against his cheek.

I walked confidently into the room just as Basil bid his return, prompting the man to turn around and rise from his chair. It was as though he was turning in slow motion, revealing his profile little by little. I stopped dead center in the middle of the office, eyes wide, and gasped in an involuntary breath of astonishment.

"Good morning." Two words. Two simple little words. And though the voice speaking was one I hadn't heard in seventeen years, it was as familiar and intimate to me as the Calvin Klein scent cloud I walked into every morning.

There stood Massimo Damiani, looking swaggeringly smug and very dapper in his charcoal gray Armani suit, Italian leather shoes, and soft streaks of silver fanning out from his temples through thick dark hair.

Though he was dressed to the nines, it wasn't his clothing snagging my attention that very moment. It was his knowing smile, the "I got you" look in his eyes, that drove me to suspect he wanted this to be a surprise.

I opened my mouth to say something and then shut it. Stunned by his presence, I couldn't decide whether to rush over and hug him or stride up and slap him. As lightning bolts of shock jammed into the top of my head, zigzagged down my spine, and I gasped for oxygen in the subtlest way a human possibly could, Max extended his hand toward me. I looked at it as though this was a new custom until Basil loudly cleared his throat, which prompted me to take the familiar hand in mine.

"Massimo Damiani"—Basil's hand swept to me—"Sofia Romano. She will be on the team assigned to the deal negotiations."

"Wonderful to see you again, Ms. Romano." Max's handshake was firm, holding mine for a second or two, then releasing. He indicated the blonde young woman who was now standing and smiling at me, with a very toothy grin. "May I introduce Mariana Serra, my administrative assistant. She will be working closely with you during these negotiations."

"It is a great pleasure, Ms. Romano," she said. "I'm looking forward to working with you."

"Pleasure to meet you, Ms. Serra, and please, call me Sofia."

"And I prefer Mariana."

Once introductions were done, I turned to Max who seemed to be positively relishing having put me on the spot. His eyes exuded confidence—irritating and intriguing me even more. "I see you still enjoy catching me off guard. And your English has greatly improved." My efforts to keep my cool composure were barely winning, and my voice oozed sarcasm.

"Working for a multinational company requires proficiency in English. But I needn't tell you about the importance of languages, do I, Ms. Romano?"

I gave him a sidelong glance of utter disbelief. "I wish you had let me know you would be in town."

"Why tell you I'd be in New York City when I know how much you enjoy surprises?"

Is he…mocking me? He's mocking me!

"If you say so. I believe I realized the importance of a great many things long ago, Mr. Damiani."

"I see you still have a long memory, Ms. Romano."

"Some memories never die, Mr. Damiani."

A palpable layer of irritation and tension overtook the room. Both Basil and Mariana watched the scene unfold like they were viewing a tennis match. Max and I, who were supposed to be figures of professionalism, sparred caustic quips of unknown meaning, which clearly left the others in the office wondering what on earth we were talking about.

After a long pause, a bewildered Basil spoke. "Are we still talking about the Eni deal?"

There was an awkward silence as all parties gathered their bearings. "My apologies, Mr. Cormier," Max said, inclining his head.

"No need to apologize. Shall we sit down?" Basil

made his way around the desk, Max sat back down in the same chair, and Mariana took a seat in another chair against the wall, her pen poised over her Day-Timer.

I stood rooted to the spot, not knowing whether to sit or turn and run.

You'll look like an unprofessional brat if you walk out. Stop considering running away as an option. Do not give him the satisfaction of thinking you're flustered by all this. The nerve of him! Clearly, he knew this would rattle me—no...rattle is too gentle a word, startle maybe...how about shock—yes, that's it, shock.

"Can you give me background into this Eni company you work for?" My tone was crisp, businesslike. "Without delving too deep into the history or getting too technical." I circled around to the chair next to Max and sat poker straight, my eyes laser-focused straight ahead.

"Certainly, Ms. Romano." Max eyed Basil, then continued with an air of confidence which annoyed me to no end. "You may remember I worked in Libya for a while—in the oil industry."

"I do remember vaguely you mentioning it," I said. "But I thought you were rethinking continuing that...career path." My silky voice held a challenge.

"Anyway"—Max arched an eyebrow and ignored my bait—"about the same time you were completing your studies at Harvard, according to your curriculum vitae, Eni signed a new agreement with Libya to explore one of the biggest oilfields in the center of the Mediterranean. I was a controller on that project, in the field. My role in the company increased until, in 1992, Eni became a joint-stock company and was listed to the Italian and New York Stock Exchange three years later when much of its capital assets were sold to private shareholders—of which I am a major holder."

"That's quite a success story." Basil arched his brows, looking thoroughly impressed. "You're what we call a self-made millionaire. A successful architect of his own fate."

"Well put, Mr. Cormier. My humble beginnings on the ground, in the field, and on the platform of an oil rig in the middle of the Mediterranean taught me some valuable lessons. It gave me a unique perspective on the corporate ladder, remembering the executives I had replaced. I've never been afraid of hard work."

Max's gaze was now fixed on me.

"When the price of oil collapsed in '98 as with other major companies, I suggested Eni turn to mergers and international acquisitions, new explorations…it set the foundations for a bona fide super company."

"So you went from a hands-on supervisor on an offshore drilling rig to a major player in the company in what—fifteen, sixteen years?" I commented briskly, tossing my hair over my shoulder in a gesture of defiance. "Very impressive, indeed. When I left Italy nearly seventeen years ago, you were a crane operator in the Libyan oil fields."

"I operated a track loader—at a refinery. Thank you." Max tilted his head in acknowledgment. "Currently, I'm working on a fledgling project—an accord with Russia to secure imports to the European Union through pipeline projects in post-Soviet countries."

"I know this much—Russia has become an energy superpower, and that has become a hot topic in the European Union," I offered. "It makes sense since their domestic production greatly exceeds domestic demand, it renders Russia the world's leading net energy exporter. I can tell you it's become a focus of international politics. Really a policy nightmare."

Now it was Max's turn to be impressed. "Very good, Ms. Romano. You know your global business affairs."

"I do work at Goldman Sachs." My expression and tone were deadpan.

"Exactly. There's where you come in. I need an investment banker who is skilled in French and Italian. Our initial negotiations are scheduled to begin next week."

I looked at Basil and then at Mariana. How could I get out of this? "There must be other investment analysts who have similar skill sets. Why not an interpreter? Why me?"

"No, in fact, there are not." He leaned in. "And why have an outsider interpret our negotiations when I know you can handle this?" I detected a thawing in his tone. "Imagine my delight when I saw your name cross my desk as a prospective candidate for this, not only for my company but for Goldman. Hundreds of jobs and billions of dollars rely on the success of this deal. And for better or worse, you know me. What I'm thinking, my intentions, the nuances, only a person who understands me could be privy to. You were the most logical choice."

I squirmed in my chair. "I highly doubt your choice had a great deal to do with logic." I secretly noted my heart rate had shot up, and I could scarcely breathe.

Basil cleared his throat, prompting me to recall my superior was in the room. *Settle. Calm down, girl.*

"Don't flatter yourself, Sofia." Max's voice was courteous but firm. "When it comes to business, I don't let my emotions get in the way. My assistant did the research. Your name came up consistently as the most suited for the task. I did suggest you as Goldman Sachs' lead negotiator, but your selection for this by the consortium to assist in this deal and help us get it to bed was a sound analytical decision."

My eyes fixed on my supervisor. "Basil." I rose from my chair and faced him. "I respectfully decline to accept this assignment."

Basil got up nearly as fast and held up an apologetic hand to Max. "Uh, please, give us one moment, Mr. Damiani…may I speak to Ms. Romano for a second?" He came around the desk and grabbed my arm, taking me to the busy hall outside his office.

Max tipped his head. "Of course, take your time."

When Basil was certain we were out of earshot, he turned to me nervously, speaking in a hushed tone. "Okay, what's going on here? Why are you turning this down? Do you know who Damiani is? He's the liaison for one of the largest oil and gas consortiums in the world, and he asked for you…*you,* as the lead for this project."

"Yes, I know, you already—"

"Then you know that as a senior analyst who is, as of now, sitting on a very long list for a VP position, this could clinch it for you at Goldman's—if you're successful?"

"I suppose."

Basil couldn't hide his exasperation. "Sofia, you're one of the best analysts I've had the good fortune to work with. This is a once-in-a-lifetime opportunity.

Why are you throwing it away? All he wants is a conference broker. You've got this. You'll work at meetings between chief executives and the like. You won't be alone. The prospectus is done. It shouldn't take longer than four, five days tops, to go through the paperwork."

"He wants a glorified interpreter." I squeezed my lips together and lifted my chin, trying to maintain my cool. "And it's only because Mr. Damiani and I have a…a history."

"A history of what?"

I rolled my eyes. "You know…a history."

It took a moment, but he finally clued in. "Oh…that kind of history." He took in a noisy breath. "Well, if I were you, I would seriously consider putting it all aside and think of your career. This is huge. Do you think anyone in the boardroom cares about what you may be *feeling*?" Basil air-quoted *feeling* and spoke it in a whiny tone.

"This is your chance to test your mettle, prove your worth for your place up in the top floor office. Are you going to let whatever happened between you and him get in the way? Think about this before you say no. You can't take something like this back."

Basil spoke wise words, but in my mind, *this* was the biggest obstacle to my accepting the job. Our paths kept crossing in this mammoth world. It wasn't as though we lived in the same city or even continent. People lived their entire lives in Manhattan who never saw each other again. What the hell was it between me and Max that whoever pulled the strings was trying to tell us?

"I'm a senior analyst now. I'll be up for a

promotion soon. What does it matter?" I finally asked Basil.

"You could be wasting away as an analyst for years. Believe me, the adage *if one is deserving, opportunities are made for you* is true, here or abroad." Basil paced as he spoke and then put a kindly hand on my arm. "I'm asking you, as a friend, to think with your head, not your heart. Think of what this could mean. Now I'm going back in. Take a moment, think carefully, and I'll see you inside." He tapped a finger on his head. "Use this."

Basil strode back into his office, chatting amicably with Max and Mariana about the lousy weather New York had been experiencing. I focused instead on my shoes as my thoughts went wild.

The first person I thought to call was James, my fiancé—dear, sweet, understanding James. But the dilemma of hesitating to accept a plum assignment because my ex-lover was at the helm of a multinational deal and I feared it would stir up old emotions didn't seem like an appropriate topic to discuss with my future husband.

I fully understood and acknowledged Basil's not so roundabout way of telling me I was a fool if I didn't snap this assignment up. All my reasoning power told me I was an idiot for even thinking of turning it down, but my heart told me differently.

I stuck my head in Basil's office and declared, "I'll be back in a minute."

I walked, first at a brisk pace, then nearly ran to Tess's cubicle.

Tess Binkley and I had hit it off immediately. We had met in the Goldman Sachs Human Resources lounge both anxiously awaiting to be interviewed for the internship program. Tess was a British national, whose daddy sat on the board of Lloyds Banking Group. If I wanted to have a heart-to-heart with my best friend, I had to hurry. They were waiting for me back in Basil's office for an answer.

Tess was on the phone. I didn't bother waiting.

"Tess," I hissed, making a cutting motion across my throat.

"Uh…right, um," sputtered Tess. "Listen, Seth, I'll have to call you back." She hung up and threw her hands in the air. "Sof, what's up?"

"Oh my God! Tess, I'm freaking out here." I sat as I tried to catch my breath.

"Take a breath, love. Calm down," she ordered, in her proper British clip.

"Okay, okay…I'm better…I'm better," I sputtered, laying my hands on my chest. "I ran here from Basil's office because do you remember that night at the Amsterdam when we had all those draughts, and I told you about the guy in Italy who I had a crazy two-week affair with, and all we did was make love and eat and drink and argue, and then I ended up leaving him?"

"Hmph!" Tess laughed, crossing her arms. "Who could forget that?"

"Well, he's sitting in Basil's office, right now." I tapped my freshly manicured fingertips on the desk to emphasize the last two words.

"Fuck off!"

"No, I'm totally serious."

"What the hell?"

"Listen, I have to get back, but apparently, he is a major player with this major Italian oil company—"

"Eni?" Tess interrupted.

"Uh, yeah, how do you know that?" I grimaced.

"Who doesn't?"

I made a face. "Anyway, they're in town negotiating a massive deal with a French oil company and the Russians. So it's a major international investment merger. He had his assistant research that I was a 'best fit' because of my language experience, and he wants me to do this special assignment." With no air left in my lungs, I took a huge breath and waited for Tess's reaction.

"Oh, wow—so don't tell me you're hesitating to take on the project."

"Wouldn't you?" I implored.

Tess raised a brow. "I would never let my emotions get in the way of my career. I'm stronger than that, and so are you."

"I am?"

"Is this Sofia Romano I'm speaking to? The woman who made the slow climb with me, both starting as interns after she completed a two-year M.B.A. at Harvard with the eventual placement as a junior broker, then analyst. You know you could be waiting for years for a corner office. This might be your chance. Opportunities are made." Tess huffed out a breath. "Let's consider the obvious. You're wavering here because, on the one hand, this project could propel you to a plum management position, yet?"

"Yet, on the other hand, there's Max—and everything that comes with him." I sighed. "I'm already sensing the dredging up of old emotions, Tess, but with these feelings, there's a whole host of others I just can't put my finger on." My eyes narrowed. "He has this confident swagger, an influential position, and this newfound self-assuredness. It makes him powerful—too powerful to resist temptation."

Tess shrugged. A corner of her mouth curled up into a crooked smile. "Would it be all that bad if you didn't—resist?"

"Seriously? Tess, I'm engaged." I thought a moment. "Is it possible I'm...no, it can't be... I'm...intimidated?"

"I don't know. But I will say you are overthinking this. And if you're going to give Basil an answer, you may want to head back."

I checked my watch. I'd been gone for nearly twenty minutes. "Oh shit. You know, if I could be sure Max wouldn't try to put a move on me, I'd take it—in a heartbeat."

My thoughts raced as I sat in Tess's cubicle considering my options. He could deny it all he wanted, but I knew him better than that. If he was right about one thing, I knew him and understood the way his mind worked.

Impatiently, I pulled my thoughts together and decided.

"Okay, my friend." I stood. "I'd better go. Thanks for listening to this crazy lady."

"Make the right move," said Tess, encouraging me with a thumbs up. "Good luck."

I strode back into Basil's office, poised, strong, and assured I could do this and if I accepted, it would be on my terms. Both men rose as I returned to my seat, opposite Basil and next to Max.

"We were about to send out the cavalry to find you," said Basil, laughing nervously.

"Well." All eyes were on me. "I have decided to accept this assignment…"

"Very good choice, Sofia," chirped Basil rising to shake my hand.

"You won't regret it…" Max was in the middle of extending his hand to me when I interrupted both men.

"…with some provisos."

Both men halted in an awkward tableau. Basil spoke first with Max subtly narrowing his eyes at me. "Go on." Basil gestured for me to continue.

I probably appeared unruffled, as I coolly folded my hands on my lap, though my insides were flipping somersaults. "First, I want to be the lead on this account. I choose the broker teams, create the schedules, and make all the arrangements for the negotiations based on the agenda provided to me by Mr. Damiani." Basil looked over to Max.

"Agreed," Max said amiably, inclining his head.

"Second, I wish to be compensated accordingly. This means bonuses from Eni for me as well as my team, in addition to our regular salary and bonuses. We can discuss the amount later."

Basil's head pivoted back and forth from Max to me as I spelled out my conditions.

"Agreed," Max repeated. I did note a smile beginning to dance around the edges of Max's mouth. I watched it flicker and fade, and I knew what he was thinking…*What a cute little thing she is, trying to play in the big leagues with the big boys.*

"Anything else?" he asked politely.

"Uh, no. I believe that's it…for now."

"Then do we have an agreement?" Max asked, peering at me as his fingers tapped on the armrest.

I looked over at Basil, who had "ulcer flare-up" written all over his features.

Then, I spoke before I was even conscious of the one syllable leaving my mouth. "Deal." I breathed out, glowing in self-satisfaction. My whole world was about to change.

Chapter Twenty-Three

The negotiations took place in one of the larger conference rooms, on the top floor of 85 Broad Street in Lower Manhattan.

Early the first morning, when Tess, Vlad, Aidan, and I arrived beforehand to prepare, Max had come in to drop off papers.

"Good morning," he said briskly.

"Morning," I replied.

"Dropping off last-minute briefs and the prospectus." He handed the papers to me, and as he did, Tess sidled up beside me and nudged me in the ribs.

"Oh, uh, Max, this is Tess, Tess, Max. Tess is on my team. That's Vlad over there and Aidan. Basil will be in and out, ensuring everything is going smoothly."

Max nodded in acknowledgment at the men but took Tess's hand. "A pleasure." His voice purred as he made eye contact.

"All mine." Tess's voice was silken.

Her eyes widened as she watched him move around the table, organizing the mandates. "Is that *the* Max?" she whispered in my ear. "Crikey—he's hot."

I ignored her. Before he left, he nodded to us both, but to Tess, he said, "We'll see you shortly."

"I'm looking forward to it," she responded all honey.

Despite my best efforts at managing my emotions,

a pang of jealousy went through me. It wriggled in my stomach like a giant earwig, unsettling my control.

My friend turned to me after Max left. "Wow—darling, he is straight away too good to waste. If you're done with him, mind if I ask him to dinner one night? Do you know if he's hooking up with someone steady?"

"Steady?" I chuckled to hide my annoyance, as I shuffled papers. "Are we back in high school, Tess? I haven't the foggiest idea."

It was nearly nine thirty, the meeting slated to begin at ten—the players assembled and seated themselves around the place cards.

"Come on, Tess," I called out to the brokers who were going over the briefs. "Vlad, Alain—it's time."

Now concentrate—relax and take a deep breath.

The Russians would begin the initial addresses.

"Dear colleagues and friends, today marks the first day of negotiations between the Union of Oil and Gas Producers of Russia, the Ministry of Foreign Affairs of Russia, and the Eni corporation of the great nations of Italy and France…"

That morning would set the tone for the entire negotiations, so it was important to get it right. To say I was nervous would be the understatement of the century.

"The Minister of Foreign Affairs of the Russian Federation, Igor Ivanov, has always paid and continues to pay close attention to the issues of economic development," the Russian undersecretary prattled on, which reminded me of the Old Man in the boardroom.

The Eni group consisted of seven senior board members and their assistants, including Max, plus two

Italian and two French representatives and their entourages. In addition, the Russian delegation was comprised of twelve: ministers, diplomats, and oil union heads, plus their assistants and their interpreters.

To prepare for the negotiations, I studied the intricacies of Italy's, France's, and Russia's foreign oil policies, with Mariana by my side the week before the talks.

Once, I feebly inquired as to Max's whereabouts during one of our sessions. Mariana had simply said he was in preliminary meetings with American shareholders in his suite at the Waldorf. She quipped something about him not liking the crass nature of Wall Street, preferring his hotel.

I smiled to myself. *Max at the Waldorf—now I've heard everything.*

"Currently Russia is one of the world's largest energy producers. Russia is not a member of OPEC and is prepared to present itself as an alternative to Middle Eastern energy resources…"

As the undersecretary spoke, Max put a hand on my forearm as I took notes. He motioned to a question he had scribbled on his pad of paper. "Ask him this when he finishes," he whispered in my ear.

I shook my head. "It's not the time yet," I answered barely moving my lips and went back to taking notes.

"Why not?" he insisted. "This is important."

"I thought you trusted me. Let me do my job."

He huffed out a breath and backed off, resting a hand against his mouth, which seemed to be stopping him from speaking out. The undersecretary continued, oblivious to our whispers.

"...I now leave the bulk of the negotiations to our brothers in the Union and look forward to continued cooperation between our two great nations. Thank you."

Applause rippled around the room as the undersecretary finished his speech with our Russian interpreters ensuring every word aligned with our copy of his opening address.

The moment the minister leaned back in his chair, satisfied he had delivered a powerful message, Max leaned into my ear as he applauded.

"Why didn't you ask him?"

I turned to face him. "Emotion has no place at the negotiating table. Look, do you trust me or not? I thought you wanted me here because I'm good."

"*You* are a good advisor—let *me* negotiate the deal," ordered Max, emphasizing the pronouns for effect.

"What do you think I've been doing at Goldman Sachs for fifteen years...twiddling my thumbs?" I replied, without flinching or losing my composure. "I've sat in on and participated in dozens of major deals. I've learned from the best here. So be sure to check your ego at the door and prepare to enter the deal-making process with a lot of business sense and discipline. There's a time and place for challenges, and yes, it would be considered a challenge, not a question. The opening statement of the undersecretary for the Minister of Foreign Affairs of the Russian Federation on the first day of negotiations is *not* the appropriate time to ask that question. There will be plenty of opportunity for such matters *later*." My eyes widened as I emphasized the last phrase.

Grudgingly, Max stood down, leaned into my ear, and whispered, "I hope you know what you're doing."

"Friends and colleagues, I believe we have earned a break," said the undersecretary. "Shall we reconvene in a half-hour's time."

I repeated the message in French and Italian, and all agreed, after which I added, "Our associates from Eni shall speak after the break. We will resume at half past eleven if we are all agreed." I breathed in a sigh of relief—then thought…four and three-quarter more days to go. Ugh.

"Well done, Sofie," offered Max, emotionless. "But I'm going to consult with the chief of Energy Solutions on the point we discussed."

"Okay. I'm going to make a phone call." I rolled my eyes and stalked off.

I was beginning to doubt my initial thoughts on the motivation behind Max asking me to be on the project—a week in Manhattan and all I'd gotten from him were memos and scribbled notes through Mariana. I hadn't even seen him until the morning of the first official meeting, where we spoke briefly about protocol but little about anything else. In fact, he had been cordial, maybe even a little aloof. I was surprised to note the nagging sense of disappointment creeping into my gut.

I grabbed a coffee from the breakfast buffet in the conference room and ducked out to call James.

"James? Hey, it's me."

"Babe!" The tone of his voice sent his smile to me. "How's it going?"

"Good. Almost got the prelims out of the way, but the Russian speaker this morning was so damned longwinded, it took up virtually the entire morning. Hopefully, the Italian won't enjoy the sound of his own voice nearly as much, and we can get down to business today sometime."

"Ha!" There was a pause. "Did that Max dude show up today?"

"Yes, he did. He's impetuous, though. Has absolutely no political savvy. Not sure how he made it to where he is."

"Interesting. What does he do?"

"His assistant tells me he is the special assistant to the executive vice president of Energy Solutions."

"Notable."

"Yeah. I don't even think he finished high school. It's quite a success story."

"Maybe he's just a savvy oil man."

"He would have to be." My mind wandered. I thought of Max, sitting around a boardroom table in a stockholders' meeting and chuckled to myself. "Look, I should be going." I sighed. "It's nearly time to go back—meaning brain overload for a while."

"You going to be home for dinner?"

"I will, but I may be late."

"I'll take care of it."

"Now I know why I love you," I cooed.

I promptly returned to the negotiations as the board members were taking their seats. It was Tess's turn to speak to the negotiations now. Max was seated next to her, me next to him, and the vice president of Energy Solutions for Eni, Elio Conti, at my side.

"Mr. Conti," I whispered to the VP. "Since today is for preliminary statements, and we have a chance to Q&A tomorrow, I suggest we hold the more divisive issues until tomorrow. I believe Tess mentioned it."

Conti leaned in. "I would agree with you, but Mr. Damiani wishes to take a different approach."

"With respect to Mr. Damiani's concerns, I advise we maintain the friendliest terms possible for as long as we can. It's the first day. Friendships in business forged today will still be here tomorrow."

Max leaned into me as he turned to face Conti. "We all agree the Russian president has different ideas regarding the future of energy in Russia and its business relationships with European nations and possibly America. I'm worried these negotiations are simply lip service, and when our lawyers finalize the deal in October, all our progress, speeches, and flesh-pressing were for nothing."

"No one can predict the future, Mr. Damiani," I contradicted. "In my experience, I've found it is the best policy to remain friendly."

Conti weighed my words carefully, then spoke directly to Max. "I agree with Ms. Romano. We wait. Tomorrow we ask about the new president and his view on the energy sector. His vision for the future." Then to me, "Thank you for your insight. I can see why Massimo suggested you from the very beginning."

Feeling triumphant, I turned to Max, who was awfully busy shuffling his notes around.

"So you suggested me at the outset? I thought your assistant chose me out of a slush pile of possible brokers."

His face flushed as he flipped through his papers. "Quiet, please," he said, gesturing to the advisor about to speak. "They're starting."

My smile widened as satisfaction warmly grew

inside me. "You're welcome," I whispered.

With a successful first day under my belt, I was more confident about my new leadership role, and once the clients began gathering their notes and the assistants began flocking to their respective advisor, I spoke in English, then alternated with Italian after every few sentences. "Ladies and gentlemen, thank you once again for a very productive first day of these week-long negotiations with our clients. I'm certain tomorrow will be as successful as today. We wish to remind all partners there will be a reception immediately following the meeting in the executive dining room adjacent to the conference room. All are welcome to attend. Good evening."

I breathed in a sigh of relief, standing as everyone began filing out, some taking my hand and thanking me as I stuffed papers into my briefcase.

Conti, Max, and their assistants were still at the table, discussing points for tomorrow's negotiations. When Conti noticed I was free, he stepped toward me and held out a hand. "A job well done today, Ms. Romano," he said.

"Thank you." I smiled cordially, shaking his hand.

"Tomorrow we discuss supplier pricing agreements and capital markets. I will have the notations delivered to your home later tonight. I'd like to tweak the wording in the documents with Mr. Damiani, before drafting the final copy. Any suggestions?" he asked.

"Well, I admit up until last week, I had only done prep research and produced reports on the topic for vice presidents or directors. But I do know people. Aside from cultural differences, we all want the same thing when it comes to negotiating in business. Listen and be understanding."

"I shall keep that in mind." He bowed slightly. "*A domani*." I watched as Conti followed the others into the reception. When I turned back to get my case, Max was putting on his overcoat and scarf.

"You're not going in?" I asked.

"No." He slipped his arm into the coat sleeve. "I have an appointment. I'll have Mariana send you the brief tonight. I will make sure I pepper it with lots of nice words." He raised his brows and smiled sarcastically at first, then stopped and took a long look at me. "You were very good today." He snapped up his coat collar, grabbed his briefcase, and headed toward the door. "Good evening."

"Good evening," I repeated quietly. But I was certain he hadn't heard as he had already disappeared into the hall, swallowed up by throngs of people on their way home.

Chapter Twenty-Four

Day Two of the Russia-France-Italy pipeline deal talks crawled by, mostly comprised of technical presentations, discussions regarding union bargaining, and effective supplier relationship management. Basil sat in on the entire morning negotiating session. This tended to make me nervous.

"Don't you have anywhere you need to be?" I whispered to him at the break.

"Simply making sure everything is going smoothly." He leaned into me and smiled cordially. "This is a rather important gathering."

"Thanks anyway, Basil. We're fine."

He nodded, and though he was reluctant to go, he agreed our team was well prepared.

Max and I sat next to one another again, and when it came time for Conti to speak on the deal, he made certain I would be the one annotating the briefs in English.

It was the speech that Max had crafted for Conti—without the hotheaded remarks raised in Max's speech at the outset. It was a clean version of his pointed question from yesterday. When I received Max's notes the night before, I called Mariana and suggested they cut the words "coercive price policy" and "blackmail or threats" from the speech. They agreed.

James and I spoke after the conferences that

afternoon, as usual, he from his law office and me from a phone in the conference room. "Today's been a day from hell, James. My eyes are stinging, my voice is hoarse from talking, and my brain is like mush." I complained, rubbing my forehead. "How is your day going?"

"Obviously not as bad as yours. Tell you what—I'll be home by seven tonight. I'll grab something for dinner, that way we can relax. Maybe some time in a warm bubble bath, sipping on cold pinot grigio?"

"Perfect. You know me too well," I said appreciatively. "Get something from Le Chinois? They have the best spring rolls."

"It'll be waiting."

I put down the receiver and looked up to see Max leaning on the wall next to me. "Oh. How long have you been standing there?"

"Sorry." He let out an impatient sigh, ignoring my question. "I need to relax. These negotiations have me so wound up I feel like I'm going to snap. I need a good strong espresso."

"Won't espresso wind you up even tighter?" I asked, raising a brow.

"Not for me. My system is screaming for a good cup of espresso. The coffee in this place tastes like dirty dishwater. Do you know a good espresso bar?"

If I say no, he might think it's rude. It's only five. Why not—it's innocent enough. "I know one. It's a few blocks away. Let's get a cab. I can use a cappuccino myself."

I plucked up my trench coat and walked around the large circular table to the door. "This way." I indicated and strode down the hall, slipping on my coat. Max followed close behind.

I bore left toward the elevators and pushed the down button. We both stared at the flashing numbers, waiting in an uneasy silence. In the elevator, we talked about the weather in France and how lovely it was at this time of year and prattled cordially as we exited the building on Broad Street and walked side by side to the curb. I raised a hand, prompting one of the cabs in the queue to pull up. Max opened the door and let me slide in first.

"Where to?" asked the driver.

"Epoca Espresso Bar on Greenwich," I replied.

We sat in silence as the cab trundled its way in stop-and-start traffic from the Goldman Sachs Building to William Street then onto Church, followed by Hudson, and barely squeaked through as the light turned, onto Greenwich Street.

"New Yorkers could give drivers in Rome a run for their money," Max commented dryly as the cab pulled up in front of Epoca. "Have you, at last, learned to appreciate an espresso shot?" asked Max as he held the café door open for me. His tone seemed a bit more relaxed now that he was out of the building. "Still with the cappuccino?"

"I have a very delicate palate," I replied walking to the counter. "Which is most likely the only part of me that's delicate."

"On the contrary." He chuckled. "You are everything a woman should be." His gaze shifted uncomfortably, from my eyes to the chalkboard menu above the massive espresso machine.

How does he do it? How does he go from cold to warm and make me feel like an insecure, confused teenager whenever I'm around him?

"You go and find a table," he said. "I'll order for us."

I complied. As he ordered our coffees and stood to wait, I watched him. I gazed at the curve of his face, the color of his hair, how he looked in his designer suit and Italian leather shoes. Clearly, it was a different Max, yet I knew now, he was very much the same. Impulsive, brash, and bordering on boastful, yet refreshingly so because of his insecurities, even under all the finery and new title and position, I knew him too well to be put off by his pride.

"Can I ask you a question?" I inquired as he set the cappuccino down on the table.

He sat to face me. "Fire away."

"How did you end up special assistant to the vice president of Energy Solutions?" I rested my chin in my hand. "I mean, one minute you're working on cranes and oil rigs and the next minute…well, here you are."

"It wasn't quite 'a minute'." Max laughed and looked out into the mellowing sky. "Conti and I met while we were both working in Libya. He liked the no-nonsense way I ran my site. He figured I could help him run the company in the same way. Once he was appointed a position as vice president of our French affiliates, I was summoned to Toulouse. It's about as high as one can climb in the energy sector's corporate ladder without a university degree. You know me—I was never much for formal education anyway."

"And that's how you became the special assistant." I stared at him, almost wordless. "I'm…I'm proud of you." I looked into my steaming cap, surprisingly unable to meet his eyes.

"Thank you. If I could, I would record what you just said…and save it."

I laughed and shook my head. "Still can't let it go, huh?"

Max chose to ignore the question, a slight shadow of amusement on his face. "And you? Never mind me, look at you. A Wall Street success story. You accomplished what you set out to do." He lifted his chin and allowed himself a slight smile. "Happy?"

I nodded. "Yes, I am. Especially with international mergers and acquisitions…they're such fertile grounds, those international meetings. I mean, besides the business aspect, of course…we learn so much from each other as if we had been seeing in 2D before, and together the ideas take on a full 3D form."

"You're the only person I know who can take a dry business deal and turn it into a diplomatic mission."

We both burst out laughing. I noticed it was something he didn't do so much anymore. I hadn't heard his laugh in nearly seventeen years, and I had forgotten how deep, warm, and rich it was. When Max laughed that afternoon, he seemed ten years younger.

"Talk to me about the deal then," he said, still a trace of laughter in his voice. "Give me your honest opinion."

"Okay. Uhm…a little business then." I licked my lips. "In keeping with the spirit of diplomacy, I'm willing to make it up to you, if you drop that guard of yours. Let me and my team do our jobs."

"I've been eating, sleeping, and breathing this deal for almost a year now. I don't want any shenanigans on the part of the Russians to jeopardize it. Yeltsin was bad enough, but this new guy…" Frustration darkened his eyes, his voice.

"No, no," I protested. "Don't brood. Hey." I touched his arm "Have you seen the Empire State Building yet?"

"I've barely been out of my hotel room and the Goldman Sachs building." He downed the last of his espresso shot.

I licked my lips nervously. "Come on—I want to show you something." I tucked my scarf around my neck and motioned for Max to follow.

****

The sun was sinking lazily below the skyline. It put on its farewell performance for the day and finished its last dance in the sky with brilliant reds, oranges, lavenders, and some otherworldly colors for which there are no names. I focused on the colors in the distance, as we stood side by side, leaning on the observation deck of the Empire State Building. The din below us didn't matter. We quietly took in the spectacular scene before us as the breezy evening took shape.

"Incredible." Max sighed, his temperament softening. "It's like a whole other world up here—away from the noise and the frenetic crowds, the tourists."

"Hmm. There's nothing like a Manhattan sunset from the top of the Empire State Building."

"A Manhattan sunset can only be surpassed by a Florentine sunset over the Arno." He turned slightly and leaned on his elbow as he focused his gaze on me. "You know all about it though, Sofia."

His stance and words wildly pulled me back to Santa Trinità bridge. I tried my hardest to ignore it, knowing full well he was expecting a reaction. It took everything I had not to offer one and chose instead to keep my gaze focused on some far-off point.

At last, he turned his attention back to the cityscape.

"It's so different from Italy here. The buildings look like stacked toy blocks." Max pointed to the horizon. "What is that one over there?"

I squinted at the structures in the distance trying to remember. "That is the Seagram's Building there. Over there is the Chrysler Building. Those two tall twin skyscrapers way down there is the World Trade Center. That's Penn Plaza. Rockefeller Center is right across there, and the bright, colorful spot down there is Times Square."

Max chuckled. "Brilliant! I'm impressed. How do you know them all?"

"I grew up a few miles away, remember? My parents used to bring me up here all the time. We'd take the ferry from Hoboken into the City, and we'd go up to the top of Rockefeller Center or here. My dad and I would compete at who could name more of the skyscrapers."

"Do you still come here with your parents?"

"No." I shook my head and looked down. "My father's gone—cancer. My mom was diagnosed with Alzheimer's disease a couple of years ago. She's in long term care, but pretty much, I'm all she has."

"I'm so sorry. You must miss your father very much."

"I do." I looked out over the Hudson. Canada geese flew in formation, heading south. "I haven't come up here since he passed. It didn't seem right."

"What about your fiancé, what's his name, Jones?"

"James. And no, I've never come here with him. We're both New Yorkers—both over it, I guess."

"Yet you brought me here?"

I smiled. "It seemed right." I wanted to look at him, into those eyes I remembered so well but didn't dare. I had no intention of letting myself be swept up again.

"I'll take that as a compliment." From the corner of my eye, I saw his gaze wander out over the vista, eyeing the skyline. "Now I have a compliment for you. I'm impressed—not only by your skills as an advisor and a banker but your intuition, perception."

"I appreciate your saying so. Self-confidence helps too, but if you're not confident, you have to pretend you are. Otherwise, people don't trust you."

"I can't see you lacking in self-confidence."

"Ah, my plan is working." I flashed a smile.

Max laughed. "I'm curious. Have you ever thought of working overseas?"

"No. Not lately anyway."

"I'll recommend you for a promotion. I truly appreciate you…advising me on the importance of timing."

"The changes were subtle but crucial. You need to have the ability to put yourself in the minds of other people."

"Hmm. True." His smile was warm and disarming, and my defenses slowly and involuntarily melted away. "And I'm glad we are talking and not fighting."

"Me too." I looked around, searching for an excuse to run, and conveniently noted the sky had gotten dark. I fittingly glanced at my watch and gasped. "Oh, my gosh—look at the time. I must go—going to be late for dinner. Come on, I'll put you in a cab." I turned, but his hand on my forearm stopped me.

"Wait…why don't we have dinner. I'm so foolish, you must be starving. We'll go to the best restaurant in Manhattan, to celebrate today's end. My treat, of course."

I smiled apologetically. "Thanks, but I can't. James is expecting me."

Max's smile faltered almost imperceptibly. "Oh, of course—your fiancé, James. When is the big day?"

I shrugged. "Yeah…we don't have a date set yet, but…" My voice trailed.

"Well, he shouldn't wait too long. Someone may come along and snap you up."

I laughed nervously. "No, I don't think so. He's right for me, you know?" I stared into his eyes. Secretly, I hoped he would ignore my last statement.

After a moment of silence, he spoke. "Well, shall we?" He made a sweeping motion toward the exit. We headed back inside.

As we waited in line for the next available elevator, a thought suddenly occurred to me. A question Tess had posed yesterday stuck in my mind. I turned to him casually. "How about you, do you have anyone special back in Toulouse?"

"I do."

At first, I stared at him, tongue-tied, then blurted, "Sounds like you're practicing for the 'big day' already."

"Actually." Max laughed. "It's not too far off."

"Really? Well, congratulations." Now it was my smile faltering.

"A few months from now. July. We've been together for a year or so. Gabriela—she's an actress.

You probably won't know her, though—"

"Hold on…are you talking about Gabriela Neri?"

The elevator pinged, and the doors *swooshed* open. We rode on what felt like a wave of tourists entering the lift.

"That's the one," Max said as the doors closed.

"You're engaged to Gabriela Neri?"

He peered down at me as we stood squished together on the elevator. "Is it so hard to believe?"

My mouth gaped open. "I'm stunned. I mean—she's a starlet. I would think…you know, the news would have—"

"We keep it quiet…not formally engaged yet. We plan to announce it when I get back. Picked up the ring at Tiffany's yesterday."

I was speechless. I was envious and confused and jealous and speechless.

"So that's where you had to rush off to." I blinked a few times and then followed up with a toasty, warm smile. "I'm so happy for you. I wish you many happy years together."

"Thank you."

The elevator slowed, and soon the doors opened. We streamed out with the swell of tourists onto Fifth Avenue, now packed more than usual, with even more people making their way home from the multitude of offices surrounding us.

I walked to the curb and put up my hand in the familiar stance one takes when in need of a cab. "This might take a while, Max. It's rush hour."

"Oh, I don't care. I have nothing to return to but stuffy notes and emails. I have a long night ahead of me. Thank you, though, for showing me a small piece of New York City."

My hand remained in the up position as I spoke. "Tell you what—if we have time, I'll take you to Rockefeller Center, to the top. There's a killer view of Central Park from there. Maybe we can even get you *into* Central Park. Taxi!"

I waved a yellow cab down like a native New Yorker. It pulled up to the curb, and Max swiftly opened the door and waited for me to get in.

"No...this one's yours. I'll get another one." My lips came together and squeezed tight.

Max politely shook his head. "You take this one. I can't leave you waiting on the street."

"Believe me, I'll be fine. I do it all the time."

He hesitated, but I pointed to the interior of the cab. "Go. Banker's orders."

Surrendering to my command, he chuckled and entered. "I'll see you tomorrow then. Good night." He shut the cab door, and I watched as his taxi disappeared into Manhattan crosstown traffic.

Damn it! I told you you couldn't do it, you stupid, stupid...

Instead of hailing another cab, I turned on my heel and walked briskly, inhaling the night air. There was no way I was taking a cab. I needed to walk. Walk all the way to my cracker box of an apartment in the low twenties. I needed to clear my head of Max's image before I went home to James.

I stuck my hands in my pockets and marched, heading south on Broadway. I loved Broadway, with the Flatiron Building in all its combined elements of French and Italian Renaissance architecture. Was it French and Italian?

My thoughts went to James and then to Max, which had become somewhat of a habit these past few days.

James would be my husband. This I knew for certain, but I'd always figured if I fell for a man, it would come as an explosion of recognition, of certainty, of passion, lust, and madness. Much like the hunger and thirst I experienced for Max.

But my love for James was more like a persistent tug, a gentle pull that drew me along from basic attraction into unexplored territory. He was good to me, stable, loving. But was this enough for me? Would he satisfy me for the rest of my life?

I sighed as I walked past the Flatiron Building, stopped for a moment, and looked up. Yes, it was French and Italian Renaissance architecture. Turning the corner on East 22nd Street, I came to our apartment building, with my keys ready, in my pocket. James always lectured me about it…for safety's sake. Would Max ever worry about me like that?

You are not going to think about him when you're with James. He deserves more from you.

Pushing the up button, I checked my hair in the mirror. Windblown…the wind on the Empire State Building. I combed my hands through my hair as the elevator got to my floor.

I let myself in and called out, "Hey, I'm home." Then, "Oh, my gosh, what?"

"I thought you might like some TLC after today. You sounded a little shook on the phone." A bouquet of pink baby roses lay in the middle of a perfectly appointed table, amid all my favorite Le Chinois dishes. Expelling a deep breath, I angled my head to James with an appreciative smile splitting my face.

"Oh, James…you're so sweet, baby." With my arms outstretched, it took only three steps to reach him from the hall to the dining table. "I love you." I gestured to the table. "See this? This is why I love you."

Putting an arm around my waist, he squeezed me affectionately. "Anything for you." He kissed my temple lovingly, and in return, I gave him a passionate, pulse-quickening kiss.

"Wow—if I knew you would've reacted this way, I'd set the table more often."

I laughed. "It's not the table—it's you. I'm so lucky to have you, James." I kissed him again, more passionately. Though he wasn't nearly as tall as Max, his arms were muscular, strong, perfect for swallowing hugs.

"I'm the lucky one." He kissed me back. "We're going to be good together, Sof."

I opened my eyes and looked straight into his deep steel blues. "Are we, James? Do you really think so? Do you love me enough that you're willing to…I don't know…step over my laundry, listen to me complain about my cramps, comfort me as I cry through sappy movies, and…tolerate me? Is our love that strong?"

"Babe, I love you enough for both of us." He smiled and took me tighter into his arms. "Hmm—what do you say we work up an appetite?" He planted a tantalizing kiss in the hollow of my neck and then added in a lower, huskier tone, "Come on, love me. Love me enough for the next couple of days."

"I'm already hungry, but I'll take you up on the invitation." There was a dreamy tenderness in his kiss which was all James. The intimacy of body to body and mind to mind. I reveled in its ardor, its sweetness, in the way it made me feel safe and cared for.

Our relationship was stable and secure. It was what I needed. It was what I wanted.

"I'm going to miss you tomorrow night, babe," said James, kissing my hands as he walked backward and led me to the bedroom.

Chapter Twenty-Five

There was no doubt in my mind when it came to my career...until two weeks ago. Despite my outward confidence, I had questions about whether I had enough stamina, skills, and grit to lead such tough negotiations. And today it seemed, was the culmination of my uncertainty. Despite everyone's satisfaction, I knew I was uncharacteristically distracted.

Day three of the grueling sessions had me walking on eggshells with every spoken word and making me take a step back and wonder why I continued to punish myself.

More fodder for the tumult happening in my mind was the fact Max was absent from the day's talks. According to Mariana, there was an emergency meeting regarding one of the oil sites with the American arm of the deal—this didn't bother me as snags often happened. What did bother me was the fact I was rattled because Max wasn't there, and despite my unwillingness to admit it, I missed him.

His presence forced me to excel. His attitude made me want to succeed and prove myself even more.

The day could not end fast enough.

I stuffed my papers in my bag as I bid Mariana a polite "*A domani.*"

"Amen to that," whispered Tess.

"Good work today, Tess." I sighed. "Cannot wait

to get home and pour myself a huge glass of merlot. Why don't you come over? We can have dinner. James is in Boston for a conference the rest of the week."

"Oh, if it were any other night, but can't, Sof, sorry. I've got a date."

"Really? Who with?"

"He's a lobbyist. You don't know him, we met at a reception last week."

"Nice guy?"

"Nice enough," she said distractedly as she freshened her lipstick. "Not thinking it's going to be long term, though—he's from Germany."

"Oh, that's too bad. Another glorious one-nighter?"

"You should give it a go sometime. Keeps things exciting."

"Believe me, I don't need any more distractions in my life. Today went by in a blur."

"Maybe it's not the deal getting to you, maybe it's the clients. Or one client in particular—"

"No," I interrupted, knowing full well what Tess was implying. "That's the dumbest thing I ever heard. What are we in high school?"

"Oh ducks, you keep denying it, but you don't see yourself when you're around him." Sitting herself down on the table edge, she peered at me with earnest eyes. "You send out mixed signals, but your gaze is always drawn back to wherever he is…whether he's right beside you or walking across the room. You're unforgiving when he screws up, which is not like you at all. It's like you're overcompensating, letting him and everyone else who cares to notice you don't give a shit about him. All this leads me to think…you do." She tilted her head, very cheeky-like.

"Well, look who thinks she's got a psychology degree." My tone was acerbic. "Have fun on your date, Tess."

"Ooh—I hit a nerve?"

"You're imagining things, my darling. I'm in a relationship. I'm engaged, for heaven's sake. Plus, he hasn't changed at all. He's far from my type—he's arrogant and impulsive and self-congratulatory. And I'm hard on him because he deserves to be knocked down a peg or two from his 'rags to riches' high horse…does he really think he's the only one in this world who's had to work to get where they are?"

Tess laughed softly. "Oh, my dear…she doth protest…you don't make love and be in love like mad for two weeks and then forget about it all. I know you. You have real feelings—and my bet is, you can't turn your emotions on and off like you turn off a tap."

I pressed my lips together hard while I thought of a response. I couldn't. Shaking my head, I hung the strap of my valise over my shoulder.

Tess smiled a knowing smile, reached over, and squeezed my arm. "There's something dangerous about him, something not quite tame or conventional. You can see it in the eyes." She slung her bag over her shoulder. "But you keep trying to convince yourself. Love you, Sof. Good night."

I stared after Tess as she sauntered out of the conference room, looking rather pleased with herself at having laid my life out before me like a buffet dinner.

She can say all the crap she wants, but she's about as far from right as she can be.

Looking around the room, I noticed I was the only one left.

I'm getting the hell out of here. This place is getting to me. Might be a good night for a walk.

I slunk back to my desk to slip on my socks and sneakers. As I was doing so, I thought about what Tess said. If it was true, then it was a good thing the talks would soon be over. It felt like I had been wrestling with my heart my entire life when it came to Max.

I stepped out of the building and took in deep lungsful of air. Taking a steady stride, I headed uptown to my East 22nd Street apartment.

It's just me here, Sofie…and it's time. High time to be honest with yourself. Otherwise, it can all sneak up on you, and you'll fuck everything up. Tomorrow and then the next day and then that's it. Get through tomorrow and the day after, and you'll be okay. You'll go back to your peaceful life with James, and everything will be like before. It's not happening again. It can't.

Just being around him, I found myself slipping back. I became a different person when I was with him, jealous, suspicious, yet some of the most intense, beautiful, lyrical moments of my life were spent in his arms. We shared a powerful, penetrating love for each other, but sometimes, love was not enough.

I had read a poem somewhere in a long-forgotten college English course that love was like a wildflower which took root spontaneously and of its own accord, refusing to be planted or cultivated like one would a garden plant.

Funny how easy it was for me to draw a comparison back then for the same reason it was so crystal clear now. I had to laugh to myself. Not only was my love for Max like a wildflower, but more like a stubborn weed. No matter how many times I tried to rip it out, it kept coming back, the root stronger than ever.

I blamed him for all this crap I was putting myself through, that insensitive bastard. Did he not think for once this little reunion may have affected me emotionally? Just because *he* had a stone for a heart. Selfish, right to the end.

I have responsibilities, obligations. I have a fiancé...but then, so does he. He's engaged—to Gabriela Neri. Gabriela...fucking...Neri. You're not even in the same league with her—what are you thinking? You are simply insane for imagining all this. You will for sure be certified and committed if you think Max has any designs on you. But what about all those signals he's sending? Am I making it up? Or reading things wrong and creating a scenario where there is nothing at all?

I stopped at Union Square and 14th at the light. A traffic cop perpetually stationed there tipped his head to me in acknowledgment. I smiled back. Green light. Go. No one passing me on the street would have guessed the tumult raging in my head.

James trusted me and loved me, yet I was entertaining wild sexual situations in my head during the day and dreaming about Max at night.

Shit. I forgot about everything I promised myself when I accepted this assignment and allowed myself to entertain the possibility of something which couldn't possibly last. Even allowing myself to fantasize about him gave validity to the feelings I had.

"Hi, buddy," I said to the homeless guy who occupied the spot in the bank alcove between East 17th and 18th. "Here, go get a sandwich." I put a five in his tattered paper coffee cup and kept walking.

He tipped his hat. "Thanks, miss, God bless."

As these insanely dichotomous thoughts of surrender, loyalty, and uncertainty raced through my head, I could hear my father's voice asking me what in the hell I was thinking.

Putting the key in the door to my apartment, I thought of how I was devoid of appetite. *Maybe cereal tonight.*

Though I secretly craved to be with Max, my moment of rational thinking had brought me back to the here and now. The two options were, I could play and regret it…or let Max send me his mixed signals and stay professional, cool, calm, and away from him and move forward with James with my self-respect and dignity intact.

Chapter Twenty-Six

It was Thursday morning, day four, the second to last day of the talks. The night had passed slowly and restlessly with vivid dreams infusing my thin sleep. They made no sense.

In one, I was running down a dimly lit marble staircase desperately trying to catch up to something, but I couldn't. The more I tried to run to the shadowy figures, the slower I became. I roused myself awake, swathed in anxiety.

Shower. Apply mascara. Pull hair into a bun. Drink coffee. Eat dry toast. Leave for work.

Be strong today and tomorrow—two more to go.

I was already seated in the conference room along with most of the French and Italian contingent, by nine a.m. Tomorrow would be light...a wrap up of the discussions, a tabling of several investment proposals, and securing an acceptable deal while still allowing the other party the impression they won. The contract would be formally signed in the fall, in Paris.

Tess was running this meeting, and I noticed in a way that creeps up on you and hits you in the face that the discussion was becoming subtly inflammatory. It seemed to me the French were getting comfortable, perhaps too comfortable.

"France shall, in good faith, respect the outcome of these initial discussions. However, there are points of interest to both our countries which must be addressed…" The CFO of Eni, France, had the floor. "…Russia's policy has often pressured the nations in the Commonwealth of Independent States to compel them to make political concessions or directed them to make political statements."

I leaned into Max. "Where is he going with this?"

"Let him talk," was all he had for me.

"…however, there are also political foundations in more than half of the incidents, and in a few cases, explicit political demands are evident. How do you address these concerns, Minister?"

"Are you kidding me?" I whispered. "Why is he doing this? He's going to blow the entire deal."

"The notes were drafted this morning," replied Max, not taking his eyes off the Russian minister. "This goes back to the issues I tried to raise at the beginning of these negotiations."

After consulting with his advisors, the Russian minister looked pleasantly at the CFO and replied, "Clearly, Europe and the United States have supplied petrol to the countries in question at below-market prices. Russia is not obligated to subsidize their economies."

Max nearly jumped out of his seat to respond after their interpreter had finished the statement. "Below-market pricing and subsidies are one thing. Using energy as a tool to be wielded against 'offending' states like Georgia and Ukraine, is another. Are we to expect the same if we pursue these negotiations?"

Say something, Tess, say something!

Tess looked over at me, her eyes urging me to speak up. I jumped in. "Gentlemen, we concede the fact below-market pricing and subsidies have been carried out by Europe and the United States. What Mr. Damiani is saying is we are concerned the credibility of our Russian friends may be questioned if they use their natural resources as a source of influence."

While I reiterated Max's pointed question, the Russian interpreter whispered in the minister's ear. He glared at Max, then at Conti, his eyes cold with indignation.

"The young lady evidently has experience with these issues. In the interest of these negotiations, may I suggest we take a short break? I could do with a good strong cup of coffee."

As everyone rose to leave the table, Max turned to me and whispered, "Thank you. Jesus Christ, the stress must be getting to me."

I nodded. "I think the minister had the right idea. Coffee?"

Max and I walked to the refreshment buffet, where Conti wasted no time. "Massimo, what the hell are you thinking? These are not political debates."

Conti grabbed a cup and poured himself a coffee, then turned to speak with another man from the panel.

"Max, I understand, but believe me, language, respect, and hierarchy are everything to them."

"Massimo, I need a word with you," Conti interrupted.

"Of course, excuse me." Max pressed his lips together, then followed Conti outside.

"Ms. Romano." I turned to see one of the senior Eni board members, reaching for a cup.

"Good morning, sir," I replied. Though I was a little rattled by Max's flare-up, I put my best face on.

"Are you satisfied with everything so far?"

He lifted his gaze as he stirred his coffee. "Yes, thank you. Your team here at Goldman has been quite helpful. Our stake in this deal could mean many hundreds of jobs. These talks must be successful."

I thought immediately Max might be admonished for his hot-headed outburst—as per usual, he could not keep his emotions in check. "Sir, I hope you're not dissatisfied with Mr. Damiani. His concerns were valid, only worded unceremoniously. He's no diplomat."

"True. I am not displeased. He is an invaluable addition to Eni and a natural at what he does. His work has been an asset to our company."

"Oh—that's a relief." I smiled, reassured.

"I like the way you stepped in to defuse the situation. It shows initiative. You have a natural ability, too. A born negotiator at heart." He laughed softly and shook his head as he finished off the last of his coffee. "You must excuse me…I am an old man, and old men are sometimes too candid, but I must say you and Mr. Damiani work very well together. You should consider attending our Paris final negotiation in October."

"I'm flattered, sir, but I can't. My work is here and—"

"Oh, I'm sure arrangements can be made. I know a few people. I'm certain we could come to some kind of—"

I suspected the flush on my face was deepening. Working in France, with Max at my side. The thought was pulling at my heart…but James.

"Thank you so much for your kind words, sir, but I'm going to be planning a wedding. My fiancé, James, and I are to be married around that time." I lied. There was no set date yet.

"Oh," he said, surprised. "Forgive me. You see—" He laughed softly. "—what I said about old men cannot be truer. Why, for some reason I thought you and Mr. Damiani were…oh, never mind, Ms. Romano. I'm making a greater fool of myself than I already have."

"Not at all, sir, but why would you think he and I are together?"

"It is obvious! I've been sitting at these talks for four days now. I listen most of the time, yes, but I also watch people. The French are world-class people watchers, you know. When I see you, when both of you are here, your eyes are on each other. But it is not only the eyes telling the story, it is what is in them." He nodded. "He cannot take his eyes from you. And you"—he shrugged—"you try your best to avoid his, but when he enters the room, you light up like the sun." He chuckled as he put his hands in the air.

"Sir, I fear you are a hopeless romantic." I laughed with him.

"Hopeless, never. Always hopeful." His gaze moved toward the door and nodded, prompting me to turn and look. Max and Conti were on their way back to the conference.

"Consider Paris, my dear." He took my hand, brushed his lips lightly against it, and walked back to his place at the table.

You are a wise old man indeed, sir. My heart melted into my chest. *Are we so obvious? Am I?*

"What was that all about?" asked Max, looking after the old man, his mouth quirked with humor.

"Nothing." The look on my face must have given away I wasn't being entirely truthful.

"Are you sure?"

"Yes." I crossed my arms over my chest. "So what happened with you and Conti?"

"We agreed to disagree on the matter until the final talks in October. In the meantime, our lawyers will have time to iron out the contracts. And I will be suggesting a high priority on uninterrupted service, with a 'notwithstanding' clause."

"Sounds like a good compromise."

"It's the best we can do for now." He looked up, then motioned toward the table. "Looks like they're reconvening."

****

The day ended with another round of applause and everyone's dignity intact.

One more day, I thought, as I organized my papers. *So why do I feel like my head is spinning out of control?*

Tess and the other brokers packed up their briefcases, just as one of the Russian interpreters stepped to the front. "Ladies and gentlemen. Minister Ivanov and the entire Russian delegation would like to invite all of you, officers of Eni, and of course, our esteemed colleagues from Goldman Sachs, as their honored guests to a banquet planned for this evening at the Plaza Hotel. Our Russian delegation has planned food, drink, and entertainment and are very keen to share our traditions and express our thanks for hosting us, as well as to demonstrate our generosity. We will tell you, our 'banquets' can last late into the night." A ripple of laughter drifted through the room. "Our minister expects everyone to attend. As a gesture of goodwill, limousines have been hired for all. You will be driven there, and of course, driven home this evening. We will drink a toast together shortly."

Applause broke out through the room. "The Plaza," I heard someone gush.

"I've never been...have you?" asked another.

I applauded like the others, but unlike the others, I wanted to get away. To escape as far as I could from Max, not because I couldn't stand to be near him—quite the opposite. Anticipation and dread sparred inside me at spending the evening with him. Underneath my collected, proud bearing, my spirit was in chaos.

"Sounds like it's going to be quite a party."

I jumped, startled by Max's voice in my ear. "Oh, yes." My voice sounded tired and less than enthusiastic. "If it wouldn't be considered rude to bow out tonight, I don't know if I'd be attending. I'm exhausted and—"

"Sofia." His tone was tender and conciliatory. "It's our last evening here. I know, it's been difficult, but"—he dipped his head slightly—"I hope we can part as friends. The last thing I intended was for you to be uncomfortable. Please, let's enjoy the evening."

As swiftly as the doubt and confusion about the evening overwhelmed me, a warm, comforting state of mind now took over. I experienced a strange numbed contentment knowing he was aware of my feelings and that he was willing to be friends. Moreover, to my surprise, I was mindful of a new lightness. Could it be so easy? Was this all I needed to hear, that he was willing to rise above our history?

If it was true, then I would be satisfied to allow relief to fill my soul—I would be content in knowing I could be his friend.

Chapter Twenty-Seven

The armada of black limousines, a few bearing diplomatic plates, pulled up to Fifth Avenue and Central Park South, where an army of attendants opened car doors and greeted the party of fifty plus. Max and I shared a limo with Mariana, Tess, the other two brokers, and Aidan and Vlad, who excitedly chatted and commended the Russians for offering a banquet in thanks for the successful negotiations.

Many times before, I had been graced with a fleeting look at the Grand Dame of Manhattan, the Plaza Hotel, but had never crossed the threshold into a whole other world of New York City, a world of lavish social affairs, and classic Hollywood films.

Upon exiting the limo, the expanse of the hotel's exterior spread before me. The red-carpeted steps begged to be ascended. Its filigreed emblem in the intricate glasswork along with the gold inlay on the black marble doorjambs exuded opulence, and were all cradled under imposing marble pillars, glass awnings encrusted with lights, and French Renaissance detail.

"Impressive," offered Max, who was by my side taking in the elegance.

"It's silly, but I feel like royalty." I sighed, trying to put every detail to memory as I walked from the limousine to the front steps. "I can't wait to see what's inside." As I took a stride toward the stairs, Max gently put his hand under my elbow.

My gaze swept to his, and he shrugged. "A princess needs a proper escort." He was dead serious. I genteelly accepted his hand.

A pleasant doorman swept open the luxurious golden door, and bade us, "Good evening, sir, ma'am. Welcome to the Plaza Hotel." Max discreetly palmed the doorman a twenty-dollar bill.

We stepped through onto mosaic travertine marble floors, reflecting soft, flattering light from the crystal chandeliers, suspended from creamy white and gold-gilded vaulted ceilings. Fresh flowers graced each accent table, intricate tapestries and original works of art adorned the walls, and elegant window treatments softened the floor to ceiling windows.

"I still can't believe I'm here," gushed Tess, standing close. The others from the Eni delegation were beginning to filter in, filling in the gaps, gathering in groups, and taking in the views. A few of the Russians mingled amiably with us, trying to recall their English and some broken French.

"Oh, there's Minister Ivanov's assistant." Tess pointed to the familiar face crossing the lobby.

"On behalf of Minister Ivanov and everyone in our delegation, I wish to welcome you to our 'home away from home.'" The pudgy-faced young man spoke in broken English, which sounded very much like the speech had been rehearsed numerous times. "It will have to do, for now. However, we sincerely extend a warm invitation for each one of you to join us in our beautiful mother country, our beautiful Russia. Please, follow me to the penthouse suites where we will share in some good food and good drink. *Nasdrovje!*"

A smattering of applause rippled amongst the onlookers and through the lobby. The party followed Nicolai, who was accompanied by one of the concierges to an out-of-the-way elevator, located in an alcove beyond the regular elevators.

"Ladies and gentlemen, we will take you in parties of ten, as unfortunately, this is the limit," said the concierge. "If you please, I will take the first group now." He pressed the up button, then spoke softly into his walkie talkie.

"This way," directed the concierge. Max, Tess, Mariana, and I along with a few of the others were next. There was tense anticipation and excited chatter as the lift began its ascent to the penthouse suite.

The elevator doors released to a security checkpoint at the floor's entrance, where somber-looking security personnel, recorded everyone's name and marked it against their list, crosschecking and ticking everyone off as we arrived.

Once through the checkpoint, the Russians wasted no time in making their guests feel pampered, spoiled, and indulged. Two servers, each with a tray of chilled shot glasses and fancy hors d'oeuvres, were on either side of the double door entrance to the penthouse suite, welcoming in each group as they entered.

When inside, there was instrumental folk music playing softly by a trio of musicians in Russian folk garb, smiling pleasantly as they stood strumming their balalaikas. In the outer reception room, a fancy spread of hot hors d'oeuvres beckoned to be nibbled. Small, colorful dishes filled the table from one end to the other, all diced and lively, pierced with fresh garlic, and swaddled in kicky vinegar. Beet tartare, dill and goat cheese meringue, deviled eggs with Russian caviar, blinis with caviar, black salmon caviar on ice served with buttered toasts, caviar, caviar, and more caviar.

"Yum! I feel like I'm in Moscow," I gushed.

"Look at the view, Sof!" Tess pointed to the expansive windows and the twinkling lights. Manhattan was laid out before us like a quilt of diamonds on black velvet.

"Look at that." Her attention was now on the staircase. "This is a duplex apartment-style suite. Luxury beyond imagination, honestly! Blimey, look—the living room and dining room open to terraces overlooking the city. I must have a look." Tess disappeared through the milling crowd to the open doors leading to the massive balcony, but not before picking up a glass of the icy vodka from a nearby waiter.

I turned to Max, catching Tess's excitement. "Oh, she's had a vodka or two," I said, feeling loads lighter. "You know, Max, it's not nearly known enough there is something fantastic about the way Russians treat their guests." My attention was drawn to a passing server with a trayful of morsels from which I plucked a canape of black caviar on toast and an icy glass of vodka.

Max watched me smack my lips as I washed down the caviar with my shot of Beluga. "Glorious!"

Max's face split into a wide grin. "I had no idea you were such a connoisseur on all things Russian." He helped himself to a canape and a shot, too.

"Hmm. When you work for an international investment firm, you develop an appreciation for international food and culture." My eyes scanned the room. Everyone was relaxed and friendly. It was over.

It was over, and it was a deal well done.

Yet among all this positive energy and sweet good feelings, a pang of tartness settled in the pit of my stomach.

Yes. It was over. Everyone would go home. The deal would eventually be finalized in Paris in the fall. It was a major coup for me, and I was feeling good about how my career would unfold as an investment banker. Now, more than ever, my eyes were set on the prize and focused straight ahead. But it was over, and Max was going home.

A pendulum inside me swung between exhilaration and sadness, and if I was going to make it through the night and look professional, I would have to find a happy medium and fast.

Max was back at my side with two fresh glasses of vodka. "Come on, let's go see what Tess is going on about." He nodded toward the balconies. We walked to the open doors and stepped into the night air. It was a quiet oasis high above the noisy traffic below. In addition to the Manhattan skyline, the penthouse suite provided sweeping views of Central Park. Max gestured toward the huge green space in the middle of the urban jungle. "You never did get to show me the park."

I smiled. "Next time."

Max didn't smile back.

Trying to split the tension, I motioned to his glass. "You're not drinking your vodka."

He snapped out of his thoughts. "It's not my cup of tea, as Tess would say."

"Oh, come on—you just don't know how to drink it properly. Focus on savoring the taste rather than shooting it back. Smell the vodka as you swirl it in your glass."

Max did as he was told, taking in a breath.

"Take a small sip and let the flavor rest on your palate for a few seconds like you taste wine. Good, now exhale through your nose to fully appreciate its grainy aroma. Now swallow it and savor the aftertaste."

Max nodded but was still unsure. "It's all right, I suppose."

"Maybe a cosmopolitan is more your speed—a little vodka, cranberry juice, Cointreau, and lime juice?"

"Sounds like a girlie drink."

"Then perhaps a vodka martini—the official drink of James Bond, 007, shaken, not stirred?"

"Now you're talking."

"Uh…some friendly advice before we go in, so you don't make an ass of yourself again." My voice was light and caustic in the same breath. "Know your limits when drinking alcohol around Russians—they'll make sure you are drowning in Beluga, so be wary."

"You can be my barometer."

"Also no one will leave until the guest of honor has left, so that's us. They won't pack it in until we do, so—"

"Don't stay too late. Understood."

A voice drifted outside from the penthouse suite, "Ladies and gentlemen, dinner is served."

"After you." Max made a motion toward the apartments.

The suite was tastefully decorated in pale blues, golds, creams, and soft grays with the overstuffed furniture finished in gold, a throwback to Versailles. The polished wooden floors were adorned with warm carpets, the walls accented with fancy wallpaper, all highlighted by crystal chandeliers, which cast endless slivers of light and shadow throughout.

Tables were set up in the main great receiving room of the suite. It took up two floors with a staircase in the far end, leading to what I assumed were bedrooms upstairs. At the head table, the upper representatives of the Russian delegation arranged themselves at their places, while the others seated themselves among the guests.

Max, Mariana, and Conti, as well as Tess and I, sat in a group at one of the long tables, along with other brokers and advisors. There were three long tables set adjacent to one another, configured in what looked like an "E" adjoining the main head table. Our hosts ensured there was a mix at the tables of a nearly even amount from each country.

The Russian minister arose once everyone was seated and raised his glass high.

"This spring," he began, "we came to New York City to build business partnerships. In New York City, we came to breathe new life into our partnership with our friends in the European Union, Eni, and France. Let us celebrate our accomplishments with food and drink. *Nasdrovje!*"

A great round of clapping and cheers rang out in the suite.

"*Nasdrovje!*" shouted Max, his glass held up.

A sumptuous traditional Russian dinner was served, including cabbage soup, borscht, beef stroganoff, and Russian kebabs. Russian beer and vodka sat on the table, which suited everyone perfectly. Brined apples, honey spice cookies, and assorted sliced cakes were served for dessert along with a long list of brandies and other liqueurs.

We enjoyed our host's hospitality, who encouraged drinking and eating and drinking again. It all carried on well into the evening, with the tea and coffee being served at nearly ten o'clock.

A few of the French and Italian advisors began rising from their seats, the most elderly being the Eni French board member who had spoken to me about Max earlier.

"You…you young people stay." He nodded toward Conti at the next table. "Old men should be in bed by now." He walked over to the Russian head table and began shaking hands, bestowing compliments on an outstanding banquet and salutations until tomorrow.

I couldn't remember when I had enjoyed myself so much. I wasn't sure if it was the union heads trying to communicate in French or Max attempting to teach them how to sing a traditional Italian song, but it was a gregarious evening fit for a college kegger.

"Oh," I wailed, holding my temples. "My head. I can't figure out if it's because I'm exhausted, or I've had one too many vodkas."

"Only one?" Tess sighed. "I'm way past one too many. I reckon it's time to go—these blokes won't stop until we get up."

"A few of the top men have already made their way out. What do you say, Conti?" asked Max.

"I'm done. I'll go and say our goodbyes until tomorrow." Conti made his way to the head table.

"Hey, Sof…you going to be okay, love?" asked Tess. "You want to share a limo?"

"I'm fine, Tess. I need to visit the powder room.

Maybe go out on the terrace, have one more look out onto Manhattan from the Plaza, and then make my way home. Cinderella's night is nearly done. Besides we're at opposite ends of the city."

"You go ahead"—Max motioned to Tess—"I'll make sure she gets in a limo safely."

Tess's eyes narrowed, ignoring Max, and focusing instead on me. "You sure?"

"Yeah, I am." I leaned forward and whispered to Tess. "Yikes, I have to hit the ladies…rather urgently."

"Gotcha. See you tomorrow." Her gaze darted to Max, unsure of how to weigh his good intentions. "You too, Mr. Damiani." She turned, and after thanking the hosts, she disappeared into the receiving room and out into the hall.

"Well, I'll be ready to go as soon as I get back, if you'll excuse me."

"Of course," responded Max. "Take your time."

Upon inquiring, a waiter discreetly pointed out the suite's powder room. Even this space was decorated to the height of luxury.

I checked myself in the mirror, then smoothed out my skirt, blouse, and blazer. I checked my face. *Oh, God—what a disaster! I've got bags under my eyes down to my knees and hardly any makeup left on my face.* Digging deep into my bag, I found my brush and makeup bag. *Hmm—brush hair, redo bun, reapply lipstick. Done.*

As soon as I exited, I spotted Max standing patiently nearby, his hands folded behind his back. "Hey." I glanced beyond him. "Where is everyone?"

"They've all left," he said.

"Oh, my gosh, I'm sorry, Max. I've kept you

waiting."

"It's no trouble. I wouldn't leave you here alone. I promised Tess I'd put you in a limousine, make sure you get home safely." His voice was uncompromising, yet oddly gentle.

A few of the men from the Russian delegation were still at the head table, smoking cigars and pouring vodka into freshly furnished icy shot glasses from nearly empty bottles of Beluga. "Let's say good night, and then we can go." We both walked over and reached across the table to shake hands. "What a wonderful evening, Minister. You have bestowed much honor on your guests."

"It was a pleasure, miss," replied Ivanov. He extended his hand to Max. "Limousines are waiting in front of the hotel. Until tomorrow, Mr. Damiani. And by the way, good work, and no hard feelings about earlier." His words were amiable, yet his icy blue eyes were cautious. His interpreter spoke, then awaited Max's response.

"Minister, you must forgive my inexperience at diplomacy." Max's voice was full of entreaty, as he tipped his head to the minister. "I was born of a poor laborer in rural Italy and raised myself from the oil fields to a consultant. I've been told I have issues with tactfulness, which I am working on. Thankfully, Ms. Romano here saved the day."

"Indeed." Ivanov's face melted, just a little. "You make a good team."

"Yes," replied Max. "It would seem this is the consensus. Good night, Minister."

Both Max and I waved our adieus and walked leisurely to the elevators, nodding to the waiters still in the banquet room, who cleared the spoils of the party and thanked the security detail on our way out.

While Max pushed the down button on the panel, I took one last look around and sighed wistfully. "Hmm, that was over way too fast."

Max nodded agreeably. "It's a beauty, all right. Though the Waldorf isn't exactly what I would call 'slumming it,' as you say in America."

"You must think I've become so shallow," I said reticently, aware of an unwelcome blush creeping into my cheeks. "Living here, in Manhattan, gawking at the view and decor in luxurious hotels."

Max studied me as if it were the first time seeing me. He spoke slowly. "I could never think such a thing. And you deserve it all, and more." His voice broke with huskiness.

I felt the warmth, the tingling in my belly, his eyes on me, bringing back memories of us. It was Max again, his aquiline nose, his dark hair, his strong jaw.

The chime of the elevator arriving brought me back to earth, prompting us to break eye contact. We stepped into the small space, and I wished for a moment to push away the thoughts racing through my mind, feeding my imagination of what could be. Then the elevator doors *swished* closed, and we both stood looking at the inside, speechless. When we realized it wasn't moving, we eased back and blurted out laughter, then simultaneously reached for the main floor button.

Our hands met at the button, my right, and Max's left, warm and familiar.

Everything around me halted as if time were swept away. Everything fell silent.

When Max looked up, his gaze caught mine, and

he froze too; the emotion in his dark eyes so intense, sexier, and more handsome than ever. His hand took mine and tucked it next to his chest, lacing his fingers through it as he wrapped his other hand around my waist, pulling me closer. He moved so his face was close to mine—so our eyes and mouths lined up.

I closed my eyes, frozen in a sort of limbo on earth where all decisions and actions were impossible. My mouth sensed the warmth of his breath, his mouth against mine, caressing me more than kissing me. "Tell me what you want, my Sofie," he murmured.

My stomach dropped away. "Oh…Max," I whispered his name against his mouth.

He waited until my eyes fluttered open, then spoke softly into my hair. "Sofie." His grip tightened around my waist. "Is this what we want?"

Suddenly, the elevator chimed. It had reached the ground floor. Impulsively, we broke our embrace before the doors slid open.

I had to fight an overwhelming urge to put my hands on him. Max took my arm, led me behind a pillar close by, and clasped my body tightly to his. "Answer me, Sofie. Do we want this?"

"You're asking me this now because you know I'm soft…" My eyes rolled back as he trailed his lips down the side of my throat. "…and pliant…and I'll give in before the practical woman in me steps in to decide I'm being swept up in the moment."

Our lips met, and it felt like nothing had changed.

"This is crazy," I said breathlessly.

"Insane." His lips trailed along my jawline.

"Max, we can't do this."

"I know, but we will."

I grasped a handful of his hair and dragged his head up until my mouth fused with his again. "This can't work."

"No way it can work." His hands were under my coat, up my back.

"This is only a temporary lapse." I braced myself against the pillar, or I would have simply slid boneless onto the shiny travertine floor.

"Say yes, Sofie," he whispered in my ear. "Is this what we want?"

Mixed feelings surged through me. I knew what he was asking, and now I understood every moment we had spent together during this deal, every denied emotion, every subtle side-glance was merely a dance leading up to this. "Yes, I suppose it is."

"Come with me tonight, then." He smoothed my hair. "Come to bed with me, and let it happen."

Devastating was his appeal. I tried to weigh the consequences of what was about to happen and in a heartbeat, thought of the quote again—every action of our lives, everything we do, touches on some chord, and like ripples on the ocean, will swell and pulse in eternity.

"Obey your heart, Sofie." His hoarse whisper broke through my thoughts, as the invitation burned in his eyes.

Taking his face in my hands, I brought his mouth to mine, pouring myself into his kiss, letting myself melt. "I will," I whispered when pulled away and repeated, "I will."

More running than walking, we stepped out into the night. The instant we were in the limousine, I pulled him close.

Max turned to the driver, who was waiting awkwardly for instructions. "Waldorf Astoria," was all Max said, then he kissed me—my lips and along my jaw, down my neck, and around my collar bone...his senses took over.

Recalling we were in a moving limousine, I put my hands on his chest and gently pushed him away, making him pay attention. "Max." I breathed in deep. "Not here." Taking his hand, I gently kissed the tips of his fingers. "You invited me to your bed. You're going to have to wait for it."

"Anything you say, my love." He swallowed hard and licked his lips as he watched me kiss his fingertips. "Anything you want."

We stumbled into his suite, already struggling, tearing at our jackets, kicking off our shoes. My hands couldn't stay off him, grasping his shirt, pulling him toward me, working at the buttons.

He grabbed my hands and pulled me toward the bedroom. He took my blouse out of my skirt, then stopped suddenly, grabbed the clasp in my hair, loosening my bun, and tousled my hair around my face. He reached out to tug on a stray wisp of hair, then caressed my jawline, and deliberately allowed his fingers to brush my throat. My breathing stopped, and a look of gratification covered his face. Then at once, he stepped back, his eyes surveyed me, every inch of me as I stood breathless in the doorway of the bedroom.

"What?" I asked, my voice a hoarse whisper, but he didn't answer.

In a split second, he reached out and grabbed my hand, pulling me hungrily toward him. He wrapped my hair around his free hand and tipped my head back gently.

I had never been more aroused.

"Are you sure you want to do this?" His dark eyes burrowed into my hazel ones. "Because once we cross this threshold, it's done. I have you for the night. The rest of your life is yours if that is what you want, but tonight, you are mine alone. No regrets, no shame."

I hid my relief at his words behind a grin. "Someone told me once that regret is a colossal waste of energy unless it's accompanied by an act of repentance."

We were so close I could see his pupils dilating. I whispered, "I promise you, Max, right now, with you, is the only place I want to be." He softened his grip on my hair. "I want you to take me to bed and I want to make love and I don't care about tomorrow."

This was all I needed to say. He swept an arm under my knees and lifted me off my feet.

With the first touch of Max's hands upon my body, I was plummeted into the past, when passion was new, and each thrill of my body was a discovery.

The room was soon filled with shadows, intertwined limbs, sweet words, sighs, and soft caresses. I felt his warm breath on my back as he kissed my skin between my shoulder blades. The familiarity of his lovemaking came back to me in a rush, the memory of us, the pleasure, and the coaxing, how he held my face.

It was our own little universe, our haven, and sanctuary. I turned to face him and looking into his eyes, and in them, there was a safety I had missed for too long.

I heard nothing but the roaring of blood in my

temples, felt nothing but the inexpressible pleasure of Max inside me, saw nothing but his face, those dark intense eyes watching me.

Then we lay quietly together, breathing, retrieving the souls we had laid out before each other. I peered around the room, and I took in the surroundings. I looked over at him, still out of breath, and brushed his soaked hair away from his face. "That was impossibly incredible. I'd almost forgotten how good we could be together…like this, I mean."

"I never did, Sofie," he replied with his irresistible crooked smile, his eyes dark and tender at the same time. He lay back, one hand still holding mine. "I feel like…like this was a gift that needed to be opened."

The words he spoke evoked new depths of emotions from me—at least temporarily. Slowly I turned and faced Max as he lay on his back. He closed his eyes. I snuggled close to him, melding my body around his.

His lips touched my forehead, and his arms slid under me pulling me close, gathering me up beside him. "It never changes, me and you, does it? Our mad, insane, out-of-body experiences." One of his fingers reached to take a lock of loose hair out of my eyes, then trailed down to my shoulder and began drawing random circles.

"I don't know about you, but my experience was anything but out-of-body…it was quite the opposite." I kissed the side of his chest and set my head back down.

A quiet filled the room. Max stopped drawing circles on my arm with his thumb—suddenly something didn't feel right. "It's not only about the body. For me, it wasn't anyway."

"I know. I was being flippant. For me either," I confessed. "This is us, just us tonight."

"So this is it then." His voice had changed. "Is it really what you want? Just tonight."

"What?" I lifted my head to look at him. "That's what you said. We both have people. I have James, and you have Gabriela."

"Oh, Christ." He got out of bed and walked over to his pants, started rummaging around in the pockets, and pulled out a pack of Marlboros. "Why mention her? Why would you do that?"

I pulled the sheet up around me, suddenly feeling very naked. "Because it's true. And what the hell?" I gestured to the cigarettes. "You're still smoking?"

"Yes, I still smoke." He looked down at his cigarette, then stuffed it back in the pack. "Shit, I forgot, this room is nonsmoking." Then back to me. "I had no idea you were so sophisticated."

"I'm not. I'm trying to be strong." I grimaced, confused. "And *you* said it was just for tonight?"

"I want to say…fuck what I said!"

My body jerked at the reprimand. This was getting dangerously close to our usual quarrel. "Are you kidding me? We're revisiting the entire disaster?"

"Be honest." He scowled. "Tell me what we did wasn't of love."

"Of course, there's love. You know I love you, but sometimes you can't see your hand in front of your face. It's not only about us…again. There's James. Gabriela." I rolled over and looked at the ceiling, shaking my head. "This is exactly what I was afraid of when I saw you in Basil's office. Didn't you think about this when you came here? That this could happen?"

"Of course I did."

My head turned to scowl at him, but his eyes were focused on the floor.

"I think, secretly," he admitted slowly. "I was hoping it would. I think I wanted to be sure I had you out of my system before I got married again."

"And do you?"

"No." He shrugged. "I don't know…I think I'll always love you."

"But can we live together? That's a whole other issue."

"Why is it an issue?"

"There's too much history. We're different people. We have established lives. We have commitments."

Max didn't say anything for a long time, then, "No guilt then. You're okay with just tonight?"

"You know, honestly"—I leaned up on my elbows—"I think I am." I thought for a while and then spoke slowly. "I think I've come to the conscious recognition we…you and me when it's only us…we are in our own universe. And in our universe, this is perfectly acceptable. Making love, being together is allowed. And nobody will ever take this from us. This will always be ours."

"I've loved you longer than I've loved anyone else," Max said quietly, then turned to face me. "Is the world going to begrudge us this one night?"

"Screw the world," I said defiantly. "It seems everything in it has worked against us to keep us apart, even though we're more suited to one another than any other human being who ever walked the earth."

He listened to my rationale, then he came back to

bed and kissed me. "The world and Fate may owe us a free pass, but I still can't deny my feelings."

"So don't." I kissed him back. "Let it go. Love me, and I'll love you back with everything I have—for tonight."

"You're right." Silence weighed heavily in the room, then he spoke. "Aren't we a pair, though."

I tilted my chin up and gazed into his eyes. "You asked me to obey my heart, and that's exactly what I did. We don't owe anybody anything. To have you here and let you go without this…it would have been wrong."

I wound my arms around his neck and pulled him toward me. Desire built up between us again, too quickly for either to build a defense. The shadows in the room intensified and kept good sense and the reality of the morning at bay the rest of the night.

Chapter Twenty-Eight

I awoke with a start and quickly swept my gaze around the room. Then I glanced over at Max, who was sound asleep, his chest slowly moving up and down with rhythmic breathing. A thin sheet covered his muscular body.

Peering from the bed through the sheer drapes, the sky outside was turning the dreamy cobalt blue reserved for the time precisely before the sun peeked over the horizon of jumbled skyscrapers. I checked the time on the antique wall clock—nearly five thirty.

With the least amount of movement and noise, I searched the bedroom for my clothes. Though I hated to leave without saying goodbye, I thought it best for both of us if I made a quiet exit. I picked up my bra from the floor, my thong from the bedpost, my skirt and blouse from the armchair, and my jacket, bag, and shoes from the floor of the foyer.

Dressing quickly, I thought of the best course of action for today. Would it be wise to see Max again, or would it be best to avoid the inevitable awkwardness at the last session? Could I bear seeing him again, pretend we were as before during the closing addresses, and part as business associates in the afternoon, or should I remember him as he was right now—my lover and the only one who would ever have my whole heart?

I checked the mirror before leaving and brushed

my hair, applied lipstick, and smoothed the little creases from my jacket. With shoes in hand, I turned to go, yet when I reached for the doorknob, I hesitated and held back.

I crept back to the doorway of the bedroom and looked in at Max as he slept. His salt and pepper hair falling carelessly across his forehead, his full mouth and strong jaw, and his shoulders, broad and muscular. Shoulders. Would our shoulders ever tire of the burden we carried? Love shouldn't be a burden, but for us, it felt like it always was.

So at peace, probably dreaming, not knowing he's going to wake up alone. This was best. Leave while he's asleep. Make it easier on him and yourself.

I leaned against the bedroom door and finally gathered the strength to turn and walk away.

When I stepped outside of the elevators into the lobby, I peered around. Two world-class hotels in one incredible night, which had now ended in the cold light of the next morning.

I walked across the carpeted floor, under the enormous crystal chandelier, out of the Waldorf front double doors, and into the uncharacteristically cool spring morning.

Gathering my jacket around me, I stepped to the next waiting cab in the queue, opened the door, and slid into the back seat, directing the driver to "301 East 22nd," then took out my cell phone and called Basil. It went to his voicemail.

"Uh, hi, Basil, it's Sofia. Listen, I won't be able to make it in today, I'm sicker than a dog. Went to the Russian banquet last night and maybe ate some bad caviar. Anyway, let Tess know, and she can take over as lead. It's only closing addresses anyway and a half day. Sorry, Basil, and thanks for understanding." I turned my Blackberry off, and the line went silent. Then I checked my messages. There were four from James. I breathed out heavily and closed my eyes, letting my head hang back on the headrest.

The cab pulled up to my apartment building. Zombie-like, I paid the driver, pulled my key from my bag, unlocked the front door, and walked to the elevator. I pushed the up button and waited. When I got to my apartment, I called James and got his voicemail.

"Hi, it's me. Sorry I didn't answer last night. I was at a banquet hosted by the Russians, and it was a pretty late night. Had my phone on silent and didn't check it until now. See you when you get home."

After I hung up, I went to the bedroom and undressed, putting everything in the laundry, then turned on the shower, adjusted the water temperature, entered the shower, and cried under the warm cascading flow.

I crawled into bed but was unable to sleep. I wrapped a bathrobe around me, made myself a cup of tea, and fell asleep on the couch.

I didn't dream at all; in fact, I would have slept the entire day if it weren't for the front door buzzer blaring incessantly. Waking with a start, I got off the couch, dashed to the door, and pressed the button. "Yes?"

"Sofie!" The voice was unmistakable. "It's Max. Are you alone?"

"Yes."

"Buzz me up."

I closed my eyes and leaned my forehead against the intercom for a long moment. He buzzed again.

"Please, I have to talk to you."

I tried to become callused. To think about how clean it would have been if he had got on the plane back to France without all this drama. How everything would have been neat and tidy. I pressed the button. "Okay, come up—I'm 601." I opened the door and went over to the window. Looking down, I saw people were wearing heavy jackets. Another cold day.

There was a soft knock. I turned, and there he was.

"How could you leave without saying goodbye?" He walked in and took a quick look around.

"How did you get my address?" I asked, my brows arched.

"Tess."

I huffed out a breath. "You have got to stop doing that."

"Why did you leave?"

"I didn't want a big production. I thought it would be easier."

"You are some coward, you know that? I thought better of you."

"Then I guess you were wrong," I said stoically.

His face betrayed his frustration with me. "Sofie, listen." Max walked to me, took my arms in his hands, and looked deeply into me. "If I asked you, would you come to Paris? The merger launches in Paris in October. Come and work for me."

"And do what? Like I said in our first meeting, there are plenty who would fit the bill." My exterior was cool, but inside I fought hard to maintain control.

"Come with me now then. Permanently. Fly back with me tonight."

"Be your personal investment banker? Drop

everything just like that and leave everything I know? No, I wouldn't." My heart felt a rip. "I don't want to call last night a mistake, but we had a lot to drink, we got caught up in the moment...both of us have made promises to other people. It wasn't right."

"You keep saying it, and maybe one day you will believe it—me I'm a realist. You said yourself, we should be together."

"Maybe in negotiating international business deals, yes...as crazy as it sounds, but us together? We've tried it before. It didn't work. All we did was fight and argue after the sex was over. We're too different."

"That's not true."

"It is!" I shrugged him off and stepped back. "I don't like the person I become when I'm with you. I already felt it coming back during the talks. The jealousy, the uncertainty. It's not who I am or what I want. And if I uproot everything and follow you to Toulouse, to Paris...leave James and leave my job here, and things go south again like I know they will...then where will I be?" My eyes begged him to understand. "I would lose everything I worked for. I can't. I'm sorry."

He looked pleadingly at me for a scrap of weakness in my resolve, but there was none.

"We're older now, more mature, and we have careers—"

"So why don't you drop everything and come here?" I challenged. "You give everything up and move here with me."

"Don't be unreasonable. Now that I've made something of myself you want me to uproot everything? You can do what you do anywhere."

I felt an unsettling twinge of anger at his

selfishness, his presumptuousness. "There you go again. I have to give everything up to follow you. When is the last time you saw your son?"

He fell silent for a long moment. "He is in graduate school in Italy…I'm based in France now. It's not so easy to—"

"Bullshit. You were hesitant to commit to coming here with me because of your son, yet I bet you haven't seen him in months. There you are…the same old pattern." My voice was stern but even. "Another relationship lost, and this is your son. How easy would I be to forget, to cast aside when something new comes along? When something better strikes your fancy, and you know it will, a new position or a woman. And after that where will I be? Where I would have been if I didn't leave to come home seventeen years ago?" Behind my eyes, tears were stinging. "Max, can't you see? It won't work." My face gave away my pain, though I tried to be strong.

He thought for a long time, then clasped his hands to his mouth, and took a deep breath. "I will tell you…you make me a better person, Sofie. But maybe you're right. Things have gotten away from us, too out of reach. And maybe I am an ass, I don't know, but I'm sorry if I am." Max stepped closer and gently took my hands. "All I wanted was for us to be happy."

I nodded slowly as the tears gathered, and my throat tightened.

"I'm so sorry we couldn't find a way." His hands slid slowly to my back and pulled me closer, so my face rested on his shoulder. I felt the scratch of his wool coat. It still smelled like the cold from the outside air.

"Me, too," I whispered. "So much me too." Trying

my hardest to hold my emotions in, I put my arms around him and held him for a long time.

After what seemed like an eternity, he put his forefinger under my chin and lifted my face. "It's all right," he said soothingly. "I'll tell you what, Sofia Romano, you pick the night, the time, and the dream." He tucked a wisp of hair behind my ear and held his hand to my cheek, kissing me tenderly on the forehead. "—and I'll be there. I will always be there. And if you ever change your mind, call me and I'll have a plane ticket waiting for you at JFK."

He breathed in deeply as I took in every detail so I could remember this moment—his touch, his voice, the delicious scent of his skin, for a long time afterward.

He held me, and I hugged back, neither of us wanting to break the embrace. I looked up and saw the briefest touch of hesitation in his eyes. His mouth came down to mine until our lips met, neither willing to stop it. Against my own will, defying my promises to myself, I kissed him, lingering and savoring every second.

When we were like this, we shared one soul and one heart, yet our last kiss embodied everything that was us, the expression of love, desire, friendship, fiery tension, and antagonism which kept bringing us together yet tearing us apart.

"When we're old and gray," I whispered on a breath barely audible and fraught with sorrow. "Maybe then, we'll make it work."

The terrible pain of our first separations brought clarity to me. We were one unit of two souls, free and united by our own choice. This way, in the positive force of the universe, love wins. That easy road other couples travel on, it leads only to mediocrity…ours was the path walked by the greatest lovers in history.

I pulled away determined not to weep, but it was no use. The sobs came, first for me and then for Max. Together we both wept, with no words, only a deep sense of loss for a life which could have been. We would be thrown together again, I was certain, in another time, in another place.

Chapter Twenty-Nine

Saint Joseph's Hospice, Present Day

Simona came to sit with Max yesterday while I picked up my husband and daughter from the train station. We dropped off their luggage and got a quick bite, and then Cara was ready to crash.

As she slept, James and I ducked down to the lobby and sipped Chianti in the hotel bar. It wasn't really a bar but a breakfast nook, with spirits and wines on the back counter, but the view from the nook's balcony took our breath away. We sat looking out at the Tuscan countryside, and James took my hand.

"Sofie," he said, and smiled awkwardly. "I'm sorry about what I said before you left. I was so frustrated and angry—more with myself than anything."

"I know." I nodded and looked away.

"I kept thinking you were on a plane and what if something happened and the last thing we did was argue."

"You worry too much. It's okay."

"I mean, everything can change in the blink of an eye. One moment we're here and the other...the other our essences are floating in the ether in the Second Circle of Hell."

I burst out laughing. "What the hell did Dante know anyway?" I said. I finished my wine. As I did,

James took my cue. He swirled the last bit in his goblet and then downed it.

James and I seemed to have a silent conversation as we stared into each other's eyes, as most couples who have been together for a long time often do.

I looked away, as his hand encircled mine. It was soft and warm, reassuring. I looked up, and he appeared uneasy.

"Look, Sof." He licked his lips and squirmed a little in his chair. I knew whatever was coming next was difficult to say. "I want to say you and Cara are the most important things—no, that's wrong, the most important people in my life. You always have been. I know sometimes I don't show it; sometimes I let the practice get to me, spend too much time working with the association; I know I don't express it enough, but…I love you more than you'll ever know. What happened in Carolina…that wasn't me. I don't know how many more ways I can say I'm sorry, but I'll keep saying it until you forgive me."

Whatever James was, he always knew how to talk to me. And beneath the talk was the love, the gentle gaze of his eyes, the relaxed nature of his face. Our talk was a salve to one another.

"I know. I love you too. Don't worry. I've had a lot of time here…to think, and…and everything will be fine." I brushed my hand against his cheek, and he immediately grasped it and kissed it. "James, you look exhausted. Come on—get to bed." I took both his hands in mine and pulled him up. "Besides, I should get back. I need to relieve Simona. Oh, she wants to meet you. Maybe we can have dinner one night? She invited us up to Pescaglia."

"Yeah," he said, looking encouraged. "Yeah, that would be nice." He wrapped his arm around my waist, and we walked to the cashier to pay for the wine.

****

As I sat once again with Max, I thought, who was I lying to, who was I hurting by denying what I felt—only me and the man I loved. As James said, everything could change in the blink of an eye.

I tried to heal the sickness I bore when I was alone—when I came across my holy grails as James had called them...an insignificant something to everyone else, a picture of a medieval wall, a menu item in a restaurant, a bottle of vodka, but only I knew it drew his memory—and I would smile and be perfectly normal, but he was there. Not in my dreams as he had promised, but inside me. And I knew I had to ask him.

I thought how many times James had wanted to vacation in Italy, but I never allowed it. And then I thought how Fate was going to laugh at our expense one last time, and I knew I had to ask him.

Max was dying, but all I could think of was the time we had together and the time we didn't. I was tired. Max was tired. But soon it would be over for him.

****

I heard the sound far off in the distance. It was a familiar one. It was the noise my phone made when it was on silent mode. A piercing pain went down the left side of my back, as my head shot up off the bedside. I had fallen asleep again. Damned sleeping position, I thought as I rubbed my neck.

I sniffed, rubbed my eyes, and squinted at Max, trying to adjust my vision to the light. His breathing was shallow, and his heart monitor showed slow and lengthy spaces between his heartbeats.

"Oh, my phone," I mumbled. Grabbing my purse, I searched until I found the quivering device. "Hi, baby?"

"Hi, Mom. Daddy and I just woke up."

"Oh good, you guys looked pretty rough yesterday," I whispered, though I didn't have to as Max had slept the last twelve hours or so with hardly a movement. "Are you settled in? Do you like the hotel?"

"It's pretty nice. Do you want me and Daddy to come there today? He said he wants to pick you up and at least eat dinner together."

My stomach clenched. "I don't know. I'll have to see how Mr. Damiani is doing." I got up and walked over to the window, still speaking in a low tone. I could nearly see our hotel from here. "Why don't you call me when you're about to leave. I'll know better then."

"Sure. Daddy's in the shower."

"Okay, hon, call me when you're almost ready."

"I will. Love you."

"Love you, too. Bye"

I watched as my phone faded to the screen saver and then to black. My gaze went to the window. The late afternoon shadows crept across the olive groves and vineyards in the distance. How strange it was to have both my family and Max in the same town.

Five days, I had been here with Max, had seen to his every need, had cooled his face with wet compresses, read to him when he slept, and wet his parched lips with a moistened sponge even before he knew he was parched. I was taking care of a sick man, but I also realized I was taking care of myself, the long-forgotten void in my soul which was always there, the dormant hunger for time with the man lying there, withering away.

I turned to put my phone back in my handbag. Max's eyes were open. Smiling broadly, I walked over to his bedside. "Hi there, handsome." I slipped my hand over his. "Can I get you something?" The shake of his head was barely perceptible, but he squeezed my fingers, then glanced at my bag.

"Who—"

"That was my daughter, Cara." My voice soft and soothing, as I brushed stray hairs away from his forehead. "She and my husband got in yesterday. I ducked out to see them for a few hours in the afternoon while you were sleeping. Simona came and sat with you while I was gone."

"Simona," he whispered. He barely spoke now and slept nearly all the time because of the powerful medicinal cocktail they gave him to control his pain. An incredible heartache filled me—soon he wouldn't even know I was here.

"Listen, Max." I spoke calmly and tenderly, in a soft, low voice. "I'm honored you asked me here— despite what I said to you when you had Victor call me last week. I'm glad you did." I waited for him to speak, but he squeezed my hand instead. I moved closer.

"Max, I need to know something. I came here for you…yet the more I think about it the more I realize…I came here for me, too. Help me, Max. You never said it—never admitted it, but I need to know. Tell me if I did the right thing…staying away, not coming back with you. Tell me I was right. Tell me the truth." The words burned in my throat. Knowing I had made the right choice was the only way I could get through this.

His hand shifted in mine. I instinctively brought it to my cheek and held it there. He let the words ride on his breath. "I was always yours in my heart, and you were mine, yet I was never for you." He coughed brutally, and I held him. I didn't care that he was brittle or weak or shouldn't move. I lifted his head from the pillow and held him until the coughing lessened. Then in a raspy weakened voice, he answered, "You were right. Did the right thing. Don't think on it anymore, Sofie."

I leaned toward him and kept my voice steady. "Thank you." I didn't care about the possibility he may have said it to give me peace. He said I made the right choice, and this was good enough for me. Still holding his hand to my cheek, I closed my eyes and let the tears flow down my face. "Thank you."

He nodded again barely moving his head, then closed his eyes.

I kept talking, not breaking the connection. "Remember we spoke a few days ago, how my husband and daughter were coming? Well, they're here." I breathed in, as I watched the blanket move up and down slowly.

"You go ahead and sleep. I'll talk if that's okay?" I waited, but nothing. "I'll take it as a yes." Rising from his bedside, I kept my gaze fixed on his breathing as I grasped the compress and water basin. "So while you were sleeping, I fell asleep, too."

I brought the basin filled with fresh water back to his bedside, squeezed the cloth, and gently dabbed his forehead. "I did a little dreaming…about us, Max. I dreamed about the piazza." I laughed softly. "I dreamed we all got on a plane and flew to Moscow. I dreamed we checked into this fancy hotel and partied with the American ambassador. Mikhail Baryshnikov was there and the minister and oh! Yeah, Tess and Conti, they were there, too. It was a crazy dream."

I looked down at him and grasped his hand again, my eyes focused on his face, his brows, his jaw, his nose. "We were young again, though, like we were in the eighties." I hummed softly. "Do you remember this song, Max? It was a song from '83. They played it constantly on the radio while I was in Florence that year. That rocking song by John Cougar…before he became Mellencamp." I softly hummed, then sang the lyrics.

He moved his fingers and squeezed my hand again, and then his lids fluttered. I sang louder. My eyes stung with tears, but I kept singing, really belting it out, and then—

"Mom!"

I flinched and spun around. Cara stood awkwardly in the doorway. "Oh my God, Cara." I put a hand over my heart and let out a huffing breath. "You nearly gave me a heart attack."

"Sorry, Mom," Cara said, timidly peeking her head in. "But I called you, and there was no answer."

"Oh, my phone's in my purse—on silent because I didn't want to—" I turned to grab my bag and saw Max's eyes were open again. My heart jolted. I turned to look at my daughter, trying to appear calm. "Where's Daddy?"

"He's in the car, double-parked." Her head twisted to look beyond me, for a glimpse at Max. "He couldn't find a spot, so he said for me to come in and get you. The nurse at the desk was on the phone, then I heard you singing so—"

"Okay, yeah." I licked my lips as my stomach tightened into knots, thinking of what I should do. "It's okay." I nodded. "It's all right, Cara."

My daughter raised her brows. "So…are you coming?"

I turned to look at Max and swallowed hard. His eyes were on Cara. Eyes wide awake and alert, revealing everything to me.

Cara with dark hair, dark eyes, and an aquiline nose, looked across the room at the man on the hospital bed, who by now was gray-haired, emaciated, hollow-faced, and jaundiced—the mere shadow of a man he once was. If they had met in his prime, she may have figured out where she got her dark hair and eyes, not from a generational trait, as I had told her.

But Max knew she was his. Even through his agony and the morphine in his veins, dulling his senses, he recognized her as his flesh and blood, though he had never seen her before, never even knew she existed.

Not a word needed to be uttered. I saw it in his eyes. He saw his face in hers, bearing resemblances to one another like two drops of water.

I inhaled and grasped Max's hand again, stepping between him and Cara. My eyes bore supplication which needed no words as I subtly shook my head "no."

Did he have the will, the strength to survive the revelation? Did Cara? James was the only father Cara had ever known. To even ponder the thought of having her or James think otherwise would be devastating. I closed my eyes and prayed.

After a long moment, Max squeezed my fingers. I

opened my eyes, ashamed, confused, and embarrassed. How horrible had I been—five days at his side and not have the balls to tell him, though it was at the forefront in my mind, of every conversation I had started with him.

I gazed down at him praying somehow he would understand why. Wishing silently he could grasp how hard I had wrestled with the dilemma of whether to tell him or not, the entire time I was here. But clearly, Serendipity, in all her bad timing and missed chances, had decided to make it right. It had been decided for me. "Please," I whispered. "No."

Max's face turned toward me, but he looked as though he didn't see me. He took a gulping breath. "I won't." His eyes were a mix of confused emotions.

I exhaled and turned to my daughter and motioned for her to step closer. "Come and meet my friend. He says it's okay." Cara hesitated, then stepped into the room. I walked toward her and took her hand, wrapping my arm around her shoulders, leading her closer to Max's hospital bed. I let Cara gauge how close she was willing to go.

Max kept his eyes open, his breathing was steady, his heartbeat steady, and his face slowly moved to form a smile as his gaze swept over Cara's face. The confusion was gone and was replaced with joy.

"Max, this is Cara. Cara, this is Max." The emotion in Max's eyes spoke what he could not say. I subtly brushed away my tears as Cara inched a little closer to Max, oblivious she was about to meet her true father for the first time.

"*Ciao*, Max," she said softly. "*Sono* Cara." Her broken Italian communicated the simplest of greetings, yet I knew that for Max, its meaning was profound.

His eyes brightened and the fingers on his hand lifted, slowly opening his hand to his daughter. Cara didn't hesitate. Pride burst inside me. After all, to her, he was only a man, terminally ill, but just a man.

"Hi, Cara." His voice broke. "I'm Max."

Cara gently wrapped her hand around his, thin onion skin covering bone, and graced him with a beautiful smile filled with warmth and compassion. Max's eyes sparkled with emotion and clung to Cara's.

"You are beautiful, like your mamma." His voice was mellow and low as he looked upon his daughter for the first time and the last. Within seconds exhaustion took over, and his eyes fluttered closed. I thought of the amount of strength and energy it must have taken from him to speak those words.

Cara gradually slipped her hand from his and placed it softly back on the bed.

"My God, Mom, he's so thin."

I nodded. "He's very sick." With a heart bursting with love, I wrapped my arms around my daughter.

Cara, taken aback at first, returned the motion, hugging me tightly, unaware of what brought on the sudden show of emotion.

"Thank you for that sweet gesture." I sniffed, not trying to hide my tears.

"No worries, Mom. I mean what kind of a person wouldn't?"

I broke the embrace and took Cara's face in my hands. "You did a good thing coming in here today."

"No worries." Cara grimaced slightly, probably wondering why I made such an issue of a simple act of kindness. "Are you staying here or coming to dinner?"

I considered whether to take a chance but, in the end, decided Max might need me. In my mind, I hoped he would see the joy in this and not hate me for the choices I had made. So I stayed.

Chapter Thirty

An hour or so passed. I paced the room before Max opened his eyes again. I had made futile attempts to rouse him, calling his name, gently shaking the bed, but to no avail. I couldn't let him pass without explaining why I had never told him about Cara.

Then he opened his eyes. Too weak to talk, but sweeping his gaze around the room, I thought maybe, he might be looking for her. He moved his fingers, so I took his hand.

"She had to go, Max." I owed him more than a simple explanation. I sat at his bedside and tried to make sense. "Listen," I started. "When we were together, that last night in New York, at the Waldorf, when you and I—"

He wasn't acknowledging me; he only turned his head slightly to the window. I stopped and followed his gaze. In the distance, the sun was low on the horizon of gently rolling hills.

"Not long after you left New York, I found out I was pregnant. I want you to know I put off getting married to James because I didn't know whose baby it was. Honestly, the baby could have belonged to either of you. And James had no idea. He thought it was his all along—he still does. Then she was born, and I knew the moment I saw her. I tried to look you up. Then I found you and Gabriela…in the European tabloids. You two were married three months after you left New York." I shrugged, tears streaming down my cheeks.

His eyes closed, this time in dismay. There was a look of sadness there which surpassed the imminence of death, the knowledge of end of life. "I couldn't do it, Max—I couldn't do that to you…or James. I never told James. I don't even think he suspected. I didn't even want to bring her to Italy…I don't know why but—"

His gaze never left the window. I looked outside, too, unsure of what to do, what else to say, praying he would forgive me—forgive and understand. We watched silently as puffy clouds gathered above the sun and small wisps moved across it just enough to accent the fierceness of its beauty, the clarity of the oranges, reds, and auburn, and the brilliance of the countryside as it burnished the day.

I gently let go of his hand and walked to the window to catch a better glimpse. A church bell tower in another village stood like a long-lost sentinel between the setting sun and my vision, a perfect alignment, with the big orange ball moving slowly down, down, down on another day, perfectly outlining the bell in the tower.

"Sofie," he whispered.

I rushed to his side. "Yes, Max." I held his hand and moved in close to listen.

"For her sake, forgive him."

Through the haze of morphine and the pain from cancer, his last thoughts were for Cara. I nodded with absolute sobriety, knowing exactly what he wanted me to do. "I promise. I promise I will." I was numb, but this, for him, I would do.

He squeezed my hand as a look of satisfaction

settled into his eyes. He opened his mouth and tried to make it work, to move breath over his lips and tongue, and make the words happen. Then finally, he whispered, "Cara."

"Yes. She is beautiful. And smart. And good." My tears mingled with my words, trying to give him a lifetime of experiences in a few words.

Max looked beyond me and to the setting sun. I grasped the bedpost and tried to move it, to align it with the sunset, but it wouldn't budge. I called down the hall. "Please, someone help me."

I waited a moment and then decided to try again. As I was struggling, Alberto hurried into the room. "Quick, help me move the bed so he can see the sunset…like this." I motioned.

"Of course," he said and grabbed the other bedpost, inching it closer to align with the setting sun.

"Okay." I sighed. "Perfect. Thanks."

He nodded and went around to check Max's IV drip. "I'll be back in an hour or so to replace the bag. How is he doing?"

"He's good now."

The nurse nodded his acknowledgment and left.

I went around the bed, so I was between Max and the windowsill. There was an old-style latch, which I disengaged, and opened the window wide. A gentle breeze flowed in over Max's face, bringing with it a fragrance of green and lavender and red earth and sounds of birds and animals settling in for the evening. Nature knew it was time to rest.

I brought my face down to Max's and looked to the sun, aligning my eyes with the church in the distance. "Look, Max," I whispered. "See how the sun peeks through the bell tower." His eyes were transfixed by the colors and the brilliance and watched as the sun sank slowly, further and further.

As I gazed out with him, I heard him faintly whisper.

"Stay with me." His breath was so weak.

"Always."

He dipped his head. I gulped down my fear—my helplessness. My throat tightened as my mind tried to comprehend the loneliness he must be bearing. Death is a heartbreaking business.

I slipped off my shoes, then carefully sat on the bed and brought up my legs, lying down beside him, moving slowly so as not to hurt him. I slipped an arm around the pillow cradling him and tucked my head, resting it above his and held his hand to my heart.

We lay there for a long time, watching the sun become smaller and weaker until it was only a sliver of pink on the hillside.

"Now that was something, wasn't it?" he murmured, his breathing farther apart and shallower than ever.

I brushed my lips over his temple and whispered, "I love you, Max. I always have."

The sky was a deepening blue, lighter where the clouds were on the horizon. We were at peace. Holding him, comforting him, I was at peace. I closed my eyes and let myself drift as I hummed a sweet song from long ago.

****

A gentle shaking roused me, and I opened my eyes to see the nurse standing at my side. "Oh, I'm sorry," I apologized, sliding my legs off the bedside. "I probably shouldn't be on the bed, but it was such a beautiful sunset, I decided to—"

Alberto put a hand on my shoulder and looked at me with empathetic eyes. He didn't have to say the words. I knew before he opened his mouth by the look on his face. The sting of tears in the back of my throat came quickly.

"Ms. Romano, Max is gone."

Stunned and suddenly feeling utterly alone, I moved off the bed to see his face. His eyes were open, looking toward the distant horizon. His expression peaceful. There was no pain in his features, only peace.

Alberto gestured to the machine. "It must have happened when you were asleep." A quiet flatline on the green screen confirmed it. The nurse reached out and gently closed Max's eyes.

Calmly with tears spilling over onto my cheeks, my only thoughts were for Max and how he had reached the end of his battle. "All right." My voice quivered. "It's done."

"I'm so sorry for your loss," said Alberto sympathetically. "Can I get you anything?"

"No, thank you. I'm fine," I said, brushing away the tears. "What happens now?"

"We will call his next of kin. I believe his brother is in Belgium. Funeral plans have been taken care of—Mr. Damiani took care of everything before he came here."

Nodding, I thought, of course, he did. He probably didn't think anyone else could do the job.

"Thank you." I glanced down and let my gaze rest on Max.

"You're welcome. We will take Mr. Damiani when

you are done. No rush." He turned and left.

I walked to the window and took in a deep breath, filling my lungs with the evening air, then taking either side, I closed the panes and bolted the latch. I turned and looked at Max, wondering what I would do next. "Thirty-seven days you say, my dear friend. May as well have been thirty-seven seconds." We were but a tiny brushstroke in a much bigger picture.

The tears came, hard and deep, almost visceral, for Max, yes, but also for the world itself, for its beauty and waste, its mingled cruelties, and kindnesses. I agonized and grieved not only for his death but for the life I would have had with him if things were different. If he were different, and I was different.

The wondering was done, the possible was gone, the ghost was gone, the permanent became ever-present.

I stayed with him for a long time, tidied his blankets, kissed his lips, combed his hair, and took his hand in mine for the last time, placing it against my cheek and resting my head on the bedside next to him. I cried until there was nothing left. And when I finished, I felt lighter, lighter than I had in years. He was at peace in the end, so I knew I could be, too.

When I sensed I could, I walked to the sink and splashed water on my face, dabbed my face with a paper towel, then grabbed my handbag, and walked.

Chapter Thirty-One

From a hidden corner in the piazza parking lot in Pescaglia, I sat behind the wheel of my rented car, watching silently as the funeral procession, bearing Max's body, slowly wound its way to the cemetery at the top of the village proper.

I asked Cara and James to wait for me at the hotel; I preferred to be alone. Though they made copious offers of moral support, I didn't want them here. I wasn't embarrassed or hiding—I needed to do this on my own. In my heart, if they were with me, it would taint mine and Max's last moments together, in some bizarre way.

It was profoundly affecting to know only the shell of the person I once loved was being buried. The man whose heart beat in my chest and whose spirit drew breath from the same soul as mine, his essence would forever be with me. It was hidden, as it always had been. And I learned to live with it, but still…it was there. I realized Max gave me the only answer to my question he knew my heart could bear.

When it was us, we were a universe unto ourselves. We were only happy if there were no one else in our world.

Once the procession disappeared into the cemetery and the casket was out of sight, I started the car, put it in gear, and headed back. The day was warmer and the oak and chestnut trees lining the road offered shade through the new leaves like sieves to the sunlight as I drove down the gently sloping incline back to the hotel. The hotel where my husband and daughter waited for me.

I knew what to do. I had healed, and I had taken care of myself, and the long-forgotten void in my soul was no longer. Max, who like the ebb and flow of waves came and went from my life, eroding, shaping, and depositing himself little by little, until everything in my life was shaped by his irregular presence.

My ghost is gone.

The hunger for time with the man who lay withered would slowly go away. When I came across a reminder of him, his memory would come flooding back, but I'd smile, and it'd be perfectly normal, and he'd always be there.

Max did for me what no one else could do, allowed me to heal, to go forward, to live with him in my heart without guilt.

And I'd do the only thing I knew to do—exactly what he asked because he asked for Cara.

Forgiving James his indiscretion was a pittance in comparison. I would tell James tonight as we walked down one of the quaint streets in Lucca after dinner. Our family, James, Cara, and I would go on. We would live a long and happy life.

Alive. I was alive. New leaves faintly rustled in the wind, and my limbs extended as I walked from my car to our hotel room. The sky over me turned sullen, but in the distance, I saw sunlight in a high mist of crystals bright and glowing, and I thought, two Chinese characters in combination comprised the word "crisis"—one meant "disaster," the other meant "opportunity."

I brushed the certainty of death aside because Max would live in my heart, strong, audacious, and swaggering, and achingly handsome until we united again. We would walk hand in hand, not old and gray as we promised each other, but young and vital, in a delicious reprieve to timelessness wherever we wish to be.

A word about the author…

E. Graziani writes books in multiple genres for adults and teens. She is the author of *Breaking Faith*, a contemporary young adult fiction novel, selected for the "In the Margins" Book Award 2018 Recommended Fiction List and one of Canadian Children's Book Centre's Best Books for Kids and Teens, and *War in My Town*, one of Canadian Children's Book Centre's Best Books for Kids and Teens and finalist in the Hamilton Arts Council 2016 Literary Awards for Best Non-Fiction. She was a reader and reviewer for Writers' Union of Canada Short Prose Competition for Emerging Writers and is a regular contributor on CHCH Morning Live Book Chat. She resides in Canada with her husband and four daughters. Visit her website for more information, events, and new releases:

egraziani1.wixsite.com/egrazianiauthor

Thank you for purchasing
this publication of The Wild Rose Press, Inc.

For questions or more information
contact us at
info@thewildrosepress.com.

The Wild Rose Press, Inc.
www.thewildrosepress.com